Middle Age Before Beauty

The Mag and Clara Balefire Mysteries

BOOK FIVE

REGINA WELLING
ERIN LYNN

Middle Age Before Beauty

ISBN- 978-1-953044-38-9

Cover design by: L. Vryhof

Interior design by: L. Vryhof

http://reginawelling.com

http://erinlynnwrites.com

First Edition

Printed in the U.S.A.

Contents

Chapter 1

"My rheumatism's acting up something fierce today." Margaret Balefire, better known as Mag, stood up as straight as she could manage after crouching to inspect the underside of a desk drawer and pressed a hand to her hip.

"Call it arthritis. Nobody uses the word rheumatism anymore." Clara Balefire, Mag's sister, ran a feather duster over a line of glass jars on a shelf in the shop they owned together. "It's outdated."

Temper flaring, Mag retorted, "Well, so am I. What's your point?"

"Besides the one on your hat?" Clara shot up an eyebrow as she surveyed Mag's current attire, which included a pair of toxic-yellow leopard-print leggings and a neon-pink tee shirt with a farting unicorn cavorting across her chest. A straw hat with a distinct point at the top perched jauntily on hair the color and texture of a dandelion clock. "I wasn't trying to make a point, just stating a fact."

"You want to hear a fact? This desk is a knock-off, and I paid too much for it because I needed one more thing that's a pain in my backside."

Because she hated seeing anyone in pain, Clara went

behind the counter and pulled out a pretty, cobalt blue glass jar of handmade liniment. "This should help with the actual pain, and I've added a little something special to make it last longer, too."

Suspicious, Mag unscrewed the cap and took a sniff. "What's in it?"

"Oh, just several types of poison. I figured if I couldn't get rid of your aches and pains, I could get rid of you instead," Clara joked.

"You're so funny I forgot to laugh."

With no sense of modesty whatsoever, Mag dragged up the hem of her top and reached around to apply the salve to the spot near her hip that pained her. "It's minty," she said. "Smells like that chewing gum you used to like."

"Is that a good thing or a bad thing?" The dusting finished, Clara fisted her hands on her hips and surveyed the shop to ensure everything was up to snuff. Outside of Mag not looking what anyone would consider professional, Clara decided the eclectic mix of antiques and personal care items passed muster and flipped the closed sign to open.

"It's just a thing. Brings back memories."

From the look on Mag's face, Clara couldn't decide if the memories were making her sister happy or sad, but she didn't want to pry when Mag was already in a foul mood. "If you'd rather go up and have a lie-down, I can take care of things here," she offered.

Prickly at the best of times, Mag took exception to the suggestion.

"The hell I will. Last time I took a nap, you sold a Koken barber chair for two-hundred bucks."

Clara shrugged. "That thing was an eyesore. It took up way too much space, and we're lucky anyone wanted it at all."

"An antique eyesore worth fifteen-hundred dollars to the right buyer, and you let it go for a fraction of what it was worth."

When Clara shrugged again, Mag's blood pressure hit numbers in the unsafe range. As a side effect, some of her magic leaked out and shook a mid-century dresser until the drawers slid open.

"Cut the crap, Mag," Clara said, but with no real heat. "You're cranky today."

"I'm cranky every day," Mag retorted. "You'd be cranky, too, if your body felt like it belonged to your grandmother." She allowed a rare moment of introspection to creep through. "I hate my life sometimes."

Sympathy etched itself all over the beautiful features Clara inherited from their mother. "If I could turn back time for you, I would because you're my sister, and I love you."

Well-known among witch-kind for her skill at hunting rogue magical creatures, Mag's reputation was probably what had led the local coven to invite the Balefire sisters to move to Harmony. Mag had singlehandedly taken out more Raythes than any ten witches combined, including the one who got a big enough piece of her to rob her of her physical youth. It was a wonder she'd survived the attack at all.

Looking at the pair of them, no one would believe the eight-year difference in the sister's true ages, which was why the non-magical residents of the sleepy hamlet of

Harmony knew the Balefires as mother and daughter.

"I know, Clarie. Just as we both know, there's nothing anyone can do to change things, so let's not talk about it again, okay? The liniment's working. You should sell this stuff." It was Mag's idea of a joke since Clara *did* sell lotions and creams as her contribution to the store they'd named Balms and Bygones. Clara ran the balms side while Mag's penchant for good antiques made up the bygones.

"What a novel idea. I'll have to consider it sometime." Clara's tone was as dry as the scented powder she'd recently added to her new personal care line. But the conversation had put Mag in a better mood, so Clara had that going for her.

Probably wouldn't last, Clara thought. With Mag, it never did.

"Why don't you come to the country club with me tonight? You're still signed up for those water aerobics classes, right? I know you had fun while doing them, and now that they fixed the heater, the pool's nice and warm. I've been going for a few weeks, and it's great fun."

Mag's left eyebrow shot up. "I signed up for those classes to catch a killer. Not to play dippity doodle with half the women in town. I've got better things to do than dunk myself in warm water like some wrinkled-up teabag."

A snort-worthy mental image, Clara thought but managed to keep a straight face. "Up to you. All I know is, killer or not, you moved easier after those sessions, and I think you should keep on with them."

Mag flicked a hand to wave the notion away. "I'm not

going."

Shrugging, Clara let it go. "You'll do whatever you want in any case. But just remember, sitting around wishing for the past won't help you feel better in the present. There's more to life than catching killers or chasing rogue hell beasts. You deserve a little fun now and then."

"Your idea of fun and mine are worlds apart," Mag said darkly. "I liked chasing rogue hell beasts a lot better than fooling around in a pool full of gossip monsters."

It wasn't until just before closing time, when her hip felt and sounded like bone rubbing against bone, that she remembered the hot tub attached to one end of the country club pool. Screw water aerobics, Mag thought. Sitting in the hot tub and watching the show would be way more fun. Who didn't enjoy seeing a bunch of silly women splashing around in unison?

Putting all thoughts of the country club out of her mind, Mag greeted the tall drink of water who walked through the door with that look in his eye.

"Looking for something special?"

"Chest of drawers for my mother. It needs to be cherry or mahogany. She likes the darker colors and bonus points if you have nightstands in a matching shade. She's redoing her bedroom but doesn't like shopping."

Grinning, Mag sized him up and decided her chances of a sale were excellent. "And you do?"

Returning her grin, he said, "Nope. Not even a little. This is my first stop, so if you could help me out, I'd be eternally grateful."

"I'm Mag Balefire, and you are?"

"Andre Cloutier."

"Well, Andre, does she have a favorite period? Modern? Victorian? Edwardian?"

The poor guy blinked twice, then admitted. "I guess."

Inwardly, Mag chuckled. "What's the budget?"

He named a figure that warmed the cockles of Mag's heart.

"Why don't we just look at some options, hm? You'll know when you see the right thing." And if she didn't have the right thing on hand, she'd at least get an idea of style and period, then make a few calls.

Wending her way through the shop, Mag pointed out a lovely Maitland Smith commode. "That's neoclassical in style. Plenty of decorative detail if she goes for that type of thing. It's a fine example. Just look at those fluted corners and that gilded molding,"

"It's nice," he said.

Nice was one of those wishy-washy words that Mag hated with a fiery passion, but the customer was always right. "It is," she said. "Too fussy?"

"A little."

Mag nodded and steered him away from the corner that housed her collection of rococo and toward a Sheraton in cherry with an understated diamond inlay down either side of the drawers. "What about something like this?"

Andre tilted his head. "It's nice but a little plain. Do you have something in between?"

"It happens, I do." Sensing a sale in the offing, Mag cheerfully navigated past her selection of mid-century modern and made a beeline for an antique Scottish mahogany dresser with claw feet, a flame pattern on the drawers, and turned column supports. "There's a touch of gold leaf on the top drawer, but it's subtle."

He looked. He leaned down to open and close each drawer. "Smooth," he said, his face giving away nothing, but Mag had heard the click that signaled she'd found exactly the right fit for the customer.

"Well-made and built to last," Mag agreed. "Now for the nightstands, I happen to have a pair of half-commodes in the same rich tones. They even have similar knobs and pulls. I can let all three pieces go for around what you're looking to spend."

"Is this place magic?" Andre couldn't believe his good fortune. The entire purchase hadn't taken much longer than half an hour.

"Something like that."

At the end of the work day, Mag went out to the little shack she called home. Not that shack was exactly the right word for the cozy set of rooms she'd magicked out of a converted shed. She didn't have nearly the same amount of space as Clara, who lived above the shop, but at least there weren't stairs to bedevil her poor hip.

Her rocking chair calling like the song of a siren, Mag dropped her cane into the umbrella stand by the door. An antique she'd nicked from the shop just because she liked it, the stand was shaped, funnily enough, like an upside-down umbrella.

Cane-less, Mag hobbled over to her rocker, sat down, and set a fire in the fireplace with the flick of a finger. As the heat rolled over her, it conjured images of basking in warm water with soothing jets pulsing gently across her sore spots.

"Drat you, Clara Balefire." Mag cursed her sister for

putting the hot tub idea in her head because now that it was there, it wouldn't dislodge, and she had to admit it would be nice just to soak awhile. Ideally, in a magical grotto conjured by her niece's faerie godmothers, but since that wasn't in the cards, she'd settle for the country club.

Rising, Mag left the chair rocking behind her as she headed for the bedroom to rifle through her dresser drawers. Her hands faltered once as a wave of dizziness washed over her, and the world began to tunnel down to black. Bearing down, Mag kept herself upright until the sensation passed. Lately, these spells had come more frequently than ever. A sign, Mag thought, that each passing day brought her time closer. She had another year, maybe two at the most, before she would shuffle off this mortal coil. The Raythe had taken a sizable chunk of her life force along with her youthful looks on that fateful day, the extent of which was something Clara didn't need to know. At least, not yet.

Shoving morbid thoughts away, Mag decided to live while she could and let out a hoot when she found the last swimsuit she'd worn before her aging accident and a vintage rubber bathing cap studded with colored flowers. Still muttering and with sharp motions, Mag snatched her favorite bespelled fanny pack from where it hung on her bedpost and stuffed the suit inside. Next, she detoured into the bathroom, came out with a striped beach towel so long she could wrap it around herself twice, and shoved that into the pack as well. The rubber cap she yanked on over wisps of white hair. She jammed her feet into a pair of fuzzy slides and topped off the look with her favorite jacket—well-worn suede with a waterfall of fringe.

Clara would hate every little thing about her sister's clothing choices, which, as far as Mag was concerned, was the entire point of them. Little else in life was more fun than watching Clara's lips go tight. For that reason, Mag waited until her sister had driven off toward the country club before fixing the image of where she wanted to go in her mind. A flicker of magic coupled with her intention carried Mag to the darkest corner of the storage closet at the back of the club's changing rooms.

To keep the shock value high, Mag decided to slip into her suit and then spring the ensemble on her unsuspecting sister right in the middle of the dip and dunk class. Hidden among the brooms and mops probably wasn't the best place to change, but Mag made it work with a strong will and another hint or two of magic. She only nearly fell over once.

Bright voices echoed from the pool area. Mag grinned, wrapped the towel tightly, tying the ends in a knot just above her chest, and headed out to make her grand entrance.

Chapter 2

"Maggie. What are you doing here?" Clara paddled to the edge of the pool as her sister approached. "You said you didn't want to come, or I would have waited for you." The implication was that Clara knew Mag had taken the easy route.

"Changed my mind," Mag said, shrugging her shoulders innocently. "But only about the hot tub, not the old fogey water ballet." She raised her voice just enough to draw attention. "You can do your synchronized splashing. I'll just be over there soaking my bones."

Mag dropped the towel.

Clara forgot to tread water, went under, and came up sputtering. "Goddess help me," she gasped.

"Chlorine in your eyes?" Mag tsked and shook her head in mock empathy.

Wet hair tangled over Clara's face. She brushed it back, got another look at her sister, and winced. "No. What are you wearing?"

"This old thing?" One hip cocked, her hand on the other, Mag looked down at the bands of material bound together with narrow straps that made up her swim attire. Tiny patches of shiny fabric struggled to contain breasts that had lost both the skirmish and the battle with gravity. Then, she hooked her thumb in one of the straps that angled down from her shoulders. "I can't believe it still fits."

As if possessed, Clara's eyes traced the V shape to its natural conclusion—a scrap of cloth barely covering what it should have. Before Clara could form words, Mag spun to show off the back.

"Does anyone have a fork? I need to poke out my own eyeballs," Clara muttered when she saw that the rear of what could only loosely be called a swimsuit mimicked the front in shape and size, not to mention scarcity of material. "Mag, half of your ass is showing."

"In more ways than one," Penelope Starr had gone pale. "There are things you see that are so horrible they stick with you forever. I think I'm scarred for life."

Half of the women in the pool stared in horror. One or two snickered. The rest found other things to look at. They were the smart ones. Mag glared at Penelope, then lazily flicked a finger in her direction.

Penelope's expression went from disdain to panic as she got busy picking at the back of her own suit. After a moment, she couldn't take it anymore and climbed out of the pool. Mag earned another glare as the younger witch crossed to the bench where she'd left her towel.

As Penelope passed, Clara noted something of a wardrobe malfunction and couldn't hold back a tiny smile. Mag's atomic wedgie charm wouldn't last long, but it wouldn't be pleasant while it ran its course. Clara should know since she'd experienced it more than once in her youth.

"If you're done with the shock and awe portion of

your day, why don't you join us? Unless you don't think you can handle the workout." Clara goaded her sister. "On second thought, maybe you should just lounge around in the hot tub. We wouldn't want to get your heart rate up too high. It might prove you actually have one."

If the zinger hit the mark, Mag's face didn't show it, which left Clara even more annoyed as she paddled back and took her place next to Mabel Youngblood. "Sorry," Clara nodded to the instructor. "Go ahead."

The drama over, at least for the moment, Mag activated the jets, sidled around the various seats until she found one with a perfect stream of pulsating water that hit the spot, and congratulated herself on the suit's impact. She'd done everything she came to do, and now she planned to enjoy the heat, the jets, and the bubbles. Sinking low, she closed her eyes and basked for maybe a minute before the sensation of being watched brought her senses to full attention.

Casually, Mag let her lids open. Just a crack so it wouldn't look like she'd noticed anything, but enough to get a feel for whose gaze might be trained in her direction. Seeing nothing out of the ordinary, she let her intuition out to play. With one notable exception, Mag's intuition had never done her wrong.

On full alert now, Mag schooled her face to maintain its lazy, almost bored expression while she sent her awareness out in every direction. She'd narrowed down the general area where her watcher must be when the sensation shut off like a light switch.

Odd. Mag thought. Probably the suit. She had come there intending to be looked at, had she not? So why did she feel all bajiggity when it happened? A question for the ages.

Settling back, she replayed the bathing suit moment in her head, laughing again at the shocked responses until an excited buzzing pulled her focus. Like almost every other woman in the pool area, Mag watched as fine an example of manhood as she'd ever seen stroll toward the pool wearing a pair of board shorts and a polo shirt with the club's name emblazoned across the front.

Ignoring the women's stares, the young man flicked a loose curl of hair off his forehead and hunkered down to look at the space below the lip where the pool water drained into the filter. Still oblivious to having stopped the aerobics class, he stood and stripped off his shirt. A sigh rose as the tan fabric revealed golden skin, washboard abs, and shoulders for days.

As Mag contemplated what she might have done with him had she still been in her heyday, the lad jumped into the pool. To a rapt audience, he surfaced and slicked his hair back while he angled for a closer look into the orifice. Whatever he saw there wasn't good because he shook his head, then placed his hands on the pool's edge and boosted himself out.

Another sigh whispered across the room as water sluiced off the pool boy's muscles. Pool boy. What a ridiculous term, Mag thought. This was no boy. This was a man. Probably dumber than a bag of eaflock hair, but at least he was pretty. She watched along with the rest as he opened a panel in the far wall, pulled out a length of hose, and shot a stream of water at whatever had lodged where it shouldn't. Finally satisfied, he returned the hose and strode off in the direction he'd entered from, pulling his shirt over his damp body. It took a full thirty seconds for activity to resume in his wake.

The second time Mag felt eyes on her, she turned her head to find the water aerobics instructor straddling the wall that separated the hot tub from the pool.

"You know, I could help you get more range of motion in that hip. Probably get rid of the cane entirely if you follow my regimen. It's a few simple exercises every day, and show up for class three times a week."

To the woman's credit, Mag's glare barely made a dent in her resolve.

"The hip's fine," Mag lied.

"I'd say pull the other leg, but we both know I don't need to. I'd add a weekly deep-tissue massage if that's enough to sweeten the deal. And I won't even charge you for the one-on-one consultation fees. Just the classes you already paid for and the massage."

"How noble," Mag drawled. "I don't trust noble. What's in it for you?" She finally pulled the instructor's name up from the dregs of her memory. "Fiona."

"Satisfaction of a job well done," came the answer, but Mag thought there was more to it than that and waited until Fiona offered up the reason. "Fine. If you must know, I'm an empath, and I know you're in more pain than you let on because I can feel it. You've found ways to overcome it when you have to, but that hip is getting worse, and those moments where you can forget the pain are decreasing all the time. If I can help you regain at least some of your mobility, most of it, if you work hard, I won't have to feel your pain anymore. But you'll have to put some trust in me."

Since the number of people Mag trusted could be counted on the fingers of one hand, she shrugged. "Tall order."

Fiona rose from her seat on the tile and swung her leg over the divider, her motion smooth and easy enough to send a spark of jealousy through Mag. "Your choice. I'm not gifted with magic, but I'm aware of it in my community, and I know you by reputation. You're one tough witch, but that doesn't mean you have to be in constant pain. If you want my help, haul your skinny self into my pool, and for the love of the sainted mother, don't wear that suit the next time you come, or the deal's off."

Mag slid sideways until she could reach the controls, turned off the jets, then sunk down until only her eyes and nose were above the water. Was she a damn fool? No. Did she want to parade her infirmity in front of the entire class? Again, no. Was it worth it if she could move around easier?

Since the answer to that one landed well across the line on the side of probably, Mag gave in and hauled her half-naked backside over the barrier. Fiona nodded approval but didn't single Mag out for special instructions and kept moving through the class.

"Let's continue with lunges. Three sets of twelve, each side, beginning with your left. And one…two."

"This is stupid," Mag muttered when her legs moved easier than she thought they should.

"The water takes some of your weight, but you're still getting a solid workout. Just be careful not to push too hard at first, or you'll be sore later."

"I'm always sore." But Mag moved with the others to

shallower water and followed along with a short series of squats. Once committed, she gave it her all. Next came bicep curls, which she didn't mind so much, and then, the dreaded high kicks. She was certain she heard her hip yelp after the first one, but it turned out to be Clara's voice breaking across the water.

"What's your problem? This should be easy for you."

"It's not the leg lifts," Clara closed her eyes dramatically. "It's you and the bathing suit from hell."

Mag snorted, but the delight carried her through the rest of the kicks and the cool-down. When the class ended, she headed back to the hot tub, noticed that she had less difficulty getting in, and cranked the jets up as high as they would go. Maybe there was something to this lark after all.

"It's something in the water, don't you think?"

All Mag wanted was the heat, the jets, and some peace. With the queen of gossip taking a seat beside her, peace was the last thing on the menu. But then again, Mag loved a good bit of gossip, even if the source of it was Gertrude Granger, who tended to smell like gingerbread all year round.

"What do you mean?"

"It's just that I feel so much better after these classes. It seems like magic, you know?"

Sliding back up to a proper seated position, Mag's chest cleared the water. Bits of her bathing suit did not.

Bless Gertrude, she took the flashing in stride, reached back to the ledge behind her, and produced a candy-cane striped towel, which she tossed at Mag. "Better cover those up. I think the club has a rule about nudity."

Mag looked down and blushed for probably the first

time in her life. She'd meant to shock, not to stupefy.

"Thanks." But Mag waved the towel away, sank back down, and adjusted the suit to cover what it hadn't.

If Gertrude had more to say about the magical pool water, raised voices stopped the conversation.

"But I *am* a member," Lydia Wayland fisted her hands on her hips and glared at the man standing at the pool's edge. "Ned Sullivan, how could you? You know me. You were at my wedding, for Pete's sake. We had the reception here. My father was on the hiring committee when you applied for this job. What is wrong with you? You can't kick me out."

His expression pained, Ned rubbed at his temple and glanced behind him toward the man who stepped out from around a corner, then said something Mag couldn't hear.

"I should have known." Her face red and infused with fury, Lydia stomped her way to the steps, mounted them, and didn't bother with a towel as she closed the distance. "What did he do, Ned? No, Wait. Let me guess. He threatened to sue the club, and rather than stand up to a bully, you're kicking me out." Lydia stood so close she dripped water on Ned's shoes.

"That guy over there is Sam Wayland. Sam is Lydia's ex-husband." The pool water amplified Gertrude's stage whisper. "He's an attorney who, according to his recently posted dating profile, likes long walks on the beach and quiet nights at home, but his main hobby is filing lawsuits and injunctions for no good reason whatsoever."

Mag had figured that much out on her own. What surprised her was the level of condemnation in

Gertrude's tone. Whether she lived in fear of getting coal in her Christmas stocking or was just *that* cheerful, the woman rarely had a bad word for anyone. Sam Wayland must have done something heinous to make Gertie's naughty list, but Mag didn't have a chance to probe for more information. She was too busy watching things play out between Lydia, Ned, and her ex.

"Sam's not the only one capable of filing a lawsuit. Did you ever think of that?" Lydia shook a finger less than an inch from Ned's nose.

"Nevertheless," Ned stood his ground. "Mr. Wayland has chosen to withdraw his sponsorship, which means your membership has been rescinded."

It's not easy to look imposing in a racer-backed one-piece, but Lydia gave it her best shot. "As a member in good standing, I sponsored him when we married, not the other way around. Did you even bother to check your records before you decided to kick me out? It's Sam who needs to leave, not me."

Ned's face reddened, and he tugged at the collar of his shirt as if it had become too tight. "As you know, Mr. Wayland purchased an equity membership last year, which altered the terms for both of you. As the equity member of your marriage, the burden of sponsorship moved from you to him. Now that you are no longer married, his sponsorship has come to an end. You are welcome to purchase an equity membership or to find someone else to sponsor your entry into the club."

"That's a loophole, and you know it."

Ned shrugged. "Nevertheless, your membership has ended, and for that reason, I must ask you to leave."

"She's not going anywhere," Miriam May, Lydia's

closest friend, headed for the steps to leave the pool. "I'll sign her in as my guest, and there's not a thing you can do about it, Ned. Don't forget, I'm also an equity member. Unless you'd like to sue me, Sam." Her tone turned the comment into a dare.

"No. Don't. It's fine, Miri. I'm going," Lydia glared daggers at her ex-husband. "Let the child have his toy. I'm done here."

"Now that you mention it," Miriam wrapped a towel around her waist. "The atmosphere in this place isn't what it used to be." If her eyes flickered toward the hot tub, Mag didn't take it personally. "I think there are better places to spend my membership dues." She turned to Ned. "I'll be in tomorrow afternoon to file my resignation paperwork. You'll need to have the refund checks ready."

"Refund checks?" Ned swallowed hard.

"According to the charter, an equity member is entitled to a prorated refund of their yearly dues should they discontinue their membership. I intend to do just that, as will my husband. So that's two refund checks. Sizable ones, I might add."

Poor Ned's day had just gone from bad to worse. "There's no need to be hasty, Mrs. May. I'm sure we can work something out."

Hands on her hips, Miriam cocked a brow and stared him down. "Is Lydia still a member here?"

Flushing, Ned looked at Sam, whose expression hadn't changed.

"I'm sorry."

"Not yet, but you will be," Miriam promised. "Come along, Lydia. I have some phone calls to make." Giving

Ned a vicious dose of side-eye, Miriam warned, "I think you'd better leave the entire afternoon open tomorrow. And keep your checkbook handy." She took Lydia's arm and pulled her toward the changing rooms while Ned shrugged and followed Sam in the opposite direction.

Furious whispers punctuated the dual exits, and within three minutes, someone had set up a betting pool for how many charter members Miriam would take with her when she went.

"You ready to go?" Clara loomed over Mag. "If you hurry up and change, I'll let you drive. Just put on a towel first. You've offended enough people's sensibilities today. Let's not have another scene."

Under other circumstances, Mag might have passed on the offer, but she figured Gertrude would return to her favorite topic: Christmas, as soon as the Lydia gossip died down. Mag wasn't quite as big a fan of the big guy and his flying poop-droppers as Gertrude.

"If I'm driving, we're stopping for ice cream."

"Sure. Sounds good." Whatever it took, Clara thought, to end the embarrassment and preserve her family name. "Let's go."

"Sorry, Gertrude," Mag double-checked her girls before stepping out of the hot tub and wrapping up in her own towel. "Looks like there's someplace I need to be. Can we talk about this later?" Or never.

So full of Christmas spirit she was affable even at the worst of times, Gertrude waved Mag off with a smile. "Go. Eat ice cream. Maybe try the peppermint stripe."

"I'll think about it." Mag escaped without a backward glance. Catching up with Clara, she said, "I left my jacket and fanny pack in the storage room. Your legs are younger than mine. Why don't you go grab it for me?"

"Nope. Getting dressed was part of the deal. You're not going out in public in that get-up. You'd freeze to death in any case."

Mag's left brow shot up. "Pretty sure I'm in public right now, so you're a little late with your prudish rules."

"I'm not a prude. I'm merely attempting to protect the retinas of those who don't deserve to have them burned to a crisp by the mental image of this," Clara gestured to include Mag's entire body, "travesty of fashion."

"What you call a travesty, I call a triumph. How many people my age can still get into a forty-year-old swimsuit?"

"Just because you can, doesn't mean you should. Not knowing the difference, Margaret Balefire, is your biggest failing. I'll wait here while you make yourself presentable." Clara held up a hand. "In clothing that doesn't look like you're auditioning for the lead in Grannie Does Dallas: The Bondage Years."

For once, Mag had nothing to say.

Chapter 3

"Gertrude looked like she was in gossip mode earlier. Anything interesting to share?" Clara clutched the door handle when Mag turned onto the main road too quickly for her liking. A thin curtain of snow filtered down from the darkened sky.

"Nah," Mag shrugged. "Gushing praise for the splash and stretch routine. That fracas with Lydia and her ex probably saved me from a discussion about proper care and feeding of Christmas elves or something. She had that light in her eyes. But I do think the peppermint stripe ice cream was a solid suggestion."

If they survived the drive. "Slow down. We have a half hour before the ice cream shop closes, and that snow's turning the road a bit slick."

Taking her hand off the wheel, Mag pulled a curious item from her pocket and handed it to her sister. Clara looked down at the toy soldier, then back up at Mag. "What's this?"

"Tire charm. And a damn fine one, I reckon. Matches the tires to the road conditions, so you always have traction. It's like driving on bare pavement." Reaching over, Mag took the toy soldier, slapped it on the dash, and added a spell to make it stick. "You're not the only one who knows how to make useful charms."

"I never said I was."

"I thought I could make more of them and see if Athena wants to sell them in her shop. She's got a petrified Phoenix heart I'd like to trade for. This might give me an edge since it's a complicated charm, and witches these days are lazy. They'd rather buy certain things than do the work to make them. I put it all down to sliced bread. That's when the world began to change."

It was Mag's driving rather than the increasingly worsening road conditions that had Clara clutching the door handle again. "Some people think sliced bread was a good thing."

Keeping one hand on the wheel, Mag used the other to wave Clara's comment away. "All these modern conveniences have made witches soft. They saw the non-magical types enjoying progress and decided to do the same. Well, that's fine and dandy, but I maintain you get a stronger spell if you prepare the ingredients yourself instead of always relying on store-bought."

"Says the woman who wants to sell driving charms to buy petrified bird parts." Clara earned a burning look. "But I do think you have a point, sister mine. The magic has a more personal element if you've harvested the herbs and whatever else yourself. More focused intention makes for more potent spells. Still, if given the choice, I'll let someone else chase down and prepare powdered dragon eggshell. That's a young witch's game."

Mag shrugged. "Okay, you've got me there, but I think my point still stands." She parked in front of the ice cream shop, slid from the seat of the old VW bus, and took three steps before realizing she hadn't grabbed her cane. She took two more before concluding she could get by without it, but habit had her turning back to grab it just in case.

Inside, Mag went for the peppermint stripe soft-serve on a cone, as did Clara, who had asked for hers to be upended in a dish and paired with a swirl of chocolate.

"I hope it tastes better than it looks because it looks like toothpaste."

Given the red stripe artistically spun through crisp white, Mag wasn't wrong.

"Doesn't taste like it." Clara spooned up a bit of both and grinned her pleasure. "Goes great with chocolate, too. I think this might be my new favorite. Except for the pumpkin and eggnog custard swirl."

"You're just as bad as I am, you know." Mag waved her cone and risked a quick flick of magic to right the frozen treat when it threatened to slide off. "You just hide it better."

Mag licked at the dripping minty goodness and headed toward the van. They were just about to pull out when the shop owner came to the door to wave at them to stop.

"You forgot this." He brought the cane out and shivered under the worsening storm. "Nasty night for it." He smiled and went back inside while Clara frowned at her sister.

"Hip not bothering you so much?"

"I guess not. Must have been the combination of your cream and the hot tub jets, but I'm feeling no pain at the moment. Maybe we should buy a hot tub for the house. There's a perfect spot for it right at the end of the garden."

"Right outside your back door, in other words." Clara's amused tone didn't phase Mag one bit.

"We could have Evian and the godmothers put in a permanent installation. I could definitely go for that. Just imagine soaking in all that lovely heat while the snow flies all around."

"The aerobics class probably helped, too," Clara pointed out.

"Not a factor," Mag dismissed. "I only did the last few minutes of the class, and don't even get me started on Gertrude's foolish idea that there's magic in the pool water."

Clara laid her spoon in her dish, then banished both to the kitchen trash in her apartment above the shop. "Gertrude thinks there's something in the water?" The notion intrigued. "Is that really so foolish? When was the last time you went without your cane?"

Mag shrugged again. "A few months, but even so, I'd have sensed magic in the water. We both would." A concession to the fact that while her strengths lay in different areas, Clara was just as powerful a witch as her sister—one Mag didn't make all that often, and then, only under extreme duress. Mag's ego was nearly as big as her talent but way more fragile sometimes.

Giving in, Clara nodded to indicate agreement, but the nod was a lie. Something was up if Mag could walk without pain. Something that bore scrutiny because, according to legend and lore, no one had ever successfully reversed the damage caused by a Raythe attack. Then again, no one else had ever survived one for more than a day. If Mag could manage one miracle, Clara figured she should try for the second.

Maybe her sister's hip pain had nothing to do with the Raythe, which would make this reprieve a nice episode, but nothing more. Or, perhaps, there was something to be done for Mag after all. If there was even a slim chance of reversing the damage and putting her sister back to her rightful age, Clara needed to know and explore the possibility. To that end, she decided to visit Gertrude as soon as she had a couple of hours of free time.

"Let it go, Clarie." Had Mag read her mind? "We've better things to do than chase our tails over something that's just a momentary fluke."

"But you'll go to the next class? And use the cream more often? And maybe we could figure out some sort of hot tub situation, or else you could just pop over to the club every day."

Heaving a sigh, Mag agreed. "I'll use the cream, and hanging out in the hot tub is no hardship."

"And take the classes."

Another sigh. "And the classes. Fiona offered some extra attention. I'll take her up on it." If she could get a massage out of the deal, so much the better. Nothing good came without some small sacrifice, at least in Mag's experience, and some of the best things came with larger losses. "Anything that would help me get around better, I would be a fool not to try."

"You've softened up some, you know." Clara meant

to compliment, but Mag took offense and purposefully whipped the wheel as she pulled the bus into their driveway.

"Ouch." Clara's arm jammed against the door, but she sucked harsh words back in. Scolding Mag only made her harder to handle.

Chapter 4

Lydia Wayland's country club ousting still occupied a prime spot in Clara's thoughts the next morning as she and Mag readied Balms and Bygones for the day.

"I knew she and Sam divorced. I didn't realize the split was so contentious. Getting her kicked out of the club was an act of pure spite, and I can't understand how the membership board allowed it."

Shrugging, Mag used a breath of magic to clear the dust off a delicate lampshade. "Amicable splits are like unicorns. You hear people talking about them but hardly ever see one. I can't tell if you're outraged about this loophole in the membership business on Lydia's behalf or because it means you have to keep sucking up to Mayor McCreepy if you don't want to suffer the same fate."

Letting out a long-suffering sigh, Clara kept her tone even. "Mayor *McCreery* sponsored our membership because we were new in town. Why do you have to read more into it than there is?"

Far less diplomatic than her sister, Mag rolled her eyes so hard it hurt. "Getting me in just added extra butter to the sauce. He sponsored *your* membership because he's warm for your form."

Clara's lips snapped into a straight line. "That's a hideous thing to say, and no one uses that term anymore."

"What are you now? The language police?" Seeing a good chance to needle her sister, Mag arched a brow. "He has a hankering for you. Does that work better?"

"No. It's worse."

Mag giggled inwardly and rattled off a list. "Is puppy love better or worse? How about he has the hots for you?"

Literal smoke wafted out Clara's ears, but Mag couldn't stop. Or wouldn't.

"He's head over heels, a smitten kitten, in over his head. He's crushing on you big time."

The more idioms Mag tossed out, the darker Clara's face became.

"You're a child, Mag."

"His idea of a perfect date with you is Netflix and chill. He wants to be friends with benefits. He's—"

"That's it." Tiny lightning sparks had joined the smoke, and Clara had had enough. "Not another word."

But Mag had one more word and wasn't about to waste it. "Thirsty."

"Keep that up, and I really will put something nasty in your liniment," Clara muttered as she turned the closed sign to open. Mag knew she'd gone too far when Clara treated her to icy silence until they closed for lunch.

"There's leftover fried chicken if you're hungry."

"Are you sure you wouldn't rather offer me a helping of fried crow?" Mag's response came with a smile that softened Clara's resolve, but only slightly.

"You wouldn't eat it if I did."

When Mag opened her mouth, Clara held up a hand. "The topic of my love life is off-limits for the rest of the day. Otherwise, go somewhere else and eat lunch."

"At least you have a love life," Mag pointed out.

"And don't try to drum up sympathy from me right now because you don't deserve it."

Contrite, Mag said nothing when pain blazed a fiery trail from her hip to her ankle as she climbed the stairs. She couldn't have spoken in any case because the sharp flare stole her breath. So much for the analgesic effects of a stint in the pool. Or maybe it hurt so badly now because she'd had a brief respite to provide contrast. With enough time and consistency, a person could get used to almost anything.

Given the choice, Mag would love to get used to a much longer respite. Oh, who was she kidding? Given a choice, she'd rather that respite not include a premature death, but it was too late for her now. Being bitter wouldn't change anything, but Mag idled at bitter, so she figured no one would expect better from her.

Preferring hot chicken to cold, Clara chose and infused a drumstick with a touch of magic flame that left it just as crispy and perfect as it had been the first time she drew it from the hot oil. No fire witch worth her wand needed a microwave to reheat leftovers.

Out of habit, Mag drained her tea, leaving the dregs behind, spun the cup six times: three widdershins, three deosil, then flipped it over to let the last of the liquid spill into her saucer.

"Want me to read yours, too?"

Clara shrugged and repeated the sequence, upending the cup with a flick of her wrist. "Might as well."

Mostly, Clara preferred to let the future unfold without knowing too much ahead of time, thereby preserving life's little surprises. But for the past couple of weeks, unease flickered like a ghost haunting the edges of her psyche.

Mag flipped her cup first, and peered into the shallow depths while rotating it slowly. "Crescent moon." She rubbed her chin. "Looks like I've got a change of plans coming up."

"Are you sure?" Clara leaned over and used one finger to tip Mag's cup down so she could see inside. "That looks like a sickle to me."

It had to Mag as well, but since the sickle was a sign of illness, she insisted it was a moon. No sense in getting Clara all riled up over something that couldn't be changed. "It's a moon, and that's the scales."

"Is it? Or is it a bird? A crow, maybe."

"It's not a crow. You used to be better at tasseomancy."

"Well, excuse me if I haven't had as much practice as you. Statues don't drink a lot of tea."

Mag spun her cup one more time, then handed it to Clara. "You've been de-stoned for months now. Time to let it go. If you look at it properly, you'll see it's the scales."

"Unbalanced, just like you, dear sister."

Tilting her head to acknowledge the zinger, Mag reached for Clara's cup. "Let's see what the future holds in store for you. Probably hearts and flowers."

Except Clara's cup had neither.

"Is that a gun?" Rising, Clara rounded the table to peer over Mag's shoulder.

"Danger," Mag agreed. "And it gets worse because that," she pointed to a blob, then turned the cup slightly, "is the wolf."

"What do you think it means?" Clara's fingertips tingled with anxiety.

"I can't say," Mag said. "You told me not to mention your love life, and the wolf can signify jealousy. Put that together with danger, and you've got a ticked-off ex somewhere."

"You know very well there hasn't been anyone serious since Sylvana's father."

Mag chortled. "Never said it had to be your ex, did I? This is what you get for juggling men."

Clara debated using Mag's atomic wedgie spell on her, but since that would set off an afternoon of retaliation, she decided to be the better witch, even if it cost her a bit of self-respect.

"There is no juggling, no jealous ex, and certainly no danger when it comes to my current dating habits."

"Picked yourself a boring man, did you?"

"If anyone is in danger, Margaret Balefire, it is you. Keep poking at me, and we'll see who's the cunning wolf and who's the one under the gun. Let it go."

Mag did. For now, anyway.

Business picked up after lunch, keeping Clara busy exchanging gossip along with lotions, soap, and the like. Mag left one ear open for anything particularly juicy as she cleaned a Rembrandt floor lamp with filigree scroll-work and onyx accents that she planned to sell for a good profit.

"Poor Ned's on the hot seat," Evanora Dupree ran her fingers through the beaded fringe of another vintage lampshade. "From what I heard, Miriam talked three additional equity members into withdrawing, so the club's out some serious bucks, and the board of directors blames Ned."

"How much money are we talking?" This was Harmony, after all, not Portland or Augusta. Or Bangor, even. Mag figured it couldn't be that much.

"Somewhere in the range of half a million. There's a town-wide betting pool on how long before he's fired." Evanora checked the price tag on the lamp while Mag considered raising her prices. If people in the area could afford to pay tens of thousands just to play golf and paddle in a fancy pool, she should be charging more for her wares. "I'll take this lamp and the one you're working on if it's not too dear."

Testing her theory, Mag named a figure five percent above the asking price she'd originally planned, and Evanora didn't even blink. "You want it delivered, that's extra."

"No need. I'll take it with me. Plenty of room in the back of my car."

Since Evanora drove a seventies-era station wagon, she'd spoken the truth. A small family could easily camp out in the back. If that is, they didn't mind sharing the space with a mischief of rats—and yes, that is the technical term for a group of rats. Mag counted six of the wily rodents as she helped Evanora stash the smaller of the two lamps, then went back inside to write up the receipt.

With business out of the way, Mag pulled the conversation back to the recent scandal. "Sounds like Ned picked the wrong dragon in that duel."

Shaking her head hard enough to set soft, brown curls bouncing, Evanora said, "He didn't have a choice. The loophole Sam found was valid, which is why the board didn't let Ned go on the spot. Miriam threatened to do more damage before the week is out, and if he can't stop the mass exodus by tomorrow, he's out of a job anyway."

Clara came up behind Evanora. "Is there any chance he'll be able to do that?"

"I can't see how unless Sam backs down, and that would not be in keeping with his character."

That was probably the nicest way Mag had heard anyone describe Sam Wayland.

"I feel bad for Ned," Clara set a sample of her new face powder on the counter near Evanora.

"I don't." Evanora huffed. "He's an adult, and he made the choice to side with Sam, so he'll have to live with the results." She picked up the powder sample and tested a smear of it across the back of her hand. "From what I've heard, Sam used Lydia's money to buy his way into the upper echelon, and that's what's got her so steamed."

"Can you blame her?" Mag wanted to know.

"No, but in her own way, she's just as stubborn as Sam, and Miriam's been annoyed with the club ever since her niece got suspended for not wearing proper attire on the links."

"What is the deal with the plaid pants and pom-pom hats, anyway?"

Given her habitually odd clothing choices, Mag had no justification for sneering at anyone else's.

"Oh, it wasn't a lack of plaid pants that put Celia in

time-out. It was the lack of pants entirely."

Clara's brows went up. "Oh, I see."

"And so did everyone else who approached the far side of the little pond near the eleventh hole. The whole thing might have been chalked up to youthful indiscretion if she'd been alone. But she wasn't, and since Celia's partner in crime remained a member in good standing, Miriam has been leading her high horse around the track, waiting for a chance to climb up and ride ever since."

"That's a lot of clothing drama," Mag observed.

Evanora's gaze flicked down Mag's body, then back up again. "You'd know all about that, I suppose." She allowed herself a delicate shudder at the memory.

If she'd meant to belittle, she'd chosen the wrong witch because Mag couldn't care less what people thought of her. "If you're going to do a thing, might as well do it right," was all she said as she took Evanora's money.

While Clara helped carry the larger lamp to the car, Mag greeted her next customer by name.

"Ellen. It's nice to see you. Are you buying or selling today?"

"Selling, I hope."

The answer came as no surprise to Mag. Over the past few months, Ellen Corbel had become a regular buyer of Clara's face cream and a seller of old furniture to Mag. On consignment, no less, which wasn't Mag's usual method for acquiring stock, but she'd made an exception in Ellen's case. Something about the woman touched one of the cold spots in Mag's heart.

"I'm glad you came in today. I sold a couple of your

pieces last week."

Delighted, Ellen grinned, her blue eyes lighting up. "Really? Which ones?"

"The hutch went to a couple from Hackinaw, and that little occasional table caught the eye of some out-of-state visitors. I got good prices for both, so I have a nice check for you."

Nearly dropping her purse, Ellen clapped her hands when she saw the amount. "I've been knitting pan-handle cozies and selling them at every craft shop within a fifty-mile radius. They're moving quite well for some reason. Between that and the things you've sold for me here, I'm really close to having enough for my dream vacation at Graceland. One more check like this will put me over the top, and a few more batches of cozies will give me some extra spending money."

Leaning close, Ellen whispered, "I'm planning to go in style. Flying first class, staying in the biggest suite at the guest house, and booking the VIP tour."

"That sounds like fun," Mag had no interest in Elvis, but she liked Ellen well enough to be mildly enthusiastic, which was as enthusiastic as Mag usually got. "But why are we whispering?"

"I'm spending my entire life savings on this trip," Ellen replied, still whispering.

Still not seeing the reason for secrecy, Mag shrugged. "Then let's make it a good one. What have you got for me this time?"

"I have a box of carnival glass that should bring in a few dollars." Ellen pulled out two photographs. "And then, there's this Victorian Davenport writing desk. The baize is a little worn in spots, but the joints are tight. It's in good condition except for missing the trim around the lock on the top drawer, and one of the pulls keeps loosening up."

Mag picked up the photo for a closer look. "It's a fine piece. I'd price it at around $550 and let them talk me down some, but I wouldn't take less than $425."

"That sounds perfect. What about this?" The second photo had drool pooling in Mag's mouth. "This one is a lady's desk that belonged to my great aunt Tessie. It's Victorian as well, I think."

Nodding, Mag handed the photo back. "The essence of the era. Eastlake. Walnut with cutout trim in excellent condition. It's worth close to three grand. I have a potential client that will probably buy it based on this photograph alone. Are you sure you want to let it go? That's a family heirloom. It should be passed down."

"Who would I pass it down to? The only family I have left is my cousin, Beryl, and a nephew with modern tastes who thinks I'm an anachronism. He's pleasant enough when he comes around, but he'd die before owning anything with age or history to it, and no one has seen Beryl since she ran off with a married man in 1983. For all I know, she's been dead for years. The desk is mine to do as I please, and I'm happy to let it go. You see, this trip is the final item on my bucket list."

"Bucket list?" Mag was unfamiliar with the term.

"Things I want to do before I die," Ellen explained. "You should make one. Goals give life purpose and meaning."

"Or stress and heart disease."

Ellen chuckled. "I suppose that could be true if you're one of those driven types. For me, it's the promise of doing something I've always wanted to do. Some of the items on my list didn't work out like I expected, and that's part of it, too."

Intrigued, Mag wondered what she'd put on her bucket list should it not be too late to make one.

"Speaking of failed attempts, I have a dulcimer you could sell. Seems my ability to learn to play wasn't in line with my desire to do so. I've heard catfights with more musical value."

Mag grinned and admitted, "For me, it was the flute. I had all the desire in the world to play and none of the talent." That flute, Mag remembered, now rested at the heart of an oak tree in the woods near her childhood home. She'd banished it there in a fit of pique after two days of tuneless bleating failed to enchant her senses. Maybe things would have been different if she'd bothered to take a lesson.

"My one neighbor says I'm wasting my time making all these plans. She thinks I should just sit back and wait to die. Don't travel, and don't have new experiences. It's sad, really."

A kindred spirit, Mag thought, as she'd heard similar sentiments a time or two.

Ellen continued, "There's nothing wrong with her, but she only leaves her house twice a month to grocery shop, and that's it. Meanwhile, my other neighbor has medical issues bad enough she uses an electric wheelchair to get around, but she doesn't let that bring her down. Not one bit. It really makes you think about what life should be like."

"I guess I'll have to think about making one of those bucket lists," Mag reached beneath the counter, came up with a sample of Clara's newest hand cream, and handed it over.

"Don't wait too long," Ellen advised. "And don't censor yourself. No dream is too big to go on a bucket list."

Mag thought hers might be, and she'd already waited too long.

Chapter 5

Red and green script scrawled across her pristine white apron announced that Gertrude was Santa's favorite ho. Clara shoved a brightly decorated cookie in her mouth to keep from commenting and followed that up with a cup of hot cocoa. Better to burn her tongue than bite it off.

When Gertrude finally whipped off the apron and sat, Clara had to take a moment to remember why she'd braved the house of all things Christmas.

"Gertrude, do you really think there's magic in the pool water at the country club?"

Confronted with the oddly abrupt question, Gertrude's face remained passive, making it difficult to gauge her thoughts. "Your sister seemed to benefit from that one dip, and I must confess to feeling a bit more spring in my step after class these past few weeks."

"I can't say I noticed anything out of the ordinary."

"Well, you wouldn't, would you? I've got a century or two on you, don't I?"

Did a soupçon of bitterness slip in there? Had she flapped the unflappable Christmas witch? Clara thought maybe she had. To smooth ruffled feathers, she conceded, "If you sensed anything in that water, you've got a better nose than I do. I never suspected a thing."

Mollified, Gertrude admitted, "I've never had so dramatic a sense of relief as Mag did, but then, I'm in remarkably good shape for my age. I only get the occasional pang or two where Margaret seems to be plagued with discomfort. She should add more hot chocolate to her diet. It has remarkable soothing properties, and adding a dash of cinnamon to the brew can evoke enough Christmas spirit to heal the heavy heart." An index card fluttered out of thin air and landed near Clara's hand. "That's my recipe."

"Thank you," Clara tucked it away. "Mag likes chocolate almost as much as ice cream."

"Happy to help." Gertrude offered her in-depth opinion on which varieties of cinnamon were best for all-around healing.

Clara only tuned back in when she heard Gertrude mention Sam Wayland.

"I'm sorry, my attention wandered. Did you say he's filed an injunction against you?"

"He thinks there should be limits on the number of lights in my holiday display." Every day was Christmas at Gertrude's house, but her yard could be seen from space from Thanksgiving through the first week of January. Okay, maybe not space, but from planes flying overhead. "Didn't quite pan out as he expected."

"How so?"

Gertrude waggled her fingers and allowed a crafty smile to alter the lines of her cheerful face. "Let's just say no one can resist my cookies when the magic of Christmas spirit is baked right in. The joy of the season makes people malleable. If you know what I mean. Plus,

I don't use the grid to power my display, so his statement on the economic impact of twinkle lights fell flat when I introduced my electric bill for last year as evidence."

"He didn't file on his own, right? One of your neighbors must have hired him."

"Pfft." Gertrude waved away the notion. "My neighbors are used to me by now, and I try to be courteous. The lights go off at ten, the music, too, and I'm generous with cookies and treats to pave the way. It's a family tradition. My grandmother lived in a gingerbread house, you know. She was a fantastic baker but an even better candy maker."

Despite all efforts to school her features, Clara felt her eyebrow cock. "Oh, really?"

"Yes, really." Gertrude huffed and rolled her eyes. "And yes, *that* house. And no, she did not cook children and eat them. Those Grimm boys should have been sued for slander."

Clara allowed a small smile. "I'm sure Sam would have been happy to defend them."

"He wasn't always such a CR, you know."

Her brow furrowed, Clara tried to think what CR might mean, and when she couldn't, she finally broke down and asked.

"Coal recipient."

"Naturally."

"It's a technical term."

Biting her lip, Clara nodded. "I see. It's a naughty list thing."

Gertrude nodded. "Anyway, Sam used to be a sweet and helpful man who cared about his community. When the bank made a mistake and tried to take Stanley Corson's farm, Sam stepped in and straightened the whole mess out. Wouldn't take a dime in payment, either."

"That was nice of him." And it didn't add up to Clara's impressions of the man at all. "I wonder what happened to change him. Do you think it had anything to do with Lydia?"

But Gertrude had anticipated the question and was shaking her head. "No. They were just the cutest, most loving couple at the time. You ask me, it had to do with his former law partner. Claudia Scanlon."

That was a name Clara hadn't heard before. "I don't think I've met her."

"Oh, you wouldn't. She left before you moved to Harmony. Right before, so that would be just over a year ago. Good riddance, I say."

"I take it the festivities are still on, then?"

Winking, Gertrude said, "Christmas is what I do, and Scrooge McGrinchypants has another little surprise coming. The coal in his stocking, if you will."

Interested, Clara leaned forward and selected another cookie from the plate while waiting for the explanation.

"This whole business of getting Lydia kicked out of the country club didn't sit well with me, so I made a call and accepted a position on the membership committee. Sam's membership is up for renewal soon. I'm not sure he's country club material. What do you think?"

Clara and Gertrude shared a look and then burst out laughing. "I think he'll never see you coming."

"Most people don't," Gertrude allowed something darker to show through her usual cheerful expression.

"They see what I want them to see."

She grinned, and the moment passed, but Clara would remember it for a long time to come.

Clara wouldn't call the desire to return to the country club pool a craving so much as a niggling annoyance she couldn't shake. Maybe Gertrude had been right when she said she felt something besides pool chemicals there, something magical. Not fountain of youth level of magic, but after seeing Mag's improvement, it was impossible to deny the water carried healing properties. An hour steeped in the crystal water had given her sister two days without pain. Two days where she said she felt twenty years younger, and for Mag, that was a miracle. One that had nothing to do with lunges and squats.

So what if the club was already closed for the night? No one had to know she was there. She didn't plan to hurt anyone, only to grab a sample of the water for testing purposes.

"Abscondius invisibilius." Activating the charm in her pocket, Clara ensured no one would see her, including any video surveillance the club might have in the pool area. With her destination pictured clearly, she shifted to the side of the pool.

Outside, in front of her cozy fire, Mag rocked and tried to ignore the siren call of hot, pulsating jets. Alone, Clara's cream took off the brunt of the pain, but it really needed the warm water to finish her off right. And why shouldn't she indulge herself? Mag wondered. What would it hurt to skim over for a quick dip?

The decision made, and because Clara wouldn't be there to get the full scandal effect, Mag chose a modest suit this time and then magicked herself directly into the soothing waters.

What Mag hadn't counted on was the lights being turned off. She couldn't get her bearings for a moment as she bobbed and floundered in the darkness, waiting for her eyes to adjust. After a few seconds of panic, Mag called herself three kinds of a fool as she cast a protective dome over the entire pool and conjured a ball of witch-light.

"That's better," she said as she spun the flaming ball in her hand and then dropped it into the water. The light turned blue, giving off a spa-like effect that made Mag smile. Happy, she conjured the unicorn pillow she'd blown up and left on her bed and was just settling herself in for a long soak when she noticed a shape standing frozen near the pool's edge.

Without thinking, Mag shot a jolt of magic at whoever had dared break into the country club.

Also without thinking, Clara deflected the attack, sent it wheeling back the way it had come, then yelled out, "It's me, you idiot." Hand on her hips, she strode toward the hot tub end of the pool and stared down at her sister. "What were you thinking? You know most of the staff are non-magical. Do you have any idea how much hot water we'd be in if you zapped one of them? And what was that, anyway?"

Since hot water had been Mag's goal, she ignored the rebuke.

"Untwist your panties. It was only a momentary binding spell. What are you doing here? Come to horn in on my fun?"

"No." Clara slipped the vial of water into her pocket and lied her butt off. "I left something in my locker. I thought I'd pop in, and no one would know."

"How's that working out for you?"

Clapping her hands on her hips, Clara stared down at her sister. "You know, you can be a jerk sometimes, and it's not like you have permission to be here, either."

Mag's chin went up. "I go where I want. No one will ever know, and it helps my hip."

Just then, the sound of footsteps echoed through the pool area. Mag and Clara exchanged a panicked look before Mag pulled Clara under her dome of invisibility.

"What was that?" Ned, the security guard, asked as he rounded the corner. He looked around the empty pool but didn't see anyone. "Must have been my imagination," he mumbled before returning to his desk.

Mag and Clara waited until they were sure Ned was gone before allowing themselves to relax.

Mag shook her head in amazement. "That was close!" She allowed a relieved sigh as she began calling balls of witchlight back to her hand. "We should get out of here before someone else shows up. Did you drive here?"

"No, I didn't drive here." Exasperation colored Clara's voice. "I didn't want anyone to see the van parked outside. It does stand out."

Chapter 6

Halfway through a nice breakfast of mixed fruit and oatmeal, Clara's toaster rang.

"What the hell?" She said out loud.

"Is that you, Clara?" A voice screeched out of the thing. "I hate phones. Can't never tell who's on the other end."

"Hagatha?" Since Clara's stomach had dropped into her shoes, breakfast was effectively over. "Is that you? Why are you calling me at home? On my toaster." A hundred possibilities swam through Clara's head, each more dire than before.

"I don't know about no toasters, but how soon can you get here? I need a ride."

It was almost time to open the shop, but Hagatha wouldn't care, and whatever she was up to would be worse without supervision, so Clara gave in and arranged to pick the old witch up at her house in fifteen minutes.

"Maggie," Clara marched through her sister's front door without bothering to knock and caught Mag watching TV. "I've got Hagatha duty. Can you open without me today? Jinx will help, or I can call Pyewacket back from Port Harbor."

How a firecracker of a witch like Margaret Balefire ended up with the laziest familiar to ever grow whiskers was a mystery to Clara. Vague as it was, the allegation hovered in the air and flipped Mag's switch.

"As if I need help flipping the sign from closed to open. Or is it that you think I'm incapable of turning the key? Go deal with Hagatha. I'll handle the stupid shop. What does the old bat need now?"

Mag was not a morning person. Then again, Mag wasn't much of an evening person, either.

"I have no idea. I also have no idea how a witch who recently whipped up a hologram using a blend of magic and current technology can't tell the difference between a phone and a toaster. These are among the many mysteries of Hagatha."

While she spoke, Clara watched Mag's television play a scene that gave her chills.

"Hey. Is that you?" Hagatha, forgotten for the moment, Clara crossed the room to get a closer look. "It is you. What's this?"

"It's nothing." Mag stomped over and jabbed the stop button on the ancient VHS player. The screen went blank. "Just let it go. I'll open the shop. You deal with Hagatha the Horrible, and we'll call that a fair trade." If her entire attitude hadn't undergone a forced change, Clara might have let the incident go.

As it was, she debated and then, with time slipping past, decided she didn't have time to spend arguing with her sister. But she made a mental note to review that VHS tape the next time she got a chance. Getting Mag out of the house alone shouldn't be too difficult.

"I'll be back as soon as I can."

"Have fun." With false cheer, Mag waved her sister away and, when the door slammed behind Clara, said, "Dodged that bullet. Come on, Jinx. You can keep me company."

White as the driven snow and fluffy as a downy duckling, Mag's familiar stared balefully at her for a full minute before slinking down off the crocheted doily pinned to the back of the overstuffed sofa. He took three steps, stretched, then morphed into a man most would never suspect spent the other half of his life as a handsome feline.

While Mag opened the shop, Clara ignored the posted speed limit on her way to find out what trouble Hagatha might be brewing. With Hagatha, ignorance was never bliss.

Sporting more wrinkles than a box of raisins, Hagatha Crow leaned on her tennis ball-footed walker at the foot of the front steps as Clara pulled in. The van had barely rocked to a stop when she magicked herself inside, her walker folded neatly behind the seat.

"I don't want to hear a word about using magic in public. I'm too damned old to climb up into this monstrosity without help and too damned ornery to ask for any. Take me to Sam Wayland's office." Whipping the seat belt into place, Hagatha crossed her arms and waited for her order to be followed. "Corner of Pleasant and Mason."

"Balefire taxi. At your service," Clara muttered and backed into the turnaround. "What do you want with Sam Wayland, if you don't mind me asking?" With Hagatha, you could never tell. Her mood could whipsaw from indulgent to annoyed at roughly the same speed a bumblebee fluttered its wings.

"I'm suing the Moonstones."

Clara nearly choked. "You can't be serious."

"As a heart attack," Hagatha cackled, the sound raising the hairs on Clara's neck.

"Those women are your coven. You can't drag Moonstone politics into open court. We'll all be branded as witches."

Which was, of course, what Hagatha wanted. Harmony's coven operated under the guise of a women's organization that allowed the witches to blend civic-minded activities with their practice while keeping the magic side of things a secret. As advancing age eroded Hagatha's filters—which Clara wasn't sure had been very filtery, to begin with—she'd decided she no longer wished to participate in the secrecy element of things. And what was good for Hagatha was good for all, so in her estimation, it was time for the coven to come out of the broom closet and wear their pointy hats with pride.

None of the other witches agreed, leaving Hagatha, as coven leader, with the power to make her desire a reality, but not the backing. What the coven needed, they had decided, was a distraction. Or a scapegoat. Enter Mag and Clara Balefire, the perfect combination of both.

Based on the Balefire name and the history that went along with it, the witches of Harmony had offered Mag and Clara the opportunity to take over the coven in a joint leadership role. What they didn't do, because none of them had the guts, was tell Hagatha she was out.

Instead of taking leadership of the coven, the Balefire sisters had ended up babysitters for an ancient witch with a grudge against her neighbors and the ability to make magical trouble on an epic scale.

Welcome to Harmony. Come on in. Put your feet up and sit awhile. Clara rolled her eyes.

"What do you hope to prove by dragging the Moonstones into court?"

Hagatha's smile chilled Clara's bones. "Not a damned thing. I'm bored. The sheep don't want me casting spells. Well, this seemed like a fun thing to do without using any magic. Let those uptight witches put that in their cauldrons and stew it."

Nothing Clara said could dissuade Hagatha, and as these things went, a frivolous lawsuit rated around 4.5 on the Hagatha Chaos Scale. It could be flying pigs again, and nothing could beat the honey pixie scandal, so there were definitely worse things Hagatha could do. Besides, any attorney worth their salt wouldn't take the case, right?

Wrong.

"Welcome, ladies." Up close, Sam Wayland was even smarmier than he'd seemed at the club. His smile didn't get within an inch of his eyes, which gleamed like a feral cat's, and if that wasn't a hint of makeup she detected on his cheekbones, she'd eat a twig out of her favorite boom. "What can I help you with?"

He focused his attention on Clara, and she didn't miss when he flicked a look toward her cleavage. It wasn't her nature to hex a man even if he'd earned it, but she did indulge in the fantasy of giving him a donkey's head. If he wanted to act like an ass, he ought to look like one, too. Rising, he reached across the desk and offered a too-long handshake that tempted Clara to wipe her hands on her pants when it ended.

"Nothing for me, thanks." Clara jerked a thumb in Hagatha's direction. "Hagatha's the one with the appointment. I'm just the driver. She made me come in here." Burned Clara's butt to admit it.

"Nice to meet you, Agatha. Are we doing a will today, then? If so, it looks like you've left it a bit late."

Choking back a snort, Clara fully expected him to sprout that donkey head and, depending on Hagatha's current mood, a tail to match. But she'd underestimated old Haggie's determination to get the job done because the old witch let the insult slide right past.

"It's Hagatha, and I don't need a will. I want to sue the Moonstones."

Wayland frowned. "For what? Did you get sick at a bake sale? I'm not sure I can help you with that type of thing. You'd want someone who specializes in smaller claims. I know someone good with personal injury."

"It's nothing to do with getting sick, Mr. High and Mighty."

Looking at Hagatha, one might not think Sam Wayland's ice was thin under his feet, and the water would not only be cold but full of things that could eat a man whole. One brow cocked, he leaned back in his chair, steepled his fingers to look important, and invited her to tell him what she wanted.

"What would you say if I told you the Moonstones are a bunch of witches and I was their leader, but they fired me for no good reason?" She folded her arms and waited for him to speak.

He didn't wait long before giving her the satisfaction. "I'd say you need to tell me more, but it sounds like we have ourselves a wrongful termination case.”

“You realize this is a civic organization we’re talking about, not some billion-dollar corporation with money to burn.” Clara couldn’t help pointing out the reality, but Wayland’s eyes already glittered with greed and Hagatha’s with revenge. He shrugged and dismissed Clara’s outrage. “And Hagatha is not only still listed as the organization’s leader, but takes an active role.” *Too* active most of the time.

“In name only,” Hagatha argued. “As you should well know.” Turning to Wayland, she said, “This is one of the women asked to come in and take my place. You shouldn’t listen to her. She’s in on it with them.”

“I’ll just leave you two to discuss this,” Clara said, leaving the room. Surely, once Hagatha clarified the financial situation, he would tell her the case wouldn’t be worth pursuing.

Ten minutes of listening through the door—no magical assist needed because Hagatha’s voice tended to carry—proved that theory wrong. Sam Wayland was just as slimy as he could be. It took nothing more than her assurance the Moonstones were sitting on some money to get him to agree to represent Hagatha in a wrongful termination suit.

“During your time with the Moonstones, did you invent or create anything the organization continues to use? We could tack on a suit for intellectual property rights.”

Clara pictured Hagatha bouncing in her seat and clapping her hands over meeting the perfect partner for causing more trouble.

“I’m sure I did. Might take me a minute to come up

with the details."

"Were you ever injured during, or as a result of, participation in organizational events? A personal injury case would hit them where it hurts."

It went on in that vein until Clara could listen no more and returned to the van to wait in the cold. Surely the county judge would throw this mess out of court as soon as Wayland filed, but maybe not. Hagatha seemed pretty pleased with herself when she'd finished her meeting and busted out in merry cackles several times on the way home.

"You don't want to do this, Hagatha. It won't help anything. There must be another way to stir up trouble." What was she saying? At least now she knew what Hagatha had planned. Turn the old witch loose, and who knew what she might come up with. "At least wait until after Yule. No sense in ruining the holiday season."

Gertrude Granger's wildly inventive holiday extravaganza drew families from near and far with the promise of enchanting light displays, freshly baked cookies, and gallons of hot chocolate loaded with oodles of marshmallows. A good many seekers of holiday fun ended up browsing through Mag and Clara's shop, so they'd be busy enough without the next best thing to a chaos demon on the loose.

"Better yet, wait until after Imbolc. February's the worst month in a Maine winter. Save this lawsuit thing for when you're really bored."

Hagatha just laughed and shook her head. "Oh, Clara, you have so much to learn about being a witch. Time is of the essence, my dear. If I waited even a month, it would be too late." Her eyes twinkled as she smiled mischievously.

"Too late for what?" Clara asked, feeling a chill run through her veins despite the room being comfortably warm.

"Ah ah ah," Hagatha said, wagging her finger at Clara. "That would be telling, wouldn't it?" She paused for a moment, looking off into the distance before continuing. "Trouble's coming. I can smell it. A man can only push people so far before they get tired of it and of him. SamWayland is a nasty piece of work, and it's only a matter of time before his actions come back to bite him." She trailed off ominously, leaving Clara to imagine what kind of dark fate might await Sam and what dark deeds he'd done to deserve it.

"So why do you want to hire him?" she asked warily. "If he's dirty, I mean."

"Why wouldn't I?" Hagatha looked genuinely confused. "He's nothing but a tool."

Clara nearly snorted because Hagatha might not understand this generation's insults, but she'd hit that one dead on. "I won't argue the point, but that's not a reason to cause trouble among your sisters in magic."

"They'll get no more trouble than they deserve."

Just what Clara was afraid of.

Chapter 7

"Mag!" Annoyed with her sister's habitual dawdling, Clara swung Mag's front door open and called out. "Aren't you ready yet? We were supposed to leave ten minutes ago."

When Mag failed to answer, Clara's mood worsened. "I'm tired of being late to everything," she muttered as she strode across the room and shoved Mag's bedroom door open. "You'd better be wearing something that doesn't look like it came out of the rag bag."

Worry didn't start to penetrate until Clara saw Mag sprawled across the bed, her breath wheezing in and out, sounding like faulty bellows.

"What's wrong?" Annoyance winked out like a star at dawn as Clara raced to her sister's side. "What happened?"

"It's nothing. I'll be fine in a minute." Mag tried to cover, but Clara wasn't having it.

"Nothing doesn't make you look like you've aged ten years since we closed for the day. It's something, and I want to know what."

The pain beginning to pass, Mag shifted her weight and struggled to a seated position on the side of the bed. "I'm just having one of my spells. I'm old, which shouldn't be front-page news. Give me a minute, and I'll be ready to go."

Pain made Mag surly, but there was more to it than that. She hated being the focus of anyone's sympathy. It might be time, she thought, to take herself off to some remote location where she could die in peace.

"Margaret Balefire, I swear to Hecate, if you don't tell me what's happening to you, I'll…get Hagatha to check you out." Clara tossed out the worst thing she could think of. Or, considering how Mag looked, maybe not. The oldest witch in living history, Hagatha Crow, had forgotten more magic than most witches learned in a lifetime.

"There's nothing she can do."

"I doubt that very much." Now that she'd thought of it, Clara decided calling on Hagatha was the best idea she'd had in a while. Probably the scariest, too. "If there's a spell or a potion or the spit of some obscure magical creature that will fix you right up, Hagatha will know about it."

Frustration lent strength enough to pull Mag to her feet. "She won't. Don't you understand? She can't. The only chance I might have had is gone. I burned the Raythe who tried to kill me. Do you see? Burned it and danced on the ashes. Without the 'hair of the dog,' I'm doomed to an early death. Let it go, or you can run along to the coven meeting by yourself and let me stay home to wallow in my mortality."

"The hell I will." It was all Clara could do to keep from crying, but Mag wouldn't respect tears shed on her behalf, so Clara let the fire of conviction burn them off. She'd save her sister if she had to pull a miracle out of her butt, and if that meant putting faith in Hagatha Crow, then that is what Clara would do. Maybe not blind faith, mind you because Hagatha created unrest as easily as a Balefire witch could conjure flame.

"Are you able to walk?"

Rising, Mag puffed up. "Of course, I can walk. It was just one of my spells, and now, it's over. I'll go to the meeting. You'll shut up about my health, got it?" She'd take a detour to the country club pool on the way home, too. Get herself set up for a pain-free night.

To that end, she suggested since they were late anyway, it might be best to take the direct route to the community center. As decisions went, this was one of her best. The sisters arrived just in time to hear someone knock on the front door.

"Who could that be?" Gertrude glanced around the room to check for absent coven members and saw that all were present and accounted for. "None of us bother to knock."

Because she was closest, Penelope opened the door a crack, peered out, then threw it wide open.

"Officer McCue. I didn't expect to see you here tonight. What can the Moonstones do for you?" Maybe he was looking for a donation to some police officer's fund. That hope broke into shards on the floor when Sam Wayland stepped into view.

Clara already knew what to expect, but Penelope had no clue what was coming as she stood between the policeman and the coven of witches. Even so, the sight of the attorney known for being a shark turned her breath shallow and set her heart fluttering with agitation.

From her seat in the far corner of the room, Hagatha

cackled and rubbed her hands together with glee. Sam Wayland had moved fast. So fast news of her wrath and her plans to seek revenge on those who wronged her hadn't had time to spread to the coven. They were all blindsided, and Hagatha couldn't be happier.

The Moonstones had been her sanctuary and refuge, where she could find acceptance and understanding. But now, with Penelope forcing her ideals on the coven, Hagatha wanted to tear it all apart.

The policeman's voice cut through the silence, his stern words starkly contrasting the abruptly silenced chatter that had preceded him. "Penelope Snow and the Moonstones?"

"You know very well who I am and what we are."

"You've been served."

Penelope slid the paperwork from the manila envelope, her jaw dropping as she read. "It's from Hagatha Crow. She's suing me and the rest of the Moonstones for throwing her out of the organization."

Her former agitation abruptly shifting to simmering anger, Penelope pointed toward Hagatha. "Given that she's in attendance at this meeting, I'd say your lawsuit has no merit." This she said for Sam's benefit alone.

"The suit," Sam looked down his nose at Penelope, "is for wrongful termination. At one point, Ms. Crow was in charge of the Moonstones, was she not?"

Clara looked around the circle of witches, their faces set in grim determination. She nudged Mag with an elbow, and the sisters stepped back into the shadows as one. Every witch in the room, Hagatha included, knew the Balefires had been invited to replace her, but that hadn't worked out the way anyone had planned.

"Why would you do this?" one of the witches glared at Hagatha. "The Moonstones haven't done anything to you. You're still here, and you're still our leader."

"In name only," Hagatha crossed her bony arms over her chest and used her chin to point toward Penelope. "She's the one calling the shots these days, and I'm not the only one suffering for it." Glancing around, her gaze finally targeted the Balefire sisters. "You two should tack onto the suit since they asked you here under false pretenses."

So much for hiding in the shadows, Mag thought as she shook her head and schooled her features to keep from revealing her thoughts. Hagatha had a point, even if going outside the magical community wasn't the best way to make it.

"That's not what happened," Penelope insisted, but without heat, because it certainly had been her plan, as every witch in the room was well aware. "I would never go behind your back," she said directly to Hagatha.

The others murmured in agreement, a feeling of strength building within the group at their show of solidarity. Penelope straightened her back, her apprehension stupidly replaced by a sense of determination. They would fight this battle against Hagatha Crow, and they would win because her sisters would stand with her.

That delusion held up exactly as long as it took for Hagatha to catch Penelope's eye and give the younger witch a wink. Against the strength of a witch with countless centuries under her belt, Penelope—even with the coven behind her—couldn't hope to compete in magical warfare. It would be stupid to try.

The policeman held up his hand for silence, his face stern but sympathetic. "You ladies will have to work your personal stuff out on your own. My work here is done." He flicked an annoyed glance at Sam before turning and walking away.

Penelope nodded slowly as she handed the papers to one of her minions. Hagatha had just declared open war on the Moonstones, and anyone who thought this was the worst it could get wasn't paying attention. With Hagatha, there was always more.

Following the officer out, Sam Wayland had one final insult to offer.

"Enjoy your meeting, ladies. It will be your last before I take the Moonstones apart piece by piece."

Her mind already spinning with plans for how they would fight back against Hagatha Crow's malicious plot, Mag flicked a finger and had the satisfaction of seeing Wayland's face change. He began to fidget.

"What did you do?" Clara's eagle eye caught the satisfied expression on her sister's face.

"Nothing much," Mag couldn't hold back a chuckle. "Just a dash of itching powder in his socks and maybe a tiny tightening spell on his boxers."

Clara shook her head slowly. "You know we're not supposed to use our craft to cause pain and suffering."

Not repentant in the least, Mag replied, "He started it."

"Hagatha started it."

Mag shrugged. What goes around comes around, and she had no problem being Karma's finger.

Speaking of the old witch, she'd risen from her seat in the corner to direct her walker toward the door. On the way past, she offered the Balefire witches a merry wink and let Sam Wayland walk her out.

"There's no way she can win!" shouted one of the coven, her eyes blazing. "We didn't kick her out of the Moonstones no matter what she says."

"That may be true," another coven member replied, "but Sam Wayland never takes a case unless he's sure he can win. He's got something else up his sleeve, or else Hagatha does."

The Moonstones exchanged worried glances. This was not a battle they could win with magic alone.

"Anyone know a good attorney?" Clara asked.

"We don't need a good attorney. We need a bad one. Someone just as sleazy as Sam Wayland. We'll have to fight fire with fire."

"Leave me out of it." Shuddering, Evanora held up both hands. "I can't stand to see us pitted against each other this way." Unshed tears glittered in her eyes. "I just can't do this." With a final shake of her head, Evanora winked away from the meeting house.

Mag snorted. "Thanks for all your help, Evanora." The sneer fell off her face when half the coven turned toward where the Balefire sisters stood. "What?"

"This is all your fault," Penelope pointed a finger toward Mag. "You're supposed to be keeping an eye on her. How could you let something like this happen? I hold you liable for everything that's happened. Maybe it's time you old witches took a step back and let us young ones be in charge."

Bedlam erupted with angry voices raised as witches took sides for or against the Balefires, the angry buzz of conversation vibrating the air. Darkly seductive, the voice of temptation drew Mag to the edge of her control. She didn't cast the spell that rose to her lips, a fact for which Penelope should thank her lucky stars, but it was a near thing.

"You're liable to lose that finger if you keep aiming it in my sister's direction." Before Mag could utter a sound, Clara drew herself to full height, which put her a solid six inches over Penelope's head.

Blanching, Penelope tucked her hand, including the offending finger, into her pocket where she hoped it would remain safe. "I only meant—"

"I know exactly what you meant." Clara took a step closer to the younger witch. "And as much as I relish the thought of teaching you some respect, we don't have time for this."

"There's no we here. There's only you. You and your sister need to fix this, or you're out."

Mag didn't cast the spell. Neither did Clara, but when they discussed the matter later, both agreed it had probably been Gertrude who turned Penelope into a fat, slimy toad. The spell only lasted a moment—a very satisfying moment if you asked Mag, and then Penelope was back to her pinch-faced self.

"That's enough, now." Mabel Youngblood put herself in the middle, just daring anyone to toss a spell in her direction. "We won't solve anything fighting amongst ourselves." Turning, she gave Penelope a level look. "You want to square off against Mag Balefire? I'll draw the dueling circle right here, right now."

If Penelope's face went any whiter, she'd turn invisible. "No. I don't. I never said—"

"Just as I thought." Mabel left her gaze locked on

Penelope's face until the younger witch looked away. "I don't know about the rest of you, but I've had all the drama I need for one night. Shall we reconvene on Wednesday?"

"You do what you want," Mag let her gaze travel the room, meeting every eye in turn. "I won't be here on Wednesday." She let her parting words hang behind her as she skimmed home.

"The same goes for me," Clara said, and followed suit.

Chapter 8

A quick dip couldn't hurt.

Oh, Mag wondered, who was she kidding? Not that there was anyone around to fall for the quick dip line. She'd pop in, do a slow lap or two, then spend an hour in the hot tub letting the jets work their magic. If she didn't, she wouldn't sleep. Not even if she slathered on an entire pot of Clara's liniment and sacrificed a virgin under the full moon. Mag would not, of course, sacrifice a virgin. She wasn't a demon. Nor would she trade her soul to one for a little pain relief.

But she had no such compunction over breaking into the country club...if you could even call it breaking in. She considered it more like appropriating pool time outside the given business hours. Nothing would get broken, no one would be hurt, and she would leave the place exactly as she'd found it. Any other twinges of conscience she buried under the intention of doing a good deed to make up for her transgression. There was that pothole in the parking lot. A little dirt and some fire to melt and spread the pavement out over it, and she'd save the club hundreds. It seemed a fair trade to her.

Get in, get out, go home, and get some sleep. That was the plan as she used a hint of magic to change from nightgown to bathing suit. Getting dressed the normal way had become too difficult over the past couple of weeks. Her joints weren't cooperating the way they used to.

Nothing was.

With the routine down pat, Mag cast a concealing spell over herself, then skimmed from her bedroom to a seated position on the steps at the shallow end of the pool. She slapped up her dome of protection, sending one ball of witchlight to the dome's apex, another into the pool, and a third into the hot tub. For fun, she tuned them to pulse through a rainbow of colors and slid into the waist-deep water.

Lifting her feet off the bottom, Mag flipped over to her back and simply floated near the ledge dividing the pool and the hot tub. The water cushioned and supported her, and suddenly Mag could breathe again. She sighed with relief and let her thoughts drift until the craving for heat drove her out of the pool.

She shivered once, then sank to her chin before sliding over to her favorite set of jets, which happened to be near the control panel. As soon as she thumbed the button, bubbles frothed and swirled. Pain slid away from her joints, leaving only a pleasant lethargy as the heat soaked into her muscles and the jets pounded against tender skin. With no need to expend energy to stay afloat, Mag let her head fall back and closed her eyes.

Finally relaxed enough that pain wasn't occupying all of her senses, Mag realized something felt off. Weird. Strange. Bad.

A pall hung over the pool and played across her nerves as if they were harp strings.

Her heartbeat kicked up a notch as her instincts began to scream that something was terribly wrong, and it had nothing to do with her illicit pool activity. Mag sidled over to the stairs, mounted them, and from that elevated vantage point, saw her instincts hadn't lied. If she'd popped in facing the other way, she'd have seen him immediately.

A man's body bobbed in the gentle wake near the filter at the pool's deep end. One she thought she recognized even from the back. If Mag wasn't mistaken, the country club had just escaped a lawsuit, and so had the Moonstones.

Now, Mag faced a dilemma. Should she admit to breaking and entering—or at least entering since she hadn't broken anything—and report her grisly find, or should she just go home and let things take their natural course? The latter was the more tempting. Instead, she settled on a third option and went home for a second opinion.

"Come with me," Mag refreshed her concealing spell to include her sister, grabbed Clara's arm, ignored the beginning of her protest, and skimmed them both to the scene of the crime.

"Holy Hecate, Mag. Did you do that?"

Furious, Mag spit, "No, I didn't do that. What is wrong with you?"

"Nothing. Just questioning your judgment recently."

"Let it go, Clara. It was a bathing suit, not a total makeover. Just let it go."

Clara sucked in a breath, let it out through her nose, then looked at Mag. "Okay, let's see if we can figure out who that is, and then we'll have to decide what to do about it.”

“I already know, and if you took a minute to look things over instead of giving me crap, you’d recognize Sam Wayland when you see him dead in a pool.”

“And do you already know the cause of death?”

Mag shot her sister a narrow-eyed look as she grabbed the rail and gingerly stepped into the water. “Let’s find out, shall we?”

“Stop. You’ll contaminate the scene.”

“Not by myself, I won’t. Get in here and help me.”

“I’m fully clothed, Mag. Why didn’t you just call the cops or set off the security alarm so someone would come? There’s no reason for us to be bobbing for dead guys in bloody pool water.”

Mag shot Clara the bird.

“Lovely,” Clara stayed on the side of the pool while Mag cast another spell on herself.

“Nondisturbitus,” she rested her palms over the surface and sent her magic through the water. “Are you happy now? I could tap dance on his head and not leave a mark. No one will ever know we were here, but I will find out what killed him.”

So much for *get in, get out, get some sleep.*

“You can argue all you want,” Mag gently bobbed in the water as she looked up at her sister. “But we both know there’s a mystery here, and we both know you’ll end up helping me solve it, so why don’t you just get on with it and save all the carping for later?”

Hands shooting up to land on her hips, Clara glared down at Mag for several moments, then sighed. “You’re right. I hate it when you’re right.”

“Sucks to be you.” Mag had zero remorse. “Help me

flip him over."

Clothes and all, Clara slid into the pool and helped Mag drag the body close enough to the shallow end to get her feet under her. "I'll do it," she said, wanting to keep her sister from straining herself. Clara heaved, but the dead weight of Sam's body resisted until Mag waded in, took hold of his pants leg, and helped ease him over.

"There's your cause of death," Mag pointed to the gash above Sam's temple. "Blunt object would be my guess."

"You're always looking for the worst possible explanation in every situation, Maggie. He could have slipped, hit his head on the tile at the pool's edge, and fallen in."

Mag shrugged. "Anything's possible, but my gut's screaming murder."

She examined Sam's body more closely, noting he wore what had previously been a neatly pressed shirt and trousers.

"It's been what? Two or three hours since he threatened the Moonstones?"

"You don't think one of us did this?"

But Mag wouldn't rule anyone out. She shrugged. "Could be anyone. Just the way he acts, you have to figure a man like Sam Wayland makes a lot of enemies. It's never a good idea to piss off a witch. Probably a worse one to piss off a coven."

"True." It was Clara's turn to shrug. "If I'm honest, I'm struggling to feel much sympathy. He wasn't a nice man." Still, Gertrude had described him differently, at least in his past, and Lydia was a decent woman. Seemed like she wouldn't choose a complete loser. "But

I like Lydia, and you know as well as I do she'll be the first person the police look at." Helping Lydia meant helping Sam. Clara sighed.

"Son of a witch," Mag let her frustrations out. "Do you know what this means?"

"That we should get dried off and call the authorities?" Clara guessed.

"You figure you can do that without telling them we were here after hours? Give that a shot and see how it goes. What I meant was it means they'll have to close the pool. Probably keep it closed until they find the killer, which means I need to find out who did this and fast."

Clara sighed again but nodded in agreement. Once Mag got her teeth into a mystery, she wouldn't let go again until she solved it. "Fine. What's one more murderer to bring to justice? It's not like we have anything better to do…like run a business, or keep a crazy old witch from blowing up the town. You do know there are people who get paid to solve crimes? They're called the police."

"Yada, yada, blah, blah, blah." Exiting the pool, Mag navigated the steps with more ease than she'd had before her brief stint in the water. "I'll do a perimeter search. You check his pockets for clues."

"Because I wanted to spend my evening feeling up a dead body," Clara muttered as she checked Sam's jacket pockets, hoping something would lead her in the right direction. His wet clothing did nothing to make the job easier.

"There's a folio with his business cards in here and a tidy little manicure kit. Probably nothing to do with his death.”

About halfway down the length of the pool, Mag spotted a smear of blood.

“This must be where he went down.” Mag’s voice echoed over the water. “Looks like he did hit his head on the side of the pool. I’ve got a blood smear and some hair.”

Working with magic, a witch used both of those things in various potions, but Clara wasn’t particularly interested in seeing or touching any of Sam’s if she could help it.

“I need my fanny pack.” Leaving Clara behind with the body, Mag flashed home to grab it from her bedpost and was back almost before her sister realized she’d gone. Armed with what amounted to a portable workshop, Mag stood and let the scene form in her mind.

“Based on the location of the smear, I’d say he came in through the side door.” Her intuition disagreed. “Feels off to me.” With purpose, Mag walked around to the other side and tilted her head to look back and calculate.

“Didn’t you say they’d changed the pool over to a salt filter system?”

“Yes, why?”

“Smells different than it used to. Less like chlorine, except I’m getting some serious bleach over here. That’s telling, don’t you think?” She circled and sniffed until she found where the sharp scent bit the hardest. “It’s fresh.”

“Okay,” Clara sounded distracted.

While Mag finished her trip around the pool’s edge, Clara dug into Sam’s pants pockets and laid out what items she found on the tile surrounding the pool.

"I've got a set of car keys, seventy-six cents in change, his wallet, a piece of folded paper that's completely waterlogged, and this." She pointed to a plastic card lying face down, glared when Mag grabbed it, and held it up triumphantly.

"It's a keycard, right? I bet he's been living in a hotel somewhere since he and Lydia went on the outs. All we need to do is figure out which room it goes to, and we've got a great place to start looking for clues."

Clara cocked her head skeptically as she left the pool and leaned over Mag's shoulder to look at the rectangle of slate gray plastic with a black stripe down one side and no other markings whatsoever.

"You're trying to fly before you've bespelled the broom. There's no hotel name on here. It could go to a storage locker, an office door, or a dozen other places. Too many possibilities to jump right to it being a hotel."

"Right." Mag stuck the card in her pocket. "We'll have to do some research."

"Margaret Balefire," Clara fisted her hands on her hips. "You cannot remove evidence from the scene of a crime. It's called tampering and is a good way to end up in jail yourself."

Cocking her head, Mag eyed her sister. "Fine." She pulled the card back out, paused for a second or two, then reached back and yanked the tag off the back of her shirt. She let it lay flat on her palm and added the card. "There's more than one way to cork a potion." She slapped her other palm over the card, and when she pulled it back, two identical cards rested where one had been.

"Slick." Clara admired the spell but didn't want her sister to get a big head. "Now you have two pieces of evidence with your fingerprints on them."

Eyes rolling, Mag pocketed the duplicate and dropped the original card near the wallet. "You'd think it was my first time solving a crime or something. Have a little faith, sister dear."

There would be no fingerprints or other traces of Balefire on anything either woman touched. Mag had already seen to that, so she emptied Sam's wallet without her conscience suffering a single pang of regret. He'd carried a small stack of credit cards, a few hundred in cash, a foil-wrapped condom, and nothing else.

"Well, that was a waste of time." Clara surveyed the detritus before a wave of her hand banished everything back into Sam's pockets.

Mag indifferently shrugged one shoulder. "I wouldn't say that. I think we've learned quite a bit." She ticked off the points as she saw them. "Sam Wayland died within days of cutting up enough of a fuss here to get someone nearly fired. In the process, he also made a fool of his ex-wife, and if that wasn't enough, he got into bed with Hagatha Crow against the Moonstones. There's no reason to think those were the only people he treated poorly lately, and there's no evidence to suggest his death was an accident."

"Nor any to suggest it isn't," Clara reminded.

"Have you lost your memory in the last two minutes? Someone used bleach to clean up something on the other side of the pool from the blood smear on the corner of the tile. I'm betting it was more blood stains. Like the kind you get when you drag a body around. Combine those, and you can't tell me you think this was an accident. I'm betting if we follow the bleach, we'll find the primary crime scene."

"Why can't you watch something besides forensic shows and soap operas on TV? Hmm? Your sense of humanity is skewed."

"And yours is all roses and sunshine. You think that's not skewed in the other direction?"

"All I'm saying is Antiques Roadshow would be a better choice."

Mag might as well have put her fingers in her ears for all the attention she paid to Clara's observation.

Clara rolled her eyes at her sister's stubbornness. "Fine. Watch whatever you want, but here's another scenario. Sam comes to the club after business hours, which is when the cleaning crew swabs the decks or whatever. Maybe he's meeting someone, maybe not. Doesn't really matter. Maybe the tiles are wet from cleaning. I don't know. But he falls and hits his head. Passes out somewhere, and no one notices. Time goes by, he comes to, crawls for help, and ends up in here. He's disoriented and probably concussed. Maybe he makes it to the edge of the pool and tries to stand, but he can't. He falls again, bangs his head a second time, and in he goes. Case closed. Accident."

"Well then," Mag clapped her hands. Let's test your theory. Shouldn't be difficult to check Sam's lungs to see if he drowned or died before he ended up in the pool."

"Okay."

Mag closed her eyes and wove a spell of discovery, murmuring words of power in a language older than time itself. As she spoke, Clara joined in, adding her magic to the weave until a shimmering light surrounded Sam's body. The light pressed against his chest, pushing out the final breath of air in his lungs, which escaped with a long, gurgling sigh.

"Did you have to do that?" Clara asked, looking at Mag and shuddering as a water bubble hovered just above the dead man's lips. "That was just plain creepy."

Creepy was a matter of personal boundaries, Mag thought, but her face stayed somber. "Only way to tell." She gestured, and Clara shuddered again as the breath sucked back into Sam's lungs with another audible sigh. "He drowned here," she said quietly.

"So you're saying this is the primary crime scene? What does that do for your theory?"

Mag's eyes narrowed as she looked around the pool area. "So he wasn't dead when he went into the pool. Doesn't mean he got there on his own. In fact, if someone was trying to stage the scene, it would be more suspicious if he hadn't drowned. I mean, whack him on the head, toss him in the pool, and clean up any blood evidence that doesn't make it look like an accident."

"I guess it could have happened that way," Clara sighed. She'd hoped to avoid another murder investigation, but clearly, that wasn't how this would go. "Still, someone had to let him in unless he had a key, which begs the question: who was he here to see?"

Glancing over at the body, Clara pursed her lips. "One thing we didn't find was a date book. Probably keeps his schedule on his phone, which we also didn't find."

"Phones," Mag huffed her opinion.

Ignoring her sister's comment, Clara glanced toward

the hallway leading from the pool. "I'll bet Sam keeps a locker here. Maybe he kept something there that can give us a lead."

The sisters headed toward the men's locker room. As they entered, Mag felt that fleeting sensation of being watched again but put it down to the situation. The air was thick with the scent of bleach, sweat, and damp towels. The lockers were lined up against the walls, and the doors were all closed.

"Which one's his?"

"How should I know?"

Annoyed, Mag skimmed back to the pool and yanked a hair from Sam's scalp. "Sorry," she muttered, even though she wasn't. After a moment's thought, she snagged a second hair, which she stored in one of the jars she carried in her pack. A sample of the pool water went into another jar. A cotton swab of Sam's blood went into a third.

Returning to the locker room, she uttered a short spell, then held the hair between her left thumb and index finger until it floated up and angled toward a doorway at the back of the room. "This way. There's another section here. Fancy lockers for the fancy members."

When the hair angled toward the third locker from the end, Mag walked up to it and placed her hand on the door. "Open," she whispered, and the door swung wide. Clara quirked a brow in surprise but didn't say anything.

Inside the locker, there was nothing out of the ordinary. A towel, a pair of swim trunks, a gym bag, and a pair of flip-flops. Clara checked the pockets of the swim trunks and found nothing. Next, she pulled out a gym bag, and as soon as Mag opened it, the smell of sweat assaulted their noses. Clara wrinkled her nose in disgust but didn't move away. Mag dug into the bag and pulled out a pair of boxing gloves, a pair of shorts, and a sweatshirt. As she began to toss the bag aside, she noticed a small piece of paper sticking out of the pocket.

She pulled it out and unfolded it. It was a local gas station receipt, and the items purchased included a pack of cigarettes and a lighter. A phone number was scrawled in pen on the back of the receipt.

Clara leaned over to take a look. "This could be something," she whispered.

Mag nodded, made a copy, and stuffed it into her ever-present fanny pack. "We'll check it out later, but for now, we should probably search the rest of the place."

"For what? If you're right, someone took great pains to cover their tracks. We need more information to narrow the search, and I don't see us getting it out of Sam, do you? Let's let the police do some of the preliminary work."

Sharp words formed on Mag's tongue, but before the first could pop out of her mouth, the sensation of being watched prickled over her again. Besides, if she kept pushing, her hip would be aching like a rotten tooth again.

"Fine. Let's get out of here."

Leaving Clara to follow, Mag returned to the pool area, where she closed her eyes to center her magic and cast a spell to return everything to the state it had been in when she arrived. Then, she doused the lights and removed her dome of protection. Mag grabbed Clara's arm in the falling darkness and relocated them to the parking lot.

"The cameras are still blocked, so we can check the lot before we leave."

"Cameras." Clara tilted her head to think. "That gives me an idea." She pulled out her phone and ignored how her sister's eyes rolled.

"What are you planning to do with that?"

"You're not the only one who knows good magic, Margaret Balefire." Whatever spell she cast, Clara didn't see fit to share the words of power with her sister as she held her phone between her palms and closed her eyes. After a moment, she held up the device and tapped the camera icon. A block of video thumbnails filled the screen. She didn't see any that showed the pool, but at least the entrances and exits were covered, and that was enough for what she planned to do. "Do you think we should check his car before we go? There might be something useful there."

"Good one." Mag offered rare praise, then took the lead as they checked the guest parking lot and found it as empty as it should be during off hours.

"Maybe he parked in the employee lot. Do we even know what he drives?" Mag grumbled.

"Silver something. Sedan of some make. I'm not sure. I saw it once, but I can only remember the color."

A single vehicle remained in the employee lot, and since it was silver, the sisters deduced that the Lexus with tinted windows and fancy rims belonged to Sam.

Clara glanced at the mud-flecked lower half of the car. "It's still wet. He'd been somewhere on a dirt road right before he died."

Mag took a look and played devil's advocate. "It's winter. Everything's wet and dirty right now."

"True, but this is more than winter wet. This is muck caked on top of more muck with a layer of muck frosting." Clara pulled out her cell phone and snapped a few photos. "We done here?"

Since the night's chill had begun to work its way under Mag's clothes, she nodded and let Clara do the shifting to save energy. When they landed in Mag's front room, the magic fire in her hearth flared to life with a roar that sent out a blast of warmth.

"Feels good," Clara held cold fingers near the heat. She found death unsettling in any form, but murder was extra chilling. Once her fingers felt pliable again, she pulled out her phone and triggered the camera app again. "For Lydia's sake," she tapped one of the thumbnails to bring up the footage from one of the inside cameras, then swiped a finger across the screen to create a living shadow and trigger the club's alarm system. Shrill tones echoed from the phone, followed only a few minutes later by the louder squawk of police sirens. They'd done what they could for Sam for the time being, so both witches settled in to watch the police arrive on the scene.

"This is better than CSI," Mag chortled. "Can you put it on the TV?"

Rolling her eyes, Clara didn't even bother with magic. She only turned on the screen-sharing app and streamed the video to Mag's set. Two hours later, men and women in various uniforms still swarmed over the area, but Clara had had enough. A breath of magic set the streaming to continue. "I'm done. I'm going to bed. If anything happens, you can tell me tomorrow."

Mag barely pulled her gaze from the screen as she waved Clara out the door.

Chapter 9

Smelling of liniment and pool water, Mag walked into the shop the next morning with far less difficulty than Clara expected after her sister's stint in the hot tub got interrupted by murder the previous evening.

"Did you go back to the pool this morning? It's a crime scene. Have some decorum."

"Untwist your undies. I didn't go near the country club." Mag's gaze met Clara's dead-on, which meant she was telling the truth. But not all of it.

"Then why do you smell like pool water?"

Mag grinned like a cat with drops of cream clinging to its whiskers. "I figured the cops wouldn't miss a few gallons."

"You stole water from the pool? You tampered with evidence?" Clara's voice rose.

The grin shifted to a scowl. "Give me at least an ounce of credit. I filtered the damn water before I took it. There's not so much as a whiff of the essence of Sam Wayland left in it. The cops aren't losing anything except enough water to fill my bathtub."

"Okay." When Mag got a snit going, she put everything into its crafting, and Clara didn't have time to work through the prickly task of dealing with one right now. "I've got a self-stirring spoon charm. Goose it a little, and you've got yourself a whirlpool."

"I'll take it."

Nodding, Clara flicked her fingers to produce a piece of paper, a pot of ink, and a quill. With spare motions, she noted down the spell, added some suggestions for how to adapt it for a bathtub, and then handed it over.

"Thanks. This will come in handy. You mind handling the shop alone for part of the day?" Mag asked after she'd reassured herself that no speck of dust marred any of her inventory. "I could run over to Ellen's for that box of carnival glass. The only thing is she's a talker, so if I go, I'll be there for a couple of hours. Do you mind?"

Since getting Mag out of the way so she could do some research suited Clara right down to the ground, she offered a token protest, then gave in without excess grumbling. Mag went off feeling like she'd scored one on her sister. As soon as Mag was out the door, Clara called for Pyewacket and waited until her familiar took human form.

"I need to grab some spell books from the sanctum back home. I shouldn't be long. Mind the shop, and if Mag gets back before I do, just tell her Sylvana needed me. That'll keep her from asking too many questions." Clara left off all mention of the other quick stop she planned. The less said the better, and what Pye didn't know, Mag couldn't find out.

The van had barely cleared the driveway when Clara activated a half-dozen charms to conceal her presence and slipped through Mag's front door. She went straight to the VCR and checked that the tape was the one she'd seen her sister watching earlier. Taking a cue from Mag,

Clara made a copy before sliding the video back where she'd found it. In his bed near the fireplace, Jinx slept through the invasion of his privacy.

With the tape still in hand, Clara shifted directly into the family sanctum at the Balefire house in Port Harbor. As always, the room registered her presence and readjusted itself to match her preferred layout. She wouldn't admit it to anyone, particularly not to her granddaughter, but although it was only a wink away, Clara missed this place more than she'd expected. It smelled of her mother even after all this time and of the magic fire from which she took her name.

Because she could, she knelt in front of the hearth and offered her hand to the flames. She smiled as the questing tongues tickled against her palms. Balefire witches knew how to play with fire. It was their element. Their strength. The source of all magic.

When she'd finished communing with her birthright, Clara mounted the stairs leading to the upper reaches of the family library, where the oldest and most obscure books of magic took up shelf space. Somewhere in this mass of information would be the answer to saving Mag's life. Not having time to scan through dusty pages of ancient tomes, Clara gathered power and cast a one-word invocation.

"Raythe."

Books flew off the shelves forming a thigh-deep stack on the floor. There were more than she'd expected. Whether that was a good thing or a bad thing, Clara couldn't say as she flipped open the cover of the one on top of the pile and studied the cramped text written in fading ink. It would take hours to pick her way through this single book, and there were a dozen more besides.

Better to take them home where she could read in peace. Clara didn't want Mag to know what she was up to for now. Going behind her sister's back would be a strike against her in Mag's book. Going behind Mag's back about something to do with Mag would mean multiple strikes, almost certainly resulting in some form of retaliation.

Shrugging, Clara summoned more magic.

"Compendium reductify." The stack of books melted and melded into a single volume. "Better," Clara said, but when she tried to lift the book off the floor, she discovered the single book weighed the same as the stack. "Almost better."

A flick of her finger sent the book to her nightstand, which collapsed under the pressure. The resulting crash scared Pyewacket so badly that she reverted to cat form and shed a whisker. Just lucky she was alone in the shop at the time.

Mindful of making a discreet entrance, Clara shifted back to her room, surveyed the damage, and shrugged. To keep her research from Mag, she reversed the compendium spell and slid each book under the edge of her bed, where they'd be hidden by the dust ruffle, before going downstairs.

"What happened?" Pyewacket had regained her human appearance, and a striking one it was. Sleek, tawny, and perfectly put together, she strolled toward her witch companion and indulged her need for attention by stroking her cheek across Clara's in a very catlike manner. "Are you hurt?"

Affectionately, Clara petted her familiar's arm. "No,

but my nightstand's toast. I sent home too many books, I guess." Keeping an eye out for Mag's return, Clara laid out the situation and asked for Pyewacket's help. "If we don't find anything in this batch of texts, I'll speak to the rest of the family. Mag says she's getting worse, and there's nothing we can do without a particular potion ingredient that is impossible to get, but we both know there's more than one way to craft a spell."

"What's the ingredient?" The curiosity of cats is no myth, and familiars are no exception.

"Essence of the Raythe who attacked her."

Pyewacket let out a low whistle. "That's a tough one after so many years."

"The time-lapse isn't even the worst of it. You know my sister and her temper. According to her account of things, she burned the Raythe and danced on the ashes."

Despite the severity of the situation, Pyewacket grinned. "That's Mag for you."

"Isn't it just?" Clara replied.

"We've had some foot traffic while you were gone. Mostly locals come to gossip. A man was found dead at the country club last night."

"Sam Wayland," Clara nodded. "I know. Mag found him when she went for an after-hours dip in the hot tub. We sounded the alarm."

"And you're just telling me about this now?" Hurt and annoyance battled for control of Pyewacket's features. Annoyance won.

"You weren't here when we got back."

"Fine. Be logical. See if I care." A smile softened the statement. "I need details."

"I don't have many. We found Wayland floating in

the pool. Drowned. Blunt force injury here," Clara pointed toward her temple. "But no evidence of a slip-and-fall."

"Murder?"

"He wasn't a nice person, so we're leaning that way." Clara shrugged and made a mental effort to picture the scene. "But I suppose he could have hit his head on the edge of the pool, then the splash from falling in the water washed away the blood, but something about that theory feels off to me."

Threading her way through the empty shop, Clara headed for the section where Mag housed her collection of outdated electronics. Perched on the shelf above a box of mismatched video game controllers, remote controls, and a jumble of wires, Clara found a small television set with a VCR built right in.

"This ought to do it." She plugged in the set and slid the tape into the slot. "If it works, anyway."

"It works. Mag tests most of this stuff out before she shelves anything."

Shushing her, Clara hit play.

"Oh," she sucked in her breath as a much younger Mag appeared on the screen. "Just look at you, Maggie."

In her prime, Mag Balefire's long legs ate the ground as she strode along a mountain path. A singing former nun was the only thing missing from the bucolic scene. Mag looked happy, Clara thought. She fairly danced along the trail, her freckled face alert and alive, her body strong and vital.

"What is this? What are we watching?" Pyewacket's eyes went round and huge when they spotted a hulking figure of a beast following the lone woman on the screen. "Look out!"

Stoic, now that she knew exactly what she was about to see, Clara did her sister the favor of watching even while her heart shattered into jagged shards as Mag grappled and stumbled. Less than five minutes in actual run time, the tape seemed to go on forever. Pyewacket gave up after two minutes, burying her face in Clara's neck and shivering, but Clara figured if Mag could stand up to the fight of her life, she could stand up to the viewing of same.

It wasn't easy, and Clara shed enough tears to dampen Pyewacket's collar.

Onscreen, Margaret Balefire battled.

Rough-skinned and scaly, a clawed hand batted Mag aside. She fell, rolled, and regained her feet just in time to be snatched off of them as the Raythe grabbed her by the throat. Its eyes blazed red as it began to drink from the well of Mag's power and life force. Pale as water, she struggled and fought until, with a final burst of magic, she proved her reputation was earned and dispatched the raging creature. It took every last ounce of her strength. Both fell at the end, but only one would rise, and when she did, she struggled to stand on shaky legs.

"Maggie." Clara breathed the name with a sob. "I never knew. She never said."

Shaking, Pyewacket clung to Clara. "She's so brave."

"She is. I wasn't there for her when she needed me most, but if there's a way to help her now, I will do whatever it takes. Mag says there's no chance for her because she dispatched the creature in a fit of rage. Maybe she did, but maybe she missed a shred."

"And you think you could find it?"

"I could try. I think I owe Maggie that much, don't you?" Reaching out, Clara hit the pause button, fixed the scene in her head, then rewound and ejected the tape. "Watch the shop. I'll be right back."

Without another word, Clara called up the magic that would take her to the place she'd fixed in her mind and shifted there between one breath and the next.

The mountain pass had looked pretty on television, but that was nothing compared to real life. Clara stood in the spot where Mag had been attacked and let herself tune in on those moments. Dread, fear, and an unnatural rage washed over her senses. She homed in on the rage. Surely that had come from the Raythe when it realized the woman in its grasp was no ordinary witch.

Following that thread of emotion, Clara found the spot where Mag had called upon the cleansing fire to rid the world of the Raythe's evil carcass. She'd done a bang-up job of it, Clara decided. Nothing grew in the places touched by the ashes. The ground lay as empty and barren as the heart of darkness spread over it.

What had she expected to find after all this time anyway? Any chunk large enough to have survived the fire would be shriveled and dried and no use to her at all.

Her tears flowing once again, Clara shifted back.

"She's right. There's nothing left. It's hopeless."

Chapter 10

"Ellen!" Mag pounded hard on the porch door and yelled through the glass, but nothing moved inside the house. "Are you in there? I've come to pick up that box of carnival glass." Probably forgot I was coming, she thought as she made her way across the front porch to peer through each window, looking for signs of life.

Seeing none, Mag stomped across the porch. "Like I've nothing better to do with my time than drive out to the back of beyond for no reason whatsoever." She got halfway back to the VW bus with the shop logo splashed down the side before a sense of foreboding began to niggle.

Ellen had one of the sharpest minds in town. She wouldn't forget an appointment. What if Ellen was in trouble and needed help? Mag decided she'd better take a second look.

"Everything all right over there?" Ellen's busybody of a neighbor stepped out on her own front porch and yelled across the road. The neighbor lady's jowls hung nearly to the collar of her paisley bathrobe. Her hair frizzed out in various directions as if she'd been sleeping on the job.

"I don't know," Mag yelled back. Sun glinted and

sparkled off the half-inch of fresh powder that had fallen in one of those fast and fierce squalls that blow in unexpectedly, turn the world white for half an hour, and then move on. The blanket of snow lay untouched except for Mag's tire tracks and footprints.

"Have you seen Ellen today? We had an appointment, but she's not answering the door."

"Nope. Haven't seen her. Probably taking a nap." Having decided Mag was mostly harmless, the neighbor went back inside but hovered near the window, watching to see what might happen next.

"I don't think so," Mag said to herself. Wallowing through knee-deep snow would send her arthritis into overdrive, and with the neighbor watching, she probably shouldn't cast a snowshoe spell to go peek in all of the windows. Instead, Mag dug around in her fanny pack for the lock-picking set she habitually carried. Hey, some women weighed themselves down with makeup, but Mag was a more practical witch.

Using her body as a shield, Mag prepared to pop the door lock, but when she touched the knob, it turned in her hand. Unlocked.

Honed to a fine point after years of hunting rogue magical beasts, Mag's intuition screamed that something was wrong. Being Mag, she trusted that inner voice implicitly, as that level of trust had saved her wrinkly backside more than once.

With a wave to the neighbor, Mag pushed the door open, then poked her head inside.

"Ellen! Are you okay?" The rest of her followed her head. "If you can hear me, I'm coming inside now. It's Mag Balefire, so don't shoot me or anything." Her voice echoed but elicited no response.

As she moved through a silence so deep not even the ticking of the clock on the wall made much of a dent in it, Mag's intuition went from niggle to scream. She was heading into something bad. Really bad.

"Don't you be dead, Ellen, you hear me?" Mag muttered as she cleared the kitchen, dining room, and living room. "Don't you be dead in the bathroom," she amended. But Ellen wasn't dead in the bathroom. She was dead in the bedroom.

Mag took in the scene with great pity welling up in her breast. She tamped the emotion down. Now was not the time for sorrow. Now was the time to record the crime scene and do what needed to be done. So thinking, she activated one of Clara's better charms. The one that allowed her to walk through any space without leaving a trace of herself behind.

Ellen lay on the floor near the window, her nightgown a pool of white against the dark, hardwood floor, a patch of blood shining wetly through silvered hair.

"What have they done to you?" Kneeling, Mag checked for a pulse just in case. Expecting none, she nearly jumped back in shock when she felt a flutter against her questing fingertip.

"Holy Hecate!" Mag stumbled to her feet and glanced frantically around the room. Clara's dratted cell phone would have come in handy right about now, but Mag wouldn't admit that to her sister for anything.

Finally, she spotted Ellen's cordless phone sticking out from under some newspapers on the table by her chair. "Don't you die on me," Mag yelled as she dialed 911. The call made, she rushed back to Ellen's side and checked again for that faint flutter of a pulse. "I'm here, Ellen. If you can hear me, I've called for help. Just hang on."

Any witch worth her salt, in Mag's estimation, carried at least some basic charms at all times. Mag wasn't what you'd call a basic witch, so she rooted around in her bottomless fanny pack until she found a packet of dried yarrow. Fresh would have been better, but there wasn't time to go home for it. Not even taking the quick route. To the yarrow, she added a pinch of chamomile for overall healing, some feverfew to help with the head pain, and some ashwagandha to reduce pain and inflammation.

"Pardon my germs," she said to the unresponsive woman as she spit into the herbs and rubbed her hands together to form a paste, which she applied to the wound. Lastly, she selected a boosting potion brewed with plenty of ginseng and used an eyedropper to feed Ellen a few drops. After each one, Mag thought Ellen's color improved slightly.

While Mag did what she could to save her friend, a siren wailed in the distance. Even if she knew enough magical first aid to get by, healing wasn't one of Mag's strongest suits. It seemed like an eternity passed before the ambulance pulled up in front of the house.

"In here," Mag yelled when she heard the door open. "Hurry!"

Mag suffered through being not-so-gently pushed aside by one of the ambulance attendants and didn't even consider casting an itching hex on the woman's socks. All of her attention stayed focused on Ellen.

"What happened here?" The second EMT asked. "Did

she fall?"

"I don't know. We had an appointment, and when she didn't answer the door, It seemed like something was wrong, so I came in and found her this way. Are the cops coming?"

Mag hadn't even considered that Ellen's injury might have been accidental. Maybe it was how her mind worked, but when she saw a body on the ground, she assumed foul play.

"For a slip and fall? Not likely."

They worked on Ellen for quite some time, checked her pupils, hooked her up to machines, got her onto a gurney, and inserted an IV for fluids. She never so much as twitched a muscle or fluttered an eyelash.

"It's bad, isn't it?" Mag finally asked.

"We're doing our best for her," said Miss Pushy Shovy.

Not one to be fobbed off with canned responses, Mag pursued the issue. "Give it to me straight. What are her chances?"

"You family?"

"I'm the only one who bothered to check on her." In her head, Mag began a countdown. If someone hadn't answered the question before she hit zero, there would be spells involved, and they wouldn't be good ones. "What are her chances?"

When the answer came, they'd begun to wheel the gurney toward the door. "I'm not a doctor, but I've seen my share of head injuries, and in my opinion, it's not good. Someone should call her family. Tell them to come right away."

It was the least Mag could do for Ellen, and if the

ambulance techs were happy to leave her in the house to make those calls, they wouldn't know if she turned her hand to some sleuthing at the same time. She certainly didn't need some puffed-up, badge-wearing lackey to tell her how to look for clues. Healing wasn't her knack, but ferreting out the truth was.

"I'll just make the calls, lock up, and meet you at the hospital."

When they were gone and the door shut tight behind them, Mag flicked a finger to lower the shades. She couldn't have the nosy neighbor popping in to ask questions while she got down to business.

The inside of Mag's fanny pack could have used Clara's touch with organization, but Mag knew where everything was without having anyone to fuss over her system. The vial she wanted contained a half-ounce of powdered rainbow. Eyes squeezed shut, Mag ran her fingers over each bottle until she found it. A few delicate motes puffed out when she pulled the stopper, and as luck would have it, she breathed them in. Her brain fogged by the image of fluffy pink clouds, Mag shook it off, loosed a series of words that would have triggered her mother's soapy mouth spell, and went back to work.

She tapped a tiny pile of dust into her hand, pinched her nose with the other hand to make sure she didn't inhale more, and blew a cloud seething with colors into the room. Handled properly, the shimmering stuff spread according to her intention. Keeping her nose and mouth buried in the crook of her arm, Mag waited until every tiny speck had time to settle. When it was safe to breathe again, she called a ball of witch light into her hand, spinning it until the rays angled down toward the floor.

The charm worked like a charm, and Mag cackled at the play on words as a series of colored footprints shivered into visibility, crisscrossing the room. Several minutes passed while Mag studied the pattern of shoe prints. She eliminated the purple ones quite quickly, as she could tell right away that they belonged to her. The pink ones had to be Ellen's since they overlapped multiple times and followed a pattern from the bed to the bathroom, closet, and dressers. A sideways flick of her palm made both colors disappear.

Next, she ruled out and wiped away the yellow and orange as having belonged to the EMTs, which left only the blue remaining. Mag bent for a closer look. The blue footprints followed a straight line into the room and back out, the paths overlapping each other, showing no wavering or hesitation of purpose.

Out in the hallway, another pinch of dust revealed two additional colors, with the blue leading straight to the front door, out onto the porch, down the steps, and into the driveway, where they both originated and terminated. That was that. Ellen's attacker had arrived by car, done the dirty deed, and left the same way.

Since neither the red nor the yellow prints tracked into the bedroom, Mag ignored those and stood near the front door contemplating her next move.

When a furtive motion drew her eye, she caught the twitch of window curtains across the street. Miss Busybody seemed to be living up to Mag's original perception. Surely the nosy old bat would have seen the would-be killer's car in Ellen's driveway.

Excited to unearth a valuable clue, Mag knocked on the neighbor's door. It opened fast, which meant she'd been watching, but only far enough to let the woman's head peek through. Clearly, Mag wasn't welcome inside.

"Ellen's been attacked." Mag saw no reason for obfuscation. Gossip went around the town of Harmony like a pea in a whistle. Everyone would know what happened soon enough. "Did you see anyone here earlier?"

"No one's been there today but you." The statement wasn't an outright accusation, but the undertones were there, and so was the ring of truth. "She ain't dead, is she?"

"Not yet. Are you sure you didn't see anyone stop by? It would have been just a little while before I got here."

"I said no, didn't I?" The door slammed shut.

Either Miss Crankypants had been lying, or there was another reason she hadn't seen anything, and Mag didn't think she'd been lying. It bore thinking about, but later. Now it was time to check on Ellen.

Mag jumped back in the van and headed to the hospital.

Chapter 11

If several driving laws were broken and one or two rules of human physics along with them, Mag didn't care. Getting to the hospital was her only goal. When she arrived, she asked the stern-faced nurse at the front desk for an update on Ellen's status.

"I'm sorry," said the nurse, "but only family is allowed to visit."

"That's not what I asked you."

"Are you a family member?"

"Not exactly, and where was her family while she was lying broken on the floor? I'm the one who found her, and I'm the one who got her blood on my hands trying to save her." Mag fisted one of those hands and slammed it on the desk, then opened it to show streaks of blood dried to the color of rust. "I want to know if she's going to be okay."

"Your friend is getting the best care we can give her, and you'll have to contact a family member for more information. That is all I can tell you."

"And you've called her family? Someone's here for her or at least on their way?" The thought of poor Ellen alone and scared drove Mag to push more than she might have.

"I'm sorry. I can't say. You'll have to contact your friend's family for more information."

With her blood pressure spiking, Mag indulged in a short but satisfying fantasy where the inscrutable nurse dangled over a fiery pit. The karmic debt wasn't worth the effort of sending the woman there, but the image of one rubber clog spinning down to flaming ash gave Mag enough stress relief to rein in the urge to make it so.

Finding Ellen wouldn't be a problem. One quick spell and Mag could walk into the operating room if she wanted to. No one would think it odd. But finding Ellen wasn't the same as getting information about her status. It would be all too easy to cast a spell on the gargoyle at the desk and force the information from her, but even with Mag's inherent disregard for any rule she thought was stupid, she wouldn't use magic on an innocent in that way. Some lines you could cross, some you could ignore, some you just had to let stand.

If her expression was anything to go by, the nurse realized she was dealing with a woman on the edge.

Just as Mag was about to turn away, an older nurse walked up behind her and put a hand on her shoulder. "It's all right," she said softly to the nurse behind the desk, "I'll take care of this." Gesturing for Mag to follow, she strode through the emergency room doors.

As they walked, the older nurse explained that Ellen had suffered a serious head injury and her chances were not good. Tears prickled behind Mag's eyes as she listened to what sounded like a death sentence for a woman she'd come to consider a friend. The kind-hearted nurse gave Mag an understanding look before patting her back gently and walking away without another word.

Mag stood there for what felt like hours before finally mustering enough courage to slide back the curtain. She found Ellen, her face nearly as white as the bandage wrapped around her head, lying still as death in the bed. Machines and monitors beeped and flashed numbers. She looked so small and fragile that Mag's throat closed up at the sight. She took a deep breath and approached the bed, taking Ellen's hand.

"Hey, Ellen," Mag whispered, her voice choked with emotion. "It's me, Mag. I'm here."

Ellen didn't respond, and Mag felt a pang of sadness wash over her. She didn't know how long she stood there, holding Ellen's hand and staring at her motionless body. It was only when a nurse came in to jot something down on a board that Mag reluctantly let go and stepped back.

"She's breathing on her own. That's a good thing, right?" Mag asked. "Does she need anything? Can I bring her something from home?"

The nurse looked at her with sympathy. "I'm sorry, honey. She's critical but stable. All we can do is wait and see, but miracles happen every day."

Mag nodded. If there was anything she hated, it was feeling helpless. It made her cranky. Or crankier than normal, anyway.

"Will you call me if her condition changes? I know I'm not family, but she does have a nephew. I intend to track him down, and it would help if I knew what to tell him."

The nurse paused long enough that Mag considered giving her a slight magical push to say yes.

"We have these rules in place for our patient's privacy, but no one should be this sick and alone. I'll make a note in her chart. We'll call if her condition changes. For now, it's best to let her rest and heal."

As she looked down at the woman on the bed, Mag's mind raced with thoughts and questions. Who had done this to Ellen? And why?

It hadn't been an accident, of that Mag was positive, but the police didn't appear to see things her way. Fine and dandy, she thought. At least they wouldn't get in her way while she did what she needed to do.

"Hear my oath. I will find out what happened to you, Ellen, if it's the last thing I do." Knowing the last statement was utter truth and entirely possible only made the vow stronger. If determination were made of something tangible, Mag's had turned to tempered steel. Ellen's attack would be avenged by her hand. That was all there was to it. The promise made, Mag left the room to make her way back through the maze of corridors. She only got lost once.

Back in the van, Mag contacted her sister.

"Where have you been?" Clara sounded harried. "I'm getting slammed here, and you should have been back at least an hour ago."

"Sorry. Ellen's been attacked. I found her and did what I could for her while the ambulance came. She's in the hospital."

Clara gasped. "That's horrible news, Mag. Is she okay?"

Mag shook her head, even though Clara couldn't see her. "No. I don't think so. She's in a coma or something. The nurses said her chances aren't good."

The busy shop less of a priority now, Clara took a deep breath. "Okay. You do whatever you need to do. I'll handle things here. What else can I do to help?"

Giving Clara grief was something Mag did without hardly thinking about it. That's what sisters were for, right? But when it came right down it, there wasn't anyone on the planet Mag trusted more.

"You're a good sister, Clara. Even if I don't say it often enough."

"Or ever, but that's okay. I feel the same about you."

Clearing her throat to eliminate any last traces of sentiment, Mag returned to her normal tone. Sentiment was fine, but it clouded the mind sometimes, and she needed to think through everything that had happened. Maybe there was a clue in there somewhere.

"I'm heading back to her place. Meet me there?"

"You've got the car."

"You are a witch, are you not? There are other ways to travel." Mag sent Clara the visual she'd need to skim directly into Ellen's kitchen.

Breaking contact, Mag set the van on the witch's version of autopilot and spent the drive to Ellen's going over every detail of what she'd seen that day to cement the details in her mind. She beat Clara to the house by a matter of minutes.

"What took you so long?"

"Very funny. How's Ellen?" It wasn't good. Clara could tell that much by the depth of Mag's scowl lines. They seemed etched nearly to the bone.

Lifting one shoulder, Mag said, "They wouldn't tell me much because I'm not a relative, but it's bad." Gesturing for Clara to follow, Mag stepped to the kitchen doorway. "See those prints?" She pointed to the splashes of blue. "I think those are from the attack."

Instantly intrigued, Clara leaned down to lay a gentle finger against one of the smears. "Powdered rainbow? Inspired."

"Yes, yes," Mag flicked one hand to brush off the compliment. "I'm a mystically magical genius. This is a well-known fact. Move on." She ignored her sister's quirked eyebrow. "What does this tell you?"

Taking care not to smudge them, Clara followed the footprints, first with her eyes, then with her body, from the front door toward the bedroom. "Well, I'd say we're looking for a man or a woman with abnormally large feet."

Mag nodded. "Man. Definitely a man. What else?"

"Is this a test?"

Annoyance flashed across Mag's features. "Are you going to help me or not?"

"Of course. Hunkering down again, Clara pointed to the cleanest print. "Our guy was wearing sneakers, and it looks like he paused just inside the door. Probably called out for Ellen, and when she answered, he went straight to the bedroom."

Because her assessment agreed with Clara's, Mag didn't attempt to pick it apart. "You know what that means, right?"

"Duh. It means Ellen knew her assailant. This is not my first time, sister dear. What do we know about her family and friends?"

Considering every word she'd ever exchanged with Ellen, Mag shared what little she knew. "Distant cousin, female, possibly deceased. No contact for years. And a nephew. Didn't sound like they were close, and I didn't think to ask if he was local. As far as friends, she mentioned two neighbors. Both women. The one across the way is probably peeking through her curtains right now. I met her. She's surly."

"Killer surly?"

"Nah." Mag shook her head. "She didn't give me the vibe. I didn't meet the other one, but I think we can let her out of the running since Ellen said she's confined to one of those electric wheelchair things." A fate Mag might share soon enough.

Clara considered all that, then tilted her head, "Got any more of that rainbow powder?" When Mag nodded, Clara reached into the cross-body purse nestled at her side, her arm disappearing almost to the shoulder, and pulled out a tuning fork. "I have an idea."

While Mag got out the rainbow powder, Clara inspected the footprints until she found the darkest, most well-defined one and dragged the tuning fork through the gathered dust until it turned blue.

"One second to set the charm," Clara held the blue fork on her palm, settled her other hand over it, and conjured the magical flame from which she took her name. A muttered spell and a flare of light later, she held nothing but the fork, which was no longer coated with color but swelling with it. "This is where it gets tricky. We need to disperse the dust and strike the tone at precisely the same time. Are you ready?"

Mag filled her palm with dust, held her breath, and nodded.

"Three, two, one," Clara struck the fork against the wall to send out a tone that set her back teeth on edge while Mag let out a steady breath that sent rainbow dust flying into the air. Both witches sneezed as the cloud lifted, dispersed, then settled again.

"What was the point of that?" Mag wanted to know. Little dancing unicorns floated across her vision, and her sleeve was covered with snot from the force of her sneezing. When Clara offered a withering glare, she subsided.

"Just watch."

Clara waited until the air no longer glittered, lifted the fork, and struck it again. Hints of blue in a variety of shades appeared throughout the house. "The newer the trace, the brighter the color."

Been there, done that tended to dominate Mag's attitude, but she wasn't above offering praise for a nice bit of magic no matter who conjured it up.

"Okay. That's pretty nifty."

Not one to rub it in, Clara merely inclined her head while accepting the compliment. "Doesn't look like the attacker returned to the scene of the crime, but he's definitely been here before."

"Bears up my theory it was someone she knew. Probably the deadbeat nephew. Why didn't I ask for his name? What is wrong with me?" Mag slammed a fist against her thigh.

"You couldn't have known." Concern joined compassion as Clara went to her sister and offered a hug. "It's no good blaming yourself for things that weren't your fault. We'll send healing light to her and do our best to figure out who did this. It will have to be enough."

Sinking into the hug, Mag laid her head on Clara's

shoulder to indulge in a rare moment of taking comfort when it was offered. And to give some back. The little digs and arguments aside, there was love and affection between the sisters. Clara would need support when Mag's time came, but this wasn't the time to think about her future. Not while Ellen's was on the line.

Breaking away, Mag got down to the business of crime-solving. "Get out that infernal phone of yours and take some pictures. I want every smudge of blue documented. The jerk's been everywhere in here, and we'll need to look for information about this nephew of hers. I'll take that on while you do the photos." Touching Clara's phone wasn't something Mag did except under duress.

"Where do you keep your photo albums, Ellen?" she muttered as she scanned the last bookshelf in Ellen's bedroom. She'd searched every drawer and cabinet in the rest of the house, and the only place left to check was Ellen's clothes closet. After opening the double doors, Mag let out a sigh.

"Clarie, I need you," she called out to bring her sister in a rush.

"What? Are you hurt?"

"No. Just short." Mag pointed to a series of small plastic bins stacked on the top shelf. "I can't reach."

"For Hecate's sake, Mag. Why didn't you just call them down to you?"

Because it hadn't even occurred to Mag to use magic, maybe, she thought, she should turn in her wand. What kind of witch was she, anyway?

"My head is not on straight today." The admission cost her some pride points, but she popped the top on the first bin to find it loaded with outdated grocery coupons. Shaking her head, she snapped the lid back down and set them aside. The next held six skeins of peach-colored yarn. She set that aside as well and kept going until the fifth one yielded results.

"Got a whole pile of photos here." She flipped one over to look at the back. "They're loose but marked with dates, times, and who's in them. I'm betting that nephew's in at least one of them."

Mag took half the pile, Clara the other.

"It feels like an invasion of privacy to look through someone else's memories." When her phone rang, Clara noted where the call originated from. "It's the hospital."

Her face turning pale, Mag said, "I gave them your number in case something happened with Ellen, and that one nurse said she'd call. Answer it."

Clara did and tapped the speaker button so that Mag could talk. The news wasn't good. Ellen had been taken into emergency surgery to relieve some of the cranial pressure from the injury. It was more important now than ever to find the nephew. Someone in her family should be there for Ellen.

"I think I've got something." Clara waved a photograph. "And you're not going to believe what I found. Look who it is."

She narrowed her eyes when Mag abruptly grabbed the photo to see for herself.

"You've got to be kidding me. That's Sam Wayland." Mag said, grabbing the photo from her sister and holding it up for a closer look.

"It is, isn't it?" Clara replied, her eyes scanning the back of the photo for more information. "This was taken at Ellen's birthday party two years ago. She wrote the occasion on the back along with names and the date."

Mag let out a deep sigh. "This just keeps getting weirder."

"I guess we can rule him out for her attack. Hard to sneak up on someone and bash them over the head when you're already dead."

"Could the two crimes be connected?" When Mag gestured with it, Clara took the photograph from her and put it back where she'd found it.

"Two people from the same family dying within a day of each other? Uh, yeah, I'd say it's more than possible. How much do you know about Ellen? Did she have money?"

Mag shrugged. "Enough to take a trip to Graceland with all the trimmings. Or she will when I sell that desk. Is that enough, do you think? Would someone hurt her for a few thousand bucks?"

"I don't know. Maybe. If she kept the money here in the house."

People did worse for less, Clara thought sadly.

Chapter 12

Arriving barely in time for the funeral, Clara pulled into a packed parking lot. "I didn't think Sam had this many friends," she said.

"Funerals are for enemies as much as they are for friends. I'm sure mine will be the same."

"Shut up, Margaret. We are not discussing your funeral today."

"You have to face facts, Clarie."

"One more word out of you, and you'll spit bubbles for a month. Do I make myself clear?"

Mag subsided. She wasn't fond of the taste of soap. Following Clara inside, she caught a sliver of conversation between two mourners she didn't recognize. They spoke too low to hear the entire thing, but she picked out enough to assume the police had made a ruling and Sam's death hadn't been accidental.

"Did you hear that? This funeral is about to get interesting."

"Looks like you were right." Mag generally was when it came to these matters, but Clara didn't plan to belabor the point and give her sister's ego too much of a boost. "But you don't have to be crass."

Rows of seating took up the center of the funeral

home's chapel, all full, and more people stood along each side. Mag shoved Clara toward a spot near the front, where she watched the range of emotions that flitted across people's faces during the service. None pulled her focus as being overly smug, but then, a smart killer would take pains to blend in.

After the service, she gave Clara's arm a shove. "Go mingle. Keep your eyes and ears open. I'll do the same. Find me in half an hour. We'll compare notes."

By the time twenty of those minutes had passed, Mag figured she'd heard every variation on the theme of Sam's death that was possible. No one seemed surprised by the murder ruling. Everyone had a suspect. Nobody seemed to know anything concrete. Finally, she made her way back to the front of the room.

She looked down at the man in the coffin as he lay there, still and silent. If she felt a pang of sorrow, it was less for the emptiness his death had left and more to do with knowing his case might be her final puzzle. Sam Wayland hadn't been a friend of hers. Nor, as unlikeable as he had been, would she call him a personal enemy. On the other hand, his ex-wife was a nice enough woman and didn't deserve the gossip and sidelong glances the people of Harmony continued to send her way.

According to the gospel of CSI and Criminal Minds, the killer was likely in this room at this very moment. Who could it be?

The man in the corner who looked soft but had hard eyes? A disgruntled witch? The manager of the country club who had nearly lost his job? A client with a losing case? Or someone else who'd run up against the man's nastier side. Maybe it was the woman who stood silently near the casket, her eyes running like a faucet.

It could be any of them. Or none.

Besides, on those TV shows, it was almost always the ex. Still, in Mag's opinion, Lydia didn't fit the type. Even if she did, she wouldn't have been able to roll Sam's body into the water by herself. The woman needed to eat something besides a steady diet of salad with dressing on the side. Lydia barely had enough meat on her bones to keep from blowing away in a strong wind. Then again, wherever Lydia went, Miriam May was sure to follow, and that woman had the constitution of a mule.

She kind of looked like one, too. Mag chuckled inwardly.

Looking back at Sam's body, something pulled Mag's focus to the coffin's edge. And that was when she saw it. Small, round, and gleaming in the dim light of the funeral home. It was a vial, its glass surface coated with a strange symbol that Mag had never seen before.

Curious, Mag reached out and took it in her hand. It felt heavier than it looked and larger. She unscrewed the cap and peered inside. The vial was filled with a deep black substance that sparkled and glittered in the light.

A potion? Or something else? Mag had to know. Gently, she withdrew the stopper.

It smelled like ink.

The mystery of the find filled her with unholy glee. Finally, something concrete to investigate. She turned the vial over in her hands, examining it closely. An aura of power emanated from or through the glass. It was as if it were alive and filled with a strange and mysterious energy. Anyone could have slipped the vial into the coffin, but for what reason?

Until she knew more about the dark substance, the possibilities were endless.

Slowly, Mag put the cap back on and glanced around, making sure that no one had seen her take it. Satisfied she had not been noticed, she reached into her pocket and pulled out a wad of the lint that had collected there. A hint of magic coupled with a strong intention turned the lint into a reasonable facsimile of the vial. She slipped the fake back into the coffin, and the real vial went into her pocket.

The sight of Sam's body made her shiver. She felt a sudden surge of sadness, which surprised Mag since she'd had no particular interest in the man when he'd been alive, so why would she waste an ounce of sentiment on him now? This excess emotion wasn't like her, and she didn't appreciate it popping up in the middle of a murder investigation.

Still, since she felt a bit maudlin, Mag figured she could use the emotion as cover. As if overcome by loss, she let her hand tremble slightly as she reached out and touched Sam's forehead gently to test for any residual magic that might still be attached to his body. Finding none, she stood a moment longer, her thoughts drifting farther away until she heard someone calling her name.

Startled, Mag shook off the sobering mood and snapped back to reality. She allowed one final, enigmatic look at the dead man's face.

"What's going on?" Clara appeared at Mag's side, her face a polite mask. "You look…funny."

"Thanks. You always know just the right thing to say.

Did you take a class, or is it a skill you come by naturally?"

Forgetting where she was, Clara began to roll her eyes, then remembered and suppressed the urge. "I didn't mean it as an insult. Did something happen?"

Mag wasn't ready to share. "Not especially. Have you noticed how no one stood up to offer a eulogy? Did no one have a decent memory of the man? Did no one care enough to share a nice thought at his funeral?" Would anyone share a nice thought at hers?

Clara Balefire had a heart like a marshmallow when it came to most people, but Sam Wayland, had he lived, would never have glimpsed that side of her. "Probably not. You met him, or at least saw him in action. I'm betting he treated most people the way he did Lydia. She's handling this quite well, I'd say."

"Doesn't hurt to have a henchman....henchwoman....henchperson. Miriam walked in a few minutes ago, so you can use whichever term sounds right to you."

Maintaining her respectful expression, Clara still managed a ladylike snort. "I'd say more like a minion, but that term evokes those yellow guys from the movies now, and they're much cuter than Miriam, so henchperson it is."

"I was just thinking Lydia couldn't have pulled off a murder like that by herself, but with Miriam's help, I can see how it would have worked."

"Minion? Really?"

Clara's gaze shifted to the woman who'd come up behind her unexpectedly. It was clear from the look on Miriam's face that she had heard both comments. She approached them slowly, her eyes hardening as she stared at Clara.

Shrugging, Clara apologized, and Miriam's gaze turned to Mag.

"And just what are you suggesting?" Her voice was low and menacing, and Mag's hackles went up just from the tone.

"I am not suggesting anything right now—just calling it like I see it. You and Lydia are tight as latex gloves, so I can see how you might have worked together to rid your friend of the albatross hung around her neck." Swiveling towards Clara, Mag's voice turned conversational. "I never did understand what anyone has against the poor albatross. I find them quite a delightful bird, really. Far too good to be compared to the likes of him." Mag tilted her head toward the coffin.

Before Mag could launch into a tale that wouldn't be appropriate for the setting, Clara poked a finger into her sister's side.

Miriam's expression softened slightly, and she sighed. "You're right, of course. But only to the point that I'd have helped Lydia get rid of Sam if she'd asked. And believe me, if she had, his body wouldn't have turned up in the country club pool. That's amateur hour. My cousin owns a pig farm, and you know what that means."

Mag did, even if Clara wasn't as savvy regarding body disposal options. Pigs will eat nearly anything, including human bones.

"But someone did kill him, didn't they? Any idea who had a motive?"

Looking around the room, Miriam lifted her left brow.

"It would probably be easier to look for someone in town who didn't. That's a much smaller number."

"Yes, of course. We were only speculating," Clara assured Miriam to smooth the moment over. "Sam wasn't…popular."

"He was an asshole. Everyone thought so. You don't need to sugar-coat it for me." Miriam glanced around the room to make sure no one was close enough to hear what she said next. "But if Lydia had anything to do with it, I'm a monkey's uncle. Or aunt. Or first cousin once removed. Whatever."

Mag's left eyebrow shot up as she decided Miriam May had a few more layers to her than it seemed.

"Tell me what you know."

"Not here." Miriam glanced around to see if anyone could hear and realized too many people were standing nearby, so she motioned for Mag and Clara to follow her somewhere else.

"Sam Wayland got what he deserved, but Lydia had nothing to do with his death," Miriam said once they'd stationed themselves behind a column where they could keep an eye on the crowd. "Nor did I." She tilted her head and measured the sisters with a look. "I do think it's funny that whenever there's a death in this town, all of a sudden, there's the two of you in it up to your ears. What's the deal there?"

Clara trod on her sister's foot before Mag could open her mouth. "Mere coincidence, I assure you."

"Pull the other one," Miriam scoffed. "Look. Sam Wayland is no loss to the world, but nobody would be dumb enough to believe he would trip and bumped his head, and who's the most logical suspect? The ex-wife, that's who."

"She didn't do it?" Mag moved her foot to keep Clara from pinching her toes again. "How can you be certain?"

Miriam's eyes rolled up toward the ceiling, "If you think me giving her an alibi would be enough to stop the gossip mill from grinding my best friend to dust, you haven't lived here long enough. People are talking about Lydia. They'd keep talking if Saint Peter left the pearly gates and came down here specifically to tell them who killed the jerk."

Clara laid a hand on Miriam's arm for comfort since the worry for her friend was coming off her in waves.

"It's just talk."

"See," Miriam all but wailed, "You don't get it. It starts with just talk, but that's only the beginning. If they don't figure out who killed him, things will change. Lydia won't get invited to someone's birthday party—to spare her feelings, of course. Just to keep things from being awkward. It won't seem like that big a deal. Not that first time, anyway, but by this time next year, Lydia won't be invited to anything, and when she passes her old friends on the street, they won't be able to look her in the eye."

It wasn't difficult to see where Miriam was headed or that she was right.

"I don't want Lydia shunned for something she didn't do. She doesn't deserve to have more trouble heaped on her head. It was bad enough when Sam was still alive. He shouldn't get to cause more pain now that he's dead. I've watched the two of you enough to know you fancy yourself amateur detectives. Say you'll pitch in and clear Lydia's name. You'll have my assistance if you want to work together. I have connections and will not hesitate to use them."

Mag considered the offer momentarily, giving Clara a long look and seeing her slight nod before she finally said, "I suppose it would be churlish to refuse."

It wasn't like Mag hadn't already been planning on it anyway, and Miriam could be helpful to the process, so long as nothing witchy slipped in while she was around.

"Can you get us a list of possible suspects by tomorrow?"

"By tonight," Miriam nodded, her expression softening slightly. "Text or email?"

Since homing pigeons weren't on the list of options, Mag stepped aside and let Clara set up the means of contact.

"I didn't kill him, and I didn't help Lydia kill him, but I'm just going to say that when you do figure out who did it, I'll buy that person a round of drinks to celebrate the favor they did for the world."

"Tell us what you really think," Mag muttered. When Miriam only smiled and walked away, the sisters exchanged a look and went back to watching the faces of everyone who approached the casket.

They hadn't learned anything new when Emily Matthews, Sam Wayland's current girlfriend, all but climbed into the casket trying to kiss him goodbye. She had been crying for most of the day, and her grief seemed genuine. But her expression changed as she looked down at Sam's lifeless body. It hardened into a mask of rage and hatred, and she turned to search the crowd. When she spotted Lydia, she stalked across the room, her hips swinging with purpose, her finger pointed in accusation.

"You did this!" Emily shouted, her voice echoing off the walls of the chapel. "You killed him! You couldn't stand that he was happy with me, so you got rid of him!"

The room descended into chaos as everyone began talking at once and trying to intervene between the two women. But it was too late; Emily had already lunged forward and grabbed Lydia by her hair to pull her towards the casket. Lydia screamed in pain and surprise as Emily slammed her against it with enough force to knock some flowers onto the floor.

Lydia fought back, slapping Emily hard across the face before anyone could stop her. The crack of skin hitting skin reverberated through the room like a gunshot and silenced all other noise immediately. Everyone in attendance stared in shock as both women stood there panting with rage, their eyes locked on each other like two predators ready to strike.

Mag and Clara rushed forward but were blocked by a wall of people frantically trying to reach the two. Miriam had moved before anyone else could, grabbing Emily from behind in a firm grip and dragging her away with surprising strength. Still screaming, Emily struggled and got loose long enough to land a solid slap on Miriam's cheek before going after Lydia again.

Whirling, Lydia landed a backhand blow that sent Emily reeling back into the crowd.

"Whoops," one man stumbled when she slammed into him, his hands shooting out to help Emily keep her balance. He gently sent her back into the fray.

Growling, she spun and locked eyes with Lydia. "You didn't have to kill him." Her fingers curled into claws, she lunged and tried to scratch Lydia's eyes out.

"Enough!" Mag's voice boomed across the room, its tone as much as the power behind it silencing everyone at once. "This is not the time or place for this. Emily, you need to calm down or leave. Lydia, are you okay?"

Lydia's eyes went dark, standing out against her pale skin. Miriam stood beside her and tried to comfort her as best she could, murmuring words of reassurance. Reassurance wasn't what Lydia needed or wanted.

It seemed like the drama had ended, but Lydia wasn't quite finished. Faster than lightning, she struck, leaving the vivid print of her hand across Emily's face.

"I didn't kill him. He wasn't worth the effort." You could have heard a squirrel fart in the silence that fell as Lydia let her gaze circle the room. Some met her look with sympathy, some with naked curiosity, some with doubt. Lydia's expression never changed.

"I didn't kill him," she repeated. "And I can prove it because I was in Bangor. On a date. With someone else." With Miriam following in her wake, she walked toward the door. Just before stepping through, Lydia turned and delivered her final statement. "I've moved on. Maybe you all should do the same."

Amid the buzz that rose, Mag and Clara exchanged another look.

Chapter 13

"That went well, don't you think?" Sarcasm dripped from her tongue as Mag's cane tapped the concrete path leading to the parking area. In all the excitement, she'd forgotten about the vial she'd taken from Wayland's casket. "Lydia's got more fire than I thought she had. I'm putting her back on the suspect list."

"Really, Margaret? That's what you got from what just happened? That Lydia is capable of murder."

Shrugging, Mag said, "Sure. What else was there?"

Clara shook her head and sped her steps to get to the van first so she could drive. Her sister might be the final word on rogue hellbeasts, but she didn't know squat about people and their emotions. Without thinking, Clara repeated the sentiment out loud.

Mag fell silent. The kind of silence that still speaks in loud tones.

"I'm sorry." Immediately contrite, Clara meant the apology. "That wasn't nice, and I know it's not true."

"Maybe it is," Mag admitted. "What did you get from today's events that I didn't?"

"Lydia still had feelings for Sam."

Scowling, Mag spun in the seat to look at her sister. "What? That can't be."

"Sure it can." Clara pulled onto the main road. "She's sad to know he's gone, and that ends any chance at reconciliation, but at the same time, she's still angry that he didn't turn out to be the man she thought he was. Then, there's Emily tossing accusations in Lydia's face—in front of everyone in town practically. Add in the fact that Sam went for a much younger model the second time around and the way he went after Lydia at the club. Then the way people looked so shocked when she said she was seeing someone. It's a lot to take. She has to be stewing in her own juices right now."

"Okay." Mag settled back and turned to face forward. "You're right. I don't have a lot of experience with love. At least not from the inside, so to speak. I missed all that, and I can see how it puts a different spin on things."

"Plus, she has an alibi, and even if she didn't, I'd know she was innocent. If Lydia still had feelings for Sam, and if she killed him, the last thing she'd do is indulge in a brawl over his coffin."

"Maybe not." Mag was grateful Clara had decided to let the conversation die before it wandered into heart-to-heart territory. Love was a wonderful thing for those who knew the good side of it, and not even her most bitter leanings would stop her from being happy that Clara had been one of the lucky few. At least once in her life. If a hint of envy sneaked in with the joy, that was something Mag could live with.

"If we want to find his killer, we'll need to dig deep into Sam Wayland's background. Any idea where to start?" Clara asked.

"No. You?"

"Not really."

Two days later, Mag still hadn't figured out her next step. During the afternoon sales lull, she slid onto one of the padded barstools she and Clara kept behind the checkout counter and swore she heard her hip sigh with relief. Clara had gone upstairs to get a snack, so Mag figured it was a good time to make some notes about the Sam Wayland case.

Not even a year ago, she wouldn't have needed to note things down on paper, but the steel trap of her mind had sprung at some point, and wasn't that humiliating to admit? Still, it helped to have a visual reference for all the people tied to Sam's death, so she drew a circle in the center of the sheet and scribbled his name inside it.

Around the circle, she drew several more, one for each of her current suspects. Lydia Wayland probably shouldn't be on the list, but without direct confirmation of her alibi, she couldn't be left out, and neither could Miriam. Which one was Mary and which one was the lamb was something Mag hadn't quite puzzled out, but the effect was the same. You never got one of them without the other following close behind.

After a second of internal debate, she added Hagatha Crow to one of the circles and hoped writing her name wasn't enough to conjure the old witch's presence. Again, Mag didn't think Hagatha had killed Sam, but could she be certain?

Witches don't kill witches. Mainly because the penalty of being immediately turned to stone deters that type of thing pretty effectively, it's a penalty that works just as well to keep a witch from killing a mortal. Most witches have no way of knowing how much magic runs through a person's blood. Anyone could have enough to generate a stoning. Since no new witch statues had appeared, either Sam's blood was clean or a mortal had killed him. Well, duh, Mag told herself, that's always the case.

And yet, some witches could smell magic in the blood. A useful knack, Mag thought. If Sam was fully mortal, one or more of the coven might know, which meant any of them could be suspects. She added the Moonstones to the list. Penelope and her pathetic minions got no special consideration other than that she lumped them into one circle together.

Next came Ned from the country club. Sam's death had probably saved his job.

More suspects would pop up. They inevitably did, but she had enough to consider for now and decided to move on. Below the suspects, she started a list of possible motives hoping they would lead to more suspects. Love, money, and revenge made up the subheadings of her list, and beneath them, Mag elaborated. For love, she jotted down Lydia and Emily's names.

It didn't take long to realize half the town might end up on her list when considering revenge as a motive. With that many suspects in the mix, listing motives probably wasn't the best way to approach the case.

With too many motives crowding her head, Mag decided to move on. She'd just begun to contemplate financial possibilities when she realized she didn't have enough information to complete that section of her list.

Next up, opportunity. Why had Sam gone to the club, and who let him in? These were the questions to which the answers should be on Clara's phone.

With the purloined video feeds in mind, Mag pounced as soon as Clara came back downstairs after her lunch break. "You got that demon device handy?"

"My phone?" Clara pinned Mag with an annoyed look. "Why?"

"Well, it occurred to me that we only looked at the footage from the security cameras starting from when we sent the police over, but what if we could rewind?"

"And watch it all again? I don't see the point."

"I meant," Mag's tone chided, "really rewind. Like to the time of the murder."

"Oh," Clara's forehead wrinkled as she considered. "I never even thought of that."

"Means isn't helping, and there are too many with motives, so I figured opportunity might be the easiest way to pry open this case."

"Let's see if it works." Clara pulled out her phone and tapped the screen to bring up the icons in a grid. "That's really clever thinking."

"Don't sound so surprised."

"I'm not." Clara let out a whoop. "Maggie, you're a genius. That worked." She'd spun the footage back two hours with the flick of a finger and let it play. "There's Ned leaving."

"And there's him coming back again," Mag pointed to a different thumbnail. "I think he's drunk or something. Did you see how he stumbled? It's hard to tell, though. This screen's way too small."

"We'll put it up on the big screen after work. Speaking of which, if you wouldn't mind watching the store, Gertrude called and asked if I had plans for the afternoon. She'd like to visit Lydia. After what happened at the funeral, it seemed like the poor woman could use some moral support. It's been a couple of days, so we figured she might be ready for company."

"Gertrude wants to know who Lydia's moving on with."

"You might be right."

"I'd like to know that myself, so this is perfect timing. Ask Lydia if Sam had any other family. Local, I mean. I'm working on the suspect list, and family always hits near the top. We need more leads. See if you can get her talking about his finances, too. And ask about enemies. Revenge is always high on the list of motives."

Sighing, Clara leaned over to observe the hen-scratched sheet. "I'm not going over there to grill her but to offer support. You do know the difference, I assume."

With an exaggerated motion, Mag rolled her eyes. "Fine. Be her best pal. You can bake her a cake with a file in it when she gets arrested. At least ask her about the keycard."

Clara returned the eye-rolling favor. "Fine. I'll see what I can learn while I'm there. Make sure to give out those face powder samples I made up. They're in a box under the counter."

"Yeah. Yeah. I'm all over it. If Gertrude brings cookies, snag one for me. Two if they're gingerbread."

"Okay." Clara watched, and when the Christmas witch pulled up in her tiny car—painted red and green naturally—left without saying goodbye. She couldn't hold back a quick smile when she saw two plates of cookies on Gertie's back seat.

Wrapped against the winter chill, Clara took one of

the plates of cookies from Gertrude and juggled it while she rang the bell and waited. And waited more.

After the divorce, Lydia had moved into a cozy little cottage-style house set back from the street at the end of a narrow driveway between two of the oldest buildings in town.

"Her car's here, and I thought I heard noises from inside. Do you think something's wrong?"

Clara hadn't, but now, she did.

"Maybe." She knocked again, louder, while Gertrude peered through a window flanking the front door. "Lydia, open up. It's Clara Balefire and Gertrude Granger."

"We have cookies," Gertrude wheedled, then lowered her voice. "I think she's in there."

Clara knocked again, then stood back from the door when she heard a muffled sound from inside. She was about to cast an unlocking charm when the door swung open.

"Can't you take a hint?"

Lydia didn't look so good, and when Clara got close enough, she decided Lydia didn't smell so good, either.

"We were worried about you." Gertrude held out the box of cookies and caught Clara's eye in a moment of silent communication.

Lydia's hair hung in lank tangles, her face was sallow, and she hadn't showered since the funeral. "I'm fine. You've done your duty; if you've come to dry the poor pariah's tears, you can forget that, too. I don't need a shoulder to cry on, and I don't need your condolence cookies."

Except she did. Anyone with eyes could see she did.

"These aren't condolence cookies," Gertrude offered one of the wrapped plates. "They're chocolate chip with hazelnuts. I have gingerbread ones in the car if you prefer. We just wanted to come by and offer our support, but if you're throwing a pity party, I can go home and get some decorations to make it more festive."

Lydia stared at Gertrude for a moment before bursting into tears and stepping back from the doorway. "You might as well come in," she whispered. "I guess I could use the company. The police think I killed Sam. They were here earlier asking questions."

"That's ridiculous," Clara said soothingly. "No one who knows you would think such a thing."

"Of course not," Gertrude added as she followed Lydia inside. "Half the town had a motive to want him dead. He wasn't the nicest person in the world."

Lydia's eyes filled again, but she blinked back the tears. "Tell that to my former friends. You saw what happened at the funeral, and Miriam didn't even take my call today. She probably thinks I'll get my murder cooties all over her."

Clara couldn't hold back a chuckle at the phrase, but the sound of her short laugh seemed exactly what Lydia needed to slough off some of the despair. "I didn't kill my ex-husband."

"I didn't think you did," Clara took Lydia's arm and led her to the sofa in the sitting room where she'd clearly been holed up for two days. It had been a neat and tidy room once, but not today. Tissues littered the coffee table and floor. The table held a flurry of empty glasses, potato chip bags, and a half carton of ice cream that had melted into a puddle on the polished wood. Mag would have a tie-dyed hissy fit if she saw that.

But Lydia wasn't finished. Her face went fierce. "But I won't lie and say I'm sorry someone else did. He was a pimple on the butt of humanity. No. I won't apologize, but I will take one of those cookies."

Gertrude beamed while Lydia yanked off the plastic and grabbed one of the sugary treats. "These were made with love and a dash of Christmas spirit. I think they'll make you feel better."

"I think you're right," Lydia grinned around a mouthful of delectable crunch and sweetness. "Just what the doctor ordered."

Lydia took a deep breath, "I'm glad you came. I guess I thought I'd feel better with him gone, but I don't. I just feel sad. I remember the day we met and all the moments in between. We were good together, at least in the beginning. I used to love him. Part of me probably still does."

"It's okay," Gertrude said softly as she touched Lydia's shoulder. "It's natural for you to feel conflicted."

Clara nodded in agreement before adding, "And it's natural to mourn for your loss."

Lydia nodded, grateful for the understanding she needed so desperately. She took another deep breath, trying to push the memories aside. "But that doesn't mean I had anything to do with his death."

"We know," Gertrude assured her. "We believe you." She looked like she wanted to ask a question but firmed her lips and held it back.

Lydia let out a small sigh of relief. It felt good to have someone on her side, especially when almost everyone else in town seemed to be against her.

Clara stood up from the couch and walked over to the window, peering out as the late afternoon sky began to darken. "Do you have any idea who did?" Of anyone in town, Lydia should be the one with the most insight.

In a futile gesture, Lydia waved her hand to include the detritus strewed through her living room. "Who had a motive?" She barked out a short laugh. "Who didn't? To meet Sam was to hate him. At least these past few years. Things were different before."

"Before?" Clara prodded when Lydia fell quiet. Her investigative senses tingled.

"Before he got into bed with the wicked witch of the Northeast."

Gertrude shot Clara a glance. Could she be talking about a member of the coven? Or worse, Hagatha?

"Who?"

The hall clock chimed as Lydia answered. "Claudia Scanlon."

"I've heard that name somewhere," Clara squinted, trying to bring the memory back.

"Sam's former partner. She left the practice right before you moved to town," Lydia waved a hand. "We were still in love then. Harmony's a small town, but there was enough business to keep Sam happy. Even in small towns, people need to make wills, buy land, or defend themselves against traffic tickets. He made a comfortable living and felt good about his role in helping the community. We were planning to have children. Until Claudia came along."

"Sam had an affair?"

"No. That would have been easier to live with. She

perverted his sense of civic pride by setting a service goal for every client that came through the door. *Do you need a will? Why not consider setting up a trust at the same time?* We're in an older community. People couldn't afford what she expected them to spend. Sam knew that when he started, but she turned him greedy. I don't think he liked the man he became, and I sure didn't."

"Seems like someone else felt the same." While Lydia continued her story, Gertrude gathered up empty dishes. She took those to the kitchen and returned with a damp cloth.

"You don't have to do that," Lydia scowled. "I can clean up after myself."

The protest didn't stop Gertrude. She merely leaned down to pat Lydia on the hand and kept cleaning.

"Tell me more," Clara prodded.

"What's to tell? They were partners, and then, they weren't. I never got all the details out of him. She filed a dissolution and left town rather abruptly." The light broke over Lydia's features. "Oh, that's suspicious, isn't it?"

"Could be." Clara caught the surreptitious motion of several items skittering to their proper places as Gertrude continued to put the room to rights. Since Lydia hadn't noticed anything strange, Clara decided not to say anything, but she caught Gertrude's eye and offered a level look. Gertrude only smiled in response.

Lydia's features lost that haunted expression as the house began to look and smell fresher. She'd needed this visit, so Clara prolonged it enough to ask a few of Mag's questions. Or maybe just one.

"Do you have any idea who would have wanted Sam dead?"

Lydia sighed. "I've thought of little else for days now. The police were here yesterday, and I'll tell you exactly what I told them. I wish I had a name for you, but there are too many to settle on one. Maybe if I had taken him back when he asked, he'd have found redemption. I feel like his death is my fault. So if you're looking for someone to blame, you're in the right place."

"Don't be an idiot," Gertrude's voice went hard. Clara whipped her head around to look at the normally-mild witch. "And don't take on responsibility for someone else's bad choices. You don't help anyone by doing that, least of all yourself. I'm not saying Sam asked for what happened to him because that would also be disingenuous, but you do him no favors by attempting to shoulder the blame for his actions."

It was the most impassioned speech Clara had ever heard Gertrude make, and to her credit, it perked Lydia up even more.

"I suppose you're right. We've only been divorced for a little under a year, but we'd been separated for the two prior, so I can't claim to have any inside knowledge of his recent caseload or anything else. We hadn't spoken in months."

"And yet, he tried to get you ousted from the club."

"Petty revenge," Lydia admitted.

"Or a bid for your attention," Gertrude's tone had softened again. "Same as a boy wants when he tugs on a girl's pigtails in the schoolyard. He wanted you back."

"Well, he picked a stupid way to try and make that happen. Most women don't respond well to public humiliation. Besides, I figured that was more of a jab at Dean Smith than at me."

"Dean Smith heads up the membership committee at the club, and while we might call it a committee, he has the last word on who joins and who doesn't," Gertrude clarified.

"And there was bad blood between Sam and Dean?"

"Going back to when Sam first moved to town." Lydia sighed and prepared to tell Sam's story, parts of which were also hers. "I was seeing Dean when Sam moved to Harmony to join his uncle's practice, and it was love at first sight. Dean didn't take the breakup well. He blamed Sam, but I can't see why he'd still be upset after all this time. He's married now, too. Happily, I thought."

"Maybe a more recent falling out? There was that business with the club memberships," Clara mused.

"Can you keep a secret?" Lydia wanted to know but then plowed on without waiting for an answer. "Sam and I had been talking right before that membership thing happened."

"Talking?"

"You know. Talking." An eyebrow waggle went along with the repetition.

"Oh," Clara nodded. "You'd been talking." There might as well have been air quotes. "What about the new girlfriend?" Jealousy could be a powerful motive. "Did she know you'd been talking?"

Lydia shrugged. "If she did, she didn't hear it from me. Plus, I suspect she'd been talking to her ex as well. Hard to blame her. He looks like he'd give excellent conversation."

"Who might that be?" Mag would want to know since it could be a break in the case.

"Mr. Hotbody." When Clara seemed mystified, Lydia elaborated. "You know the guy who cleans the pool at the club." She nodded when Clara caught on.

"He's pretty, that one."

"But not dumb." One of Gertrude's cleaning passes allowed her to drop her opinion into the conversation.

"No?"

"She's right," Lydia confirmed, "Denton Bell has an MBA from Harvard."

"And now he's a pool boy?"

"Not exactly," Gertrude cocked her head and smiled indulgently. "He owns a chain of pool companies. But he takes care of the country club to keep himself humble. Or so he says, and he still finds the time to visit me every Christmas. He likes my cookies."

For a moment, Clara couldn't tell if Gertrude meant her actual cookies or if they were a euphemism for something else. Before she could stop it, a mental image formed that would require industrial chemicals to bleach out.

"And I think that's all I needed to know about that," Clara said.

"I'd already decided things weren't going anywhere with Sam. The membership incident was payback."

"No," Clara shook her head. "It was proof."

"See," Lydia sat up straighter than since they arrived. "You get it. That he would stoop so low was all the proof I needed to know I'd made the correct choice. I wasn't lying about my alibi, either. I've been seeing someone else for a few weeks. Someone from not here. I find I'm a bit soured on the dating possibilities around here."

"Why did Sam move to Harmony? Do you know?"

"He'd lost his parents to a drunk driver, and his uncle had recently been diagnosed with cancer. Uncle Charlie figured he could groom Sam to take his place, and for several years, that's exactly what Sam did. We began to build a life here. Then Claudia showed up, and everything went to hell."

When Clara would have pressed for more details about Sam's family, Gertrude cut in, "It's getting late. Do you want us to stay with you for a bit longer?"

Lydia shook her head, a small smile on her face. "No, I'll be okay. Thank you both for coming by. It means a lot."

With more finesse than Clara expected, Gertrude herded her out the door.

"I had more questions, you know."

"Lydia needed a break. I think she'll be okay now, but I plan to call Miriam May and give her a piece of my mind." Gertrude's tone held ominous notes as she dug through her coat pockets for the keys to her car.

"Oh, I don't think that will be necessary," Clara said, her gaze riveted to the figure stalking along the icy sidewalk. "Hello, Miriam. Are you on your way to see Lydia? We've just left her, and she was very upset because she couldn't reach you today."

"I'm sure she was. I had some errands to do, but I'm here now. You haven't been badgering her, have you?"

"We came to offer cookies, support, and a listening ear. If that's badgering, I guess so."

Mollified, Miriam nodded. "Okay. You get a pass."

The frustration in her voice spurred Clara to comment. "I take it others haven't earned a pass."

"There are some nice people in this town, and then, there's the rest." Miriam's hand fisted. "I'm not one of the nice ones, but I protect my friends."

"But you don't kill for them."

"Not as yet," Miriam allowed a feral smile. "But the day isn't over." With that, she turned to mount Lydia's front steps.

Chapter 14

"Why aren't you dressed already?"

Mag looked down at her clothes, then back up at her sister. "Did you drink your lunch or something? Aren't we supposed to watch the surveillance footage tonight?"

"Not until later, and those are not workout clothes." Since Clara wore a sports bra under a tank top with skintight leggings, Mag could only assume that was what she meant by workout clothes.

"No, they're not. What's your point?"

"I have an exercise class at the country club tonight, and you have your massage. You knew that," Clara said, exasperated.

"Is there water in the pool?"

"No."

"If all I'm getting is poked and prodded, why would I want to bother?"

Clara sighed but managed to keep her expression neutral. "To get out of the house? To talk to friends? To investigate a murder? To get your back rubbed? Just get ready. You'll enjoy yourself once we get there."

"What could you possibly find enjoyable about prancing around with a bunch of witches and bitches?" Mag scoffed. "You know, I can see every inch of you under those clothes. You might as well have just painted that outfit on."

"Says the woman who went into the pool wearing a suit that looked like it was made from the seat of a lawn chair and a couple of rags left over from Woodstock," Clara all but growled.

Mag raised an eyebrow, but Clara continued her sales pitch undaunted. "Never mind the clothes. We could use this opportunity to get some information from Ned without arousing suspicion. Maybe he knows something to help us figure out what happened to Wayland."

"Fine. I'll go."

With Mag in the driver's seat—because she wouldn't have it any other way—they set off for the country club together, bickering all the way. Ultimately, Clara joined the class while Mag elected to try the sauna. Once inside, she chose the far corner of the room and added a magical boost to the steam so it would billow and hide her from view. Then, she waited.

It didn't take long for her patience to be rewarded. At the approach of chattering voices, she shrank back even more and listened.

"I'll petition the board if I have to, but they're not setting off fireworks at the end of June. Not when I already have to deal with them for the fourth, anyway. Mr. Flufferdoodle can't stand the noise. It took me half the day to get him out from under the bed last year."

"Good luck with that. It's the club's hundredth anniversary. You know they're planning to go all out for it, and you only get one of those."

"I don't care. I'll take them to court if I have to, even if I have to go to Bangor to find an attorney. Sam

Wayland picked the most inconvenient time to die."

Mag rolled her eyes at the entitlement of thinking of a man's death in those terms.

"I heard they had to fish his brains out of the pool, and that's why they drained it."

When Mag couldn't see the speaker, she realized her plan had a minor flaw and added a two-way mirror effect. If she hadn't been trying to stay still, she'd have patted herself on the back for that one. Genius, if she said so herself. As her vision cleared, she recognized Evelyn from the bakery. An inveterate gossip with, in Mag's estimation, no recognizable filter.

"That's not what I heard." The second speaker was Evanora Dupree, who knew perfectly well what had happened to Sam Wayland but enjoyed her position as a large cluster on the town grapevine.

"He had it coming." Mabel Youngblood leaned in close and lowered her tone. "Nasty piece of work he was."

That seemed to be the consensus as far as Mag could tell. In the days following Wayland's death, she hadn't heard enough good words about the man to fill a thimble. How did someone become so morally bankrupt? Mag wasn't above bending or breaking the rules if it suited her needs. But only to protect, never out of spite or an intention to harm. Sam Wayland, it seemed, had enjoyed far fewer scruples.

"He helped me once," came the timid voice of the fourth woman who had entered the room. All heads turned. "And I'll never forget it."

"Do tell," Evanora encouraged while Mag cocked an ear to hear every detail.

"My ex tried to take my kids away from me. It was horrible the way he had everyone convinced I was a bad mother. All to keep from paying child support. Lydia heard what was happening, and the next thing I knew, Sam knocked on my door and offered to be my knight in shining armor."

When Mag realized her expression mirrored the rest, she pulled her brows back to their habitual scowl. Not that anyone could see her, but even so. Still, she let a smirk cross her lips when Evelyn muttered something about him being more of a donkey's ass.

"That's redundant," Evanora chirped.

"Apparently, so was he," Evelyn replied.

Twitters followed until the fourth woman interrupted. "It's not funny. He treated me with respect and fought hard for me and my children. He won, by the way, and then he wouldn't take a penny for his work. Sam Wayland was a good man, and you're just a bunch of mean women." With that, she rose and flounced to the door, letting in a blast of cooler air and swirling the steam behind her. Thankfully, Mag remained hidden behind her bespelled cloud.

"I guess she told you," Mabel said as the door slammed shut. Evelyn shrugged.

"Even a lying dog can do something nice occasionally."

"I suppose." Evanora sighed. "Doesn't make him less of a dog, and I know it's not nice to speak ill of the dead, but there must be more than a few people who are not sorry he took a header on the edge of the pool."

"Where have you been? He didn't take a header. The police say it wasn't an accident. The question is, who did it? I'm sure there are plenty who would have helped him along if they had the chance."

What followed was, in Mag's estimation, pure gold. When she left the room, she'd added several items to her list of suspects and motives for murder. Given his proximity, Mag put Ned, the manager, at the top.

Meanwhile, Clara's luck ran on similar lines. While she sweated her way through the class, Sam's death was the topic of the day. To her surprise, some women had nice things to say about him.

She'd just emerged from the showers when Mag exited the steam room.

"You get anything?" Mag asked.

"Loads. You?"

"Some."

"Fiona's waiting for you. I'll take a steam and see you after. We can compare notes then." Clara walked inside and closed the sauna door behind her with finality leaving Mag to join Fiona.

Minutes later, hands of velvet over iron pressed and kneaded Mag's muscles until they wanted to scream with both pain and relief. She couldn't help it when her body twitched.

"There's tension in your lower back. Probably from compensating for that hip," Fiona prodded a particularly tender spot. Mag yelped, then got annoyed with herself for showing weakness.

"It's not that bad."

"Really?" Fiona prodded again, and while Mag held back another yelp, she twitched. "It's not a weakness to ask for help when you need it or to admit that something hurts."

Just the sentiment Mag didn't want to hear.

"I don't need the philosophizing, just do what you do, and we'll see if it's worth anything first."

Where another woman might get testy at being told to mind her own business, Fiona allowed a chuckle. Margaret Balefire wasn't her first cantankerous client. Probably wouldn't be her last.

"You're holding grief in your muscles."

"Quit giving me grief, then."

The hands working at Mag's muscles went lax for a moment, then Fiona chuckled. "Do you always deflect? Or is the prickly exterior just for my benefit?"

"I am what I am," Mag said, wincing at the bolt of pain Fiona teased from her hip. "A cranky, selfish old lady who'd rather stab you with a knitting needle than look at you."

Fiona's hands stilled. "What I see in you, Margaret Balefire, is a heart of fire encased in glass. Your fire burns to protect and light the way for others, but the glass keeps anyone from getting too close."

Feeling like a butterfly on a pin, Mag shrugged off Fiona's healing touch. "I think our time is up."

"Yours will be if you don't let the fire melt that glass. Letting people see who you really are doesn't make you vulnerable. It lets them love you better."

"Love is a weakness."

Her hands gentling, Fiona let out a single sigh. "It's not, but I suppose you'll have to figure that out on your own." Gentling her hands, she did what she could for the elderly witch and rubbed away the pain.

Mag sighed at the relief and turned the conversation to other interests. Namely murder.

"When are they planning to open the pool again? Looks like the police are done with it." The tape had gone since her last visit. Not that Mag would have let a little police tape slow her down.

"Sam Wayland. Almost as much trouble dead as he was alive. Maybe more."

The utter disgust in Fiona's tone got Mag's curiosity up. "What did he do to you?"

"I lost my business when he helped a former customer file a lawsuit against me. It didn't amount to anything because her doctor stood up for me in court, but the legal fees ate my savings, and the defense took up so much time I couldn't keep up with my business. I had to shut down and take a job here. They pay well enough, and I like the work just fine, but it's not the same."

"Sounds like you're not sorry he's gone."

Her fingers paused mid-knead. "I suppose I should be, and I'm not fully bereft of compassion, but I won't miss the fact that he'd begun to worm his way onto the board here. I know I won't lose my job now, at least."

Chalk up another motive. Sam seemed to generate them like baby rabbits.

"I'm sure I'm not the only one he'd have been gunning for if he'd managed to score a slot. Ned's only holding onto his job by a thread, and he'd have been on the chopping block. Anyone who won a case against him ended up on Wayland's list."

"Did he lose often?"

"Not often enough, in my opinion, but it did happen occasionally. Ned was already looking for something else before the whole blowup the other day."

"You're not the only one glad to see the back of him,

then."

"I wouldn't go so far as to say I'm glad he's dead. Just that he's not getting on the board."

"All the same. Who else was he gunning for?"

Fiona shrugged. Mag felt the motion more than saw it in her peripheral vision. "I don't have all the details."

Mag sensed the *but* coming. "But a member of the finance committee was caught with a girl on the back nine. From what I heard, she was barely of age, and still, she took the brunt of it."

"Celia May?"

"Then you already know what happened."

"I know a little."

"Elliot Sinclair kept his job at the credit union while Celia took the brunt of the gossip. After that, some of the club's female members took a dim view of him. I'm not sure why it took them so long. It wasn't such a big surprise he'd go after a young woman considering he hit on anything with boobs."

"Including you?"

Fiona's fingers paused, then the massage continued. "I have boobs, don't I?"

Mag chuckled at Fiona's dry tone. "Not your type?"

"Not even close."

The white sheet whispered across Mag's skin as Fiona slid it up to cover both hips and went to work on calves that hadn't been sore before but gave off little twinges when prodded.

"Ow," Mag said when Fiona hit a particularly tender spot.

"Sorry."

"I don't think you are." Not when her fingers kept

sending up more flares of pain.

Fiona grinned, enjoying the challenge. "You're right. I'm not. But you'll thank me when you can walk without wincing."

Mag grunted in response, trying to focus on the pain and not the memories that swirled in her mind. Memories of the last time she had felt this vulnerable and exposed. The accident left her with a body constantly in pain and a heart that was too afraid to let anyone get too close. It was easier to push people away than to risk being hurt again.

But Fiona's hands on her body, molding and soothing her muscles, were making it harder and harder to hold onto that fear. It was like the heat from a fire trying to melt away that protective glass around her heart. And for the first time in a long time, Mag felt a flicker of something she had long thought was lost: hope.

"Just relax," Fiona patted Mag on the back of her calf. "Let the tension go from both your mind and your body. Just let it drift."

As Fiona worked, Mag let her mind wander away from the murder investigation. Sam Wayland may have been a snake, but that didn't mean he deserved to die. And whoever had killed him was still out there, possibly even among the members of the club.

But for now, she let herself be lost in the sensation of Fiona's hands on her body and thought maybe she should work up a bucket list like Ellen's.

What, Mag wondered, would she like to do before she died?

Finding a way not to die so soon topped the list, but since that wasn't exactly in her control, Mag considered more mundane activities.

There wasn't a corner of this world or several others that Mag hadn't seen if the mood took her. Travel wouldn't make the list, so what else did people get excited about? Since nothing came to mind, Mag asked Fiona.

"What's the one thing you'd like to do before you die?"

Not even missing a beat, Fiona answered, "Burn that bathing suit you had on the other day."

"Funny." Mag rolled her eyes. "But really. Do you have a bucket list? I'm looking for ideas."

Fiona paused a moment to think to prove she took the question seriously. "You mean like visit the Dali Lama or climb Everest?"

Since Mag had done both...or maybe it didn't count as climbing if you used magical means of travel, she shrugged. "If that's your thing."

"It's not," Fiona decided. "Not at all. I don't even think I have a thing."

"Come on," Mag insisted. "Everyone has a thing."

"Okay, fine. If you insist, I think I'd like to touch a penguin."

Mag evaluated and found it a fine response. "The little buggers are pretty cute."

"And we're done." With a final flourish, Fiona re-draped the sheet. "Take a minute while I wash my hands, and then I'll help you sit up."

"I can sit up by myself. I'm not that feeble yet." When she began to do just that, Fiona laid a restraining hand on her arm.

"We did a lot of deep tissue work to relax your

muscles. You'll undo some of my hard work if you get up too soon. Make sure to drink plenty of water for the next few hours."

Maybe it was like mixing a potion. Sometimes you needed to let things rest a minute.

"Fine." Lying back, Mag cooperated with more grace than usual because she felt just that good. Good enough, she was tempted to conjure up a penguin and make Fiona's wish come true. Of course, that wouldn't do, but she'd keep it in mind for the future if these massages continued.

Mag found Clara sitting in a chair outside the massage room when she came out. "Come with me."

"Why?" Clara wanted to know. "Where are we going?" Mag declined to answer. Instead, she strode towards the manager's office and knocked on the door. "Follow my lead."

Full of curiosity, Clara did.

Not waiting for a response, Mag pushed the door open and walked inside. At his desk, Ned looked up with an expression of equal parts surprise and wariness when he saw them standing together. He recovered quickly, offering them a polite smile as he leaned back in his chair.

"What can I do for you ladies?"

His face, Clara noted, showed strain around wary brown eyes, and it didn't look like he'd paid much attention to his shaving that morning because he'd missed a small patch of whiskers on his chin.

"We'd like to buy a charter membership," Mag stated, settling in the chair opposite his desk. On any other day, his look of skeptical disbelief might have earned him a tongue-lashing, but today, Mag only smiled. "Can you make that happen?"

"I could, of course. You realize it's quite an expensive prospect."

"You don't think we're good for the money?"

Dressed in a bespoke suit, his hair expertly and expensively coiffed, Ned barely managed to keep his thoughts from being painted all over his face. Mag looked like she'd crawled out of a Salvation Army drop-off bin from the seventies, and Clara still wore her workout gear. He would swear on his sainted mother's name these women could not afford the fees. He'd have been wrong. Dead and epically wrong.

He cleared his throat. "It's my job to help you choose the level of membership that's right for you."

Mag tagged Clara's ankle with her foot and ignored the sidelong glance it cost her, but Clara got the hint.

"It's just…you see… Mayor McCreery sponsored our membership, and after what happened to Lydia…" she let the words trail off while she watched Ned's face deepen a shade or two.

"That was an unfortunate incident, to be sure." Ned lifted a hand to loosen his collar. "But I can assure you, it was a one-time thing specific to the parties involved."

"It seems as if you were instrumental in the situation. Maybe you could explain what happened. It would help us with our decision."

When Clara fixed her warm gaze on his face, Ned took a slightly deeper breath and began to pick his way through an explanation that wasn't much more detailed than what the Balefires already knew.

"Once it was brought to our attention, we altered our

membership rules to eliminate the loophole and ensure nothing like this ever happens again. You don't need to worry about a thing."

"If you don't mind me saying," Clara injected a load of sympathy into her voice, "you still seem worried. Sam's death must have come as quite a shock."

Without seeming to think about it, Ned pinched the bridge of his nose. Probably had a headache from stress, Clara thought and sent soothing thoughts in his direction.

"And maybe brought you some small measure of relief," she said softly.

"Between us, I've had better weeks."

Since Mag wasn't as good with people, she kept her mouth shut and let Clara handle the sympathy routine with her usual skill and style. Should she wish to, Clara could charm the birds from the trees with only the power of her voice.

"It might help to talk about it. Your taking the time to talk with us has made me feel better, and I'm happy to return the favor. People say I have a listening ear. A weight shared is a burden lifted."

Ned smiled. Clara Balefire was a hard woman to resist. And yet, he did. Sort of.

"We regret the loss of one of our members. Small communities become like family over time, so an accident like this hits harder and deeper. To mitigate some of the loss, I've set up a sponsorship memorial in Sam's name. We'll fund one family and one personal membership each year."

"Isn't that a nice thing for the club to do?" Clara said. "Such a good indication of how they value their members.”

Mag covered the snort that slipped out with a cough.

“Oh, this isn’t a club decision. It’s something I’ve decided to do out of my own pocket,” Ned clarified.

Interesting, Clara thought. Guilty conscience at work? Maybe.

“Commendable, I’m sure.”

Several seconds passed while Clara debated what question to ask next, but before she formed a firm idea, the door swung open behind her.

“Sullivan, I need…sorry. I didn’t know you were with someone. Ladies.”

The newcomer nodded to each of them in turn. Mag recognized him from Wayland’s funeral. The soft man with the hard eyes who’d stared at the casket but never approached.

“Meet Mag and Clara Balefire.” Ned made the introductions. “They stopped in to discuss their membership. In light of recent events, this has become a common occurrence.” When he looked back at Clara, Ned’s smile looked less genial than before. “Mrs. and Miss Balefire, I’d like to introduce Ben Worthington. Ben oversees our membership office, so he’s the right person to answer all your questions.”

The implication being that Ned no longer wanted to bear the brunt of Sam Wayland’s fallout.

“Of course, of course.” Worthington put on a smile to match his jovial tone, but again, Mag observed it didn’t reach his eyes. “What can I do for you?”

“We simply wanted some assurance of our options should something happen to our sponsor. It seems your policies are…more flexible than we’d been led to believe. We have enjoyed our time here and wouldn't want to see our membership jeopardized over something as trivial, let's say, as a falling out among friends."

Worthington's eyes fired at the mere suggestion of impropriety, but his voice stayed smooth as peanut butter on warm toast. "Now, now. The Wayland situation was unfortunate, but it has been handled. You have nothing to fear. Just put that worry right out of your head and don't think about it again."

"I feel ever so much better."

If the men missed the ripe sarcasm in Mag's voice, Clara didn't and barely suppressed a snort.

"Glad to be of service," Worthington's voice was dismissive.

"Well, you must be very busy. We'll just get out of your way. Come now, Mother. It's long past time for your nap."

Mag burned her with a look but followed Clara out the door willingly enough. "He did it," she said once the door had closed behind them.

"Maybe."

The air carried a deeper chill when they walked into the parking lot—the kind that promised snow before morning. Mag felt a wave of dizziness wash over her, and she stumbled slightly, bracing herself against Clara's arm.

"Are you all right?" Clara asked, steadying her with a hand on her back.

Mag shook her head, feeling weak and disoriented but defaulting to annoyance. "I'm fine. Just a little slip. What's for supper, anyway? I'm probably weak from hunger."

Clara rubbed small circles on Mag's back to comfort her as they walked slowly across the parking lot. "Then we'll get you home, where I can ply you with soup and tea. That should help you feel better in no time."

But Mag didn't make it to the van before she had another weak and dizzy spell, swaying unsteadily on her feet until Clara decided it didn't matter if anyone saw her doing magic and flashed them into their seats.

"Hold on, Maggie. We're going home." Fear turned Clara's guts to ice, her hands clammy, and set her heart thumping in her chest.

"I said I'm fine." Mag's voice sounded weak even to her. "Maybe we'd better postpone watching those videos, though."

"You're not fine, and neither am I." Clara drove far enough to be out of sight of the club and shifted the entire van into their driveway. By the time she got Mag into bed with a steaming bowl of soup, her decision was cemented in as much stone as she once had been.

Clara meant to save her sister and wouldn't count the cost.

Chapter 15

"Did you want to look at that footage?" Since it was the one day of the week when the shop was closed, Clara had other plans, but she didn't want Mag to get agitated.

What Clara didn't know was that Mag also had plans for her day. Still, the footage might be worth the time.

"You got your phone with you?"

"I do." Since she'd already pulled her phone out, Clara brought her fingers together over the screen in a grasping motion, then flicked them out to send the image thumbnails to Mag's television. "It works with commands. Pause, rewind, fast forward—that type of thing."

Mag grinned. "Almost impressive."

"Bite me." Clara also allowed a grin, but only because it felt good to see Mag on her feet and feeling sassy. "Besides, it gets better." Another finger flick expanded each thumbnail until the grid filled the screen. The first image picked up where they'd left off, with a still shot of Ned returning to the club. With a flourish, she reversed the rest to that same time marker and then said, "Play."

Not to be outdone, Mag cast an expansion spell that increased the size of the viewing area by more than double. "I got the left side. You watch the right," she said.

After a minute or two, when nothing moved on the screen, Clara boosted the playback speed by fifty percent. A few seconds later, Mag yelled, "Stop!"

"Pause," Clara said.

"Can you just play that one?" Mag pointed to the frozen image of the rear entrance closest to the pool area. "Reverse it a little, and then let it play."

"Sure." Clara made it happen.

"Do you see what I see?" Mag clapped her hands and would have capered around the room if not for her hip. "That's Fiona. Pause. And that's Fiona rigging the door to keep it from locking."

"It is," Clara agreed. "I wonder why."

"Why she'd rig the door? Or why she'd kill Wayland?"

"Seems like one would answer the other."

"I suppose," Mag shrugged. "There was a lawsuit that cost Fiona her business."

Nodding, Clara set the videos on play again. "That would do it, I suppose, but I think we should keep watching. Just in case it wasn't her."

Since Fiona wasn't ringing Mag's bell, she flicked her hand in a circle to indicate they should get on with it.

"There's the membership guy. What was his name again?" Mag couldn't bring it to the front of her memory.

"Worthington. Ben, I think. And that guy with him is Elliot Sinclair."

Mag remembered that name. "He's the one who got caught in the tall grass with Miriam's daughter. According to Fiona, he hits on anything with boobs. I wonder if that includes Ben Worthington?"

"Probably," Clara snorted. "His are bigger than mine." She clapped a hand over her mouth. "That wasn't very nice."

"No, but it was accurate. He's got mean eyes."

"I noticed." The memory was enough to turn Clara sober. "I take it he's on the list."

"Far as I'm concerned," Mag continued watching the videos, "they all are. The problem is that the more I learn about Sam Wayland, the less I care who did him in."

"I care that Lydia might be arrested." Diplomatic as usual, Clara wouldn't admit she felt the same. "But if the police have access to these videos, they know she wasn't there that night. Her alibi holds up."

"She could have been," Mag pointed out. "We didn't go back far enough to know for sure."

"She wasn't." Not wanting to get into an argument, Clara set a charm to leave the videos running and excused herself. Mag didn't argue and waved her sister out the door.

In her workshop, with the vial of pool water resting on the table before her, Clara leaned her elbows on the scarred wood and dropped her chin into her cupped hands to think. Divining potion ingredients without a recipe called on several skills not every witch possessed. Magical chemistry wouldn't be easy, it wouldn't be fast, and it wouldn't be fun, but if anyone could figure out what was in the pool water, Clara thought she was the witch for the job.

Patience and a logical approach to separating ingredients were key, so Clara thought as she began with a whispered spell to send pool-maintenance chemicals into one of the small bowls she'd set out for that purpose. She wrinkled her nose at the sharp scent and used a flick of magic to send the bowl across the room where the chemical stench wouldn't impede her ability to work. Getting rid of anything unnatural was the easy part since none of the stabilizers or other chemicals, including the type of chlorine generated by the new salt filter, existed in nature.

"Now, we'll see what's what." Clara often talked to herself while she brewed and mixed her cosmetics, but she relied on her familiar, Pyewacket for this type of work. "Take a sniff. Tell me what you think."

On the windowsill, a dying fly buzzed and spun in lazy circles. Since there was nothing Pyewacket loved better—in her cat form, of course—than a delicious sky raisin, the fly drew her attention away from the task at hand.

"Pye! Pay attention. The fly can wait."

Siamese in her cat form, Pyewacket looked no less regal in her human one as she hastily bent her head and inhaled to detect the scent of magic.

"It's diluted, but I'm getting hints of something."

Clara held her fingertip over the opening and tipped the vial up to let a drop of the liquid pool on her skin, then slid her tongue across the moisture. "No taste." The faintest echo of a deep musical note sounded in her head, but that could have been just nerves, she supposed.

Following suit, Pyewacket concurred. "Still, there's something."

Because she agreed, Clara divided the water into two smaller vials, stoppered, and set one aside in case her first attempt failed, then poured the remaining one into another of her testing bowls.

"Aqua Divimentum" A flick of her wand and the power of her intent sent only the water from one bowl to another, hoping to leave any other ingredients behind. "Well, that would have been too easy," she muttered as she confronted the empty bowl.

"Can't have that," Pyewacket agreed with a touch of acerbic humor.

Shrugging, Clara tried again. "Revelio." She tapped her wand on the edge of the bowl, but other than a ripple caused by the motion, nothing happened.

Wrinkling her nose, Clara exchanged a look with Pye and tried a third spell. "Separatimo simulus." Water fountained back to the other bowl leaving behind a small, green puddle and, in the center, the tiniest drop of something golden and gleaming.

"That had better not be what I think it is," She said as she brought the bowl up to her nose for a gentle sniff, then delicately dipped the tip of her pinky into the droplet and touched the sticky sample to her tongue.

"Hagatha!" Clara scowled. "I should have known."

"Pixie honey." Pyewacket wasn't asking. Hagatha's honey pixie hive and colony had been the most recent of the old witch's obsessions. One that had turned the entire town upside down before Mag and Clara discovered what Hagatha had been up to and made her send the pixies back to their native land. Or at least most of them. There'd been one who bonded with Hagatha and either refused to leave or had found a way to return for visits—Clara wasn't entirely certain which, but the why of it wasn't important.

"Among other things." Clara magically sent the drop of honey into a fresh vial, then contemplated the green puddle left in the bowl.

"What other things?"

Clara tipped the bowl so that Pyewacket could see. "Something herbal for the base, I'd say. I'm getting hints of verbena, nettle, and St. John's wort. Nothing special there. Mostly herbs with healing properties, but there's more, and some of that more is concerning." As she named each herb, Clara removed it from the mixture. With each extraction, the brew changed color.

"Blood, maybe?" Pyewacket asked as the green slowly leeched into a pale pink. " Blood and something else."

"That's my theory as well. Blood magic used on the unsuspecting goes against everything we stand for." With a flick of her wrist, the blood coagulated into a single droplet, which she sent into a vial, leaving nothing in the bowl but a shallow puddle of clear liquid that wasn't water.

"And this must be the mystery ingredient. Or ingredients, I suppose." Pyewacket stuck her face in the bowl and sniffed deeply. "Odorless."

"Of course it is," Clara grumbled and stared into the bowl while she decided what to do next. "We can agree the enchantments added to this water were intended to be beneficial."

Pyewacket shrugged. "I'd agree with you, except that Pixie honey carries addictive properties. That's shady."

Her fingertips tapping on the tabletop, Clara nodded. "It is. Or maybe the potion requires more than one exposure to be effective, and the honey's meant to draw people back so it can work."

"Did you feel the pull?"

Chestnut curls bounced when Clara shook her head. "Mag did. Does, I suppose. She thinks I don't know how many times she's gone back, but I do."

When properly matched, a witch and her familiar complete each other in all things magical. Pyewacket picked up on Clara's thoughts as if they were her own. "You think you weren't as affected by it because you were in less need of relief."

"It's a theory."

To test the theory, Clara rose, went to the windowsill, and retrieved the dying fly. Pyewacket's eyes glazed over, and if she'd been in the proper form, her tail would have twitched.

"Don't even think about it," Clara shuddered and warned as she retrieved an eyedropper from a nearby drawer and used it to apply the solution to the fly.

"Could be meant for people," Pyewacket commented when it continued to buzz and spin on its back. "Could be too late, too."

Clara shrugged but kept watching as she tried to work out the ratio of potion to water in her head and then scale that up to figure how much had gone into the pool. Then again, a drop this size with a good expansion spell would do the trick, so maybe the math wasn't worth the effort. While she arrived at this conclusion, the fly righted itself.

"Would you look at that?" Clara breathed.

She would never learn, however, whether the effects were short-lived or long-term.

"Was that strictly necessary, Pye?" She said as the fly

disappeared between furry lips.

A woman again, Pyewacket blushed. "I couldn't help it."

Clara shook her head in disgust but figured it was best to focus on the problem and not the stumbling blocks, except for the fact that the current problem and biggest stumbling block led back to Hagatha Crow and Maypole the honey pixie, which meant a visit to the old witch. If Hagatha hadn't created the mystery potion, she'd at least supplied the honey and, with some prying, might be willing to give Clara a name.

Clara was sure she could save her sister if she could bolster the potion's healing properties with something more permanent than pixie honey. If it meant bearding old Haggie in her den, Mag was worth the effort.

Meanwhile, in her tiny house, Mag had finished her nap. Despite Clara's warning to stay in bed, she'd risen and gone into research mode with the mysterious vial from Wayland's casket.

It would have surprised Clara to see her sister enter a deeply meditative state, holding the glass between her palms, but Mag's methods tended to be more intuitive than clinical.

"Magic," she muttered. "And plenty of it, but what kind?"

Still holding the vial, she surveyed the artifacts she'd laid out in a semi-circle before her. The items represented each type of elemental magic: earth, wind, fire, water, and metal, for a start. She'd also added what she could find from her collection of the darker arts and included that performed by other practitioners as well.

"Worst one, first one," Mag said as she chose a piece of cloth from a necromancer's shawl impregnated with magic and held it firmly in her other hand. The vibes didn't match at all. "Phew. Guess he won't be coming back from the dead."

Clara wasn't the only Balefire who talked to herself sometimes.

Having run through her repertoire without getting a strong hit, Mag took the next step, pulled the stopper, and separated the contents into a second container bespelled to be inert. Holding the empty bottle in one hand, she let the other hover over the dark substance.

Only one sparked of magic, and surprisingly, it was the vial. The only reason Mag could think of to cast a spell on a vial was to hold something volatile. Poison, maybe? But the liquid still smelled and looked like ink. Poisoned ink? But why? Devil's ink? Had Sam done a deal with a demon? No, those were written in blood.

None of it made sense to her as she repeated the round of testing talismans against the ink-black liquid. Nothing. Nor did it react when she poured some into a smaller vessel, pricked her finger, and fed the substance some blood. No response.

Impatient, Mag called the blood back to her, watched it reabsorb into her finger, and fed the ink a taste of conjured fire. Liquid boiled away, leaving a dusting of lampblack. Definitely ink, and an old-fashioned one, too, she decided.

Eyes narrowed, Mag considered her next move. Why

would the ink be kept in a bespelled container if it wasn't dangerous? Or had the container been bespelled for another reason? And would finding the answer bring her any closer to knowing why she'd found it where she did? Frustrated with her lack of results, she banished the ink back to the bottle and sent the bottle to sit on a high shelf where it could sit and mock her efforts.

Chapter 16

Her hands plunged into a sink full of warm, soapy water, Clara absently washed the pasta pot while watching bright patterns of light splash across the sky from Gertude's Christmas display. Aurora Borealis had nothing on Gertrude Granger when the holiday season was upon her. Providing joy to strangers was Gertrude's way of generating Christmas spirit. That Gertrude had figured out a way to bottle that spirit was just one of the reasons Clara intended to drag Mag out to see the show.

It seemed as if half the state had shown up to view the spectacle during the week, but Mag hadn't wanted—or worse, hadn't been able—to walk over for a tour.

"We'll see about that," Clara decided as she finished the washing up, then went downstairs to her workroom behind the shop where she had a batch of salve already brewing for her sister. She'd added several drops of the distilled essence from the pool water—minus the pixie honey—the same herbs, and a dash of cayenne pepper to the mix. The salve turned a rosy peach color which deepened to salmon as it cooled.

Pocketing the small jar, Clara went back upstairs to exchange cotton socks for a pair of bespelled wool ones that would protect her feet from the evening chill.

Thinking Mag might appreciate the same, Clara selected a second pair, added the charm, and then prepared to approach the lion in her den.

"Come on, Maggie. It's a beautiful night. Come out for a walk with me. I'm betting Gertrude's lights can be seen from space, so it's a spectacle you won't want to miss. And," she cut off any protest before Mag could utter a word. "I have some new salve for you to test for me. I'll add it to the new line if it does what I hope, but I need a guinea pig."

None of those reasons were ones Mag couldn't resist, but Clara had one more carrot to put before the mule. "And I thought we could stop for ice cream on the way home." She pulled out the container of salve and tossed it in her sister's lap while ignoring Mag's annoyed expression.

"You're not letting this go, are you?" Mag resigned herself to an evening of dealing with a crowd while cold seeped into her bones.

"We need some cheer around here." And some hope, but Clara wouldn't let Mag see hers was flagging. "Wear these. I'll wait while you change." The socks joined the salve. "Unless you need help putting on the salve."

As expected, the subtle suggestion she might not be fully up to snuff forced Mag to prove Clara wrong.

"I was watching my stories."

"You can watch those anytime. Gertrude's going all out this year. You don't want to miss it."

"You don't know. I might." But Mag was already up and limping toward the bedroom to change out of her nightgown.

"Well, I want to go, and you're going with me. Don't

forget the socks. You'll thank me later."

"I'll thank you to mind your own," Mag muttered as she shut the door behind her. The salve went on easily and provided more relief than she'd expected, which went some way toward easing her lousy mood. The heat penetrating her toes and working its way up her body pushed her toward cheerfulness. Where had these socks been all her life?

Not trusting the pain to stay relieved, Mag dressed with the speed of magic and joined Clara in the front room. "I'm keeping these socks."

Delighted, Clara reached in her pocket for the matching hat, complete with a cheery pom-pom on the top. "Good. This goes with them, and here are the mittens as well."

Mag caught the hat when Clara tossed it, yanked it on over the fluff of her hair, and felt the immediate warmth washing down her body to meet the heat sliding up from her feet. "If you've got a set of wool panties in your pocket, I'll take them." The constant heat would feel wonderful on her hip.

Clara's face colored slightly. "I don't think I've ever seen a knitting pattern for underwear. They'd probably be itchy."

Mag shrugged. "I'm sure I'd survive. Shall we?"

Clara nudged Mag in the side with an elbow and said with an amused smirk, "Well, let's go have fun then! I'm sure Gertrude will appreciate some company."

Mag and Clara strolled through the streets of Harmony, their conversation ranging from the latest gossip to Clara's prized boots— pointy-toed ankle huggers with chunky heels and a tarnished buckle. Mag rolled her eyes and joked, "I swear if you trip over another pebble, I'm leaving you here," as Clara stumbled over an imaginary crack in the pavement. The duo continued along until they reached Gertrude's house, and as they approached, they heard a strange noise coming from somewhere on the grounds. Mag whispered to Clara, "I hope she isn't practicing her bagpipe skills again!"

"She might be," Clara said with a smirk. "Or else fifty cats are fighting in there."

Mag shook her head. "Gertrude doesn't do cats. Cats like to tear up tinsel. You know she has a partridge as a familiar, right?"

Surprise stilled Clara in her tracks. "I did not."

"It lives in a pear tree in her backyard."

"Get out!"

"Hand to Goddess," Mag swore. "Maybe it teamed up with the seven swans a-swimming and the six geese a-laying, and they're all in there having a honk fest. That would be something to see."

"I don't think partridges honk." Clara laughed. "And if they did, I doubt they'd honk to the tune of—is that Jingle Bells?"

"What sound does a partridge make?" Now that the conversation had gone in that direction, Mag couldn't help wondering. "I think it's Frosty the Snowman."

"I can't tell, exactly. But I can find out what sound a partridge makes." Clara pulled out her phone, did a quick search, and then the two witches stood on the sidewalk and listened to the results. "I'd call that more of a squawk than a honk. Either way, it doesn't sound anything like bagpipes."

Bagpipe serenade notwithstanding, the crowd milling around Gertrude's house was even bigger than the year before. Mag and Clara weaved through the buzzing throng until a hand landed on Clara's arm.

"Lydia's been cleared." Miriam May leaned in close to keep anyone from overhearing. "The guy she'd been seeing finally gave a statement, and the wait staff at the restaurant verified she was there at the time of Sam's death."

"That's good news."

"You got anything better?"

Clara shook her head. "Not yet."

"Let me know if and when." Miriam stalked away.

"Rude woman," Mag sniffed. "There's Gertrude. Over there by the…when did she add the merry-go-round?"

"No idea," Clara rubbed the wrinkled spot between her brows. "It wasn't there a few days ago when I stopped in to ask a question."

If Mag intended to ask what that question had been, she didn't get a chance because Gertrude had spotted the sisters and rushed to join them. "What do you think? Isn't this my best display ever?"

The pipe organ inside the merry-go-round was the source of off-key honking one might mistake for an inexperienced witch playing the bagpipes.

"What's it playing?" Mag asked.

"What else?" Gertrude pointed toward the horses, which, now that they were close enough, the Balefire sisters could see were actually reindeer with red, lighted noses. "Rudolph."

"I guess we were both wrong," Clara admitted with a private smile for her sister.

Gertrude beamed with pride as she gestured to her display; the twinkling lights illuminated her features, and her eyes were wide with enthusiasm while she spoke about each carefully crafted element. Her hands moved frantically in the air as she exaggerated each detail of the decorations as if they were her own children. "Oh, and this one is my favorite," she grinned, pointing at an old-fashioned bulb shaped like Santa's head. "It's just so...perfect!"

Most of the paint had worn off the bulb's raised surfaces, leaving Santa's face mostly white with creepy lines around the eyes and mouth. It was the stuff of nightmares, but Clara didn't make the observation out loud.

Aside from the honking carousel, children's laughter joined joyous shouts as they ran around the lawn in awe. Families looked on with wide eyes, their expressions filled with wonder as they took in the magical decorations that had transformed Gertrude's yard into a place of enchantment.

"Oh my goodness! It's like something out of a fairy tale!" one mother exclaimed, her voice trembling with delight. Her little boy tugged at her sleeve and pointed excitedly at a snowman coated entirely with glitter dust, which sparkled in the night sky. His face lit up in glee as he raced towards it, his tiny feet crunching over the blanket of snow that had fallen the night before.

With every passing minute, more children scrambled around, marveling at each decoration they encountered - from life-sized nutcrackers to delicate icicles dripping down from trees like glass tears. Everywhere you looked was something new and wonderful.

"You've truly outdone yourself this year," Clara said warmly.

Even Mag couldn't help but chuckle as she saw Clara admiring the swath of twinkling lights suspended without wires like stars in the night sky. "You know, I think we might have to steal that idea for our place," Mag said with a mischievous grin.

Clara rolled her eyes playfully. "You always were the one with sticky fingers," she said, but there was a hint of amusement in her voice as she teased. Seeing her sister get into the Christmas spirit meant Mag still had hope. And she didn't see anything wrong with celebrating Yule and Christmas at the same time. Clara considered herself a progressive witch, and Mag hadn't ever been one to adhere to custom solely for the sake of it being expected.

As they continued to explore the decorations, Mag noticed that Gertrude had disappeared. "Where did she go now?" she asked Clara, looking around for the older witch.

"I don't know," Clara said, her brow furrowed in confusion. "She was here just a minute ago."

"You can go look for her," Mag said as she snagged a spot on a nearby bench. "I'll be right here resting my hip."

Clara took one more turn around the yard, calling Gertrude's name as she went, then slipped inside the house to check for her. She was about to give up and head back outside when she heard a faint noise coming from upstairs.

It probably wasn't nice to sneak up on Gertrude, but Clara barely gave that a second thought before hurrying up the stairs, her footsteps muffled by the thick carpet. As she reached the top of the staircase, she saw a pale light glowing from beneath a door at the end of the hallway. She approached the door cautiously, unsure what she might find on the other side.

As Clara pushed open the door, she was greeted by the sight of Gertrude sitting in front of a large cauldron, her eyes closed in deep concentration. The room was filled with the scent of cinnamon and nutmeg, and the walls were adorned with intricate symbols and runes picked out in shades of red and green.

"Gertrude," Clara said softly, not wanting to startle her. "What are you doing?"

Gertrude's eyes fluttered open, and she turned to face her friend with a serene smile. "Just a little bit of holiday magic," she said, gesturing to the cauldron before her. A series of bubbles rose from the depths to pop as they met cooler air.

Approaching the cauldron. As they peered inside, Clara saw it was filled with shimmering golden liquid that seemed to dance and twirl, generating half the room's light.

"What is that?" Clara figured she already knew but needed confirmation.

"Nearly distilled Christmas spirit," Gertrude said, her eyes sparkling excitedly. "A potion for happiness and joy. It's made with the very finest holiday ingredients—love, laughter, and a pinch of magic. Takes nearly a month to make, so I start right after Thanksgiving when the first lights go up in town."

Nodding, Clara opened her mouth to ask another question but was stopped when the bubbling sound of the potion reduced dramatically.

"Ooh." Capering around the cauldron, Gertrude clapped her hands with glee. "You're just in time to see some serious poop."

At about that time, a tiny bubble rose from the pot. Clara sucked in a breath, drawing the sparkling mote toward her. When the bubble landed on her hand, she both heard and felt the gong of church bells as if she stood inside one while someone struck it with a mighty hammer.

"Ow!" Clara shouted.

With her attention riveted to the cauldron's contents, Gertrude muttered, "Sorry. The spirit is strong this year."

Strong? Clara wondered as the noise continued to reverberate through her brain. The bells faded to a single note after a moment, or maybe several of them. One Clara recognized. Her eyes narrowed as she contemplated Gertrude.

"It was you."

"What?"

"Don't play with me, Gertrude. I took a run at the contents of the pool water today, and this," Clara gestured toward the cauldron, "was part of it. You doctored the pool water, didn't you?"

Furious, Gertrude drew herself up to her full height. "I did no such thing, and you've no right to accuse me."

"I know what I know. That is the same magic I found in the pool water."

Gertrude deflated. "I suppose it's possible, but it wasn't me."

"Then who?"

With a sigh, Gertrude confessed a name. "Hagatha."

"I should have known." Clara slapped her palm against her forehead to stave off the headache that threatened to build behind her eyes. "It's always Hagatha. Why didn't you tell me?"

Her wand flashed in the light as Gertrude used magic to gather the contents of the potion into a single vial.

Distracted, Clara stared. "That's all you got for your work? That's not even half an ounce."

"A drop goes a long way when it comes to holiday cheer."

"And you didn't realize that's what was in the pool water? Or were you covering for Hagatha?"

"Could you blame me if I was?" Gertrude's face had fallen back into its peaceful lines.

"No. I guess not." Crossing Hagatha was a nasty business and only undertaken by the foolishly naive or just the very foolish.

"Besides, I've developed a tolerance over the years. This entire vial diluted by a pool full of water wouldn't touch me in the slightest. I'd need to add essence of Santa for that, and I only gave Hagatha half a drop."

"Essence of Santa?" The question popped out. "You know what? I don't want to know." Frowning, Clara decided to let Gertrude off the hook. Even if she'd sold the diluted spirit to Hagatha, what had been done with it wasn't her fault. Besides, for the first time since the Balefire sisters had moved to Harmony, Hagatha had done a nice thing. Sort of. At least Clara hoped there hadn't been some sort of retaliatory magic attached to the potion.

Since there was only one way to find out, she

determined to keep mum with Mag and talk to Hagatha secretly. What could go wrong with such a plan?

Only everything.

Chapter 17

The flare of pain in Mag's hip made the next morning nearly unbearable. The only thing that got her out of bed was taking a magical peak at the country club pool and finding it refilled. Looking at the time, she figured she had an hour before the club opened. Just long enough for a rejuvenating dip if she didn't waste time getting dressed. Two seconds later, she was soaking under a charmed dome and feeling less pain. Worth it.

As she basked in the pounding jets, her mind drifted back to Ellen. The poor woman, Mag thought. All she wanted was a trip to Graceland. Instead, she ended up with a bashed-in head. It wasn't right, and it wasn't fair.

And so, Mag decided to do something about it. And if Mag chose to do a thing, she'd do it right. Still sitting in the hot tub, she pondered and worked out a solid plan.

Back home and feeling no pain, she stood in front of the mirror, put her hands over her face, and called on the magic that formed at her core.

The glamor settled over her features like a thin glaze, altering hair color and tightening skin to stretch over subtly altered cheekbones. If Ellen was getting her dream vacation, why shouldn't Mag also take a break from her advancing life?

When she had it right, Mag closed her eyes, turned her magic inward, pressed palms against cheeks, and bound the glamor to her skin, making it a part of her.

A different woman stared back at her from the glass when she took her hands away. Turning this way and that, Mag decided she approved. Looking at her now, no one would see a pathetic old witch on her last legs, and shaky ones at that. A break from pity was just what she needed, and giving Ellen this trip was as good an excuse as any to take that break. Neither of them had much time left, so they might as well make every second count.

Lost in thought, she didn't hear the door open and jumped when her sister spoke.

"Margaret Balefire, what have you done to yourself?"

"What?" Instantly defensive, Mag glared.

"That hair. You look like Ronald McDonald's love child."

Mag turned back to the mirror. "I like it. Red hair suits my coloring, and it's fluffy. Makes my head look smaller."

"It looks like a home perm gone wrong, and no one in their right mind wants their head to look smaller." Grabbing the brush from Mag's dresser, Clara tamed the rioting curls adding magic to make them sleeker, softer, and more appealing.

"It's a glamor, not a freaking crime against nature."

Clara sighed. "Where were you planning to go looking like that?" Two days had passed since Mag had had one of her "spells," so some of Clara's worry had subsided, but not all.

"Graceland. I'm taking Ellen while she still has time."

"Ellen?" Clara's brow furrowed. "Isn't she still in a

coma? They won't let you take her to Graceland in a coma, and what good would that do her anyway? She wouldn't even know she was there."

When Mag merely lifted one eyebrow and fixed her sister with a level look, Clara clued in.

"You can't." Eyes going wide, Clara shook her head. "You can't take her on a spirit journey. She's not one of us. It would require enormous magic to move a tethered human spirit that far by yourself."

Without so much as a whisper of movement, Mag sent the fire in her hearth, a remnant of the mighty Balefire, the source of magic, roaring up the chimney like a burst from a jet engine. The sound of it filled the room.

"I am a Balefire witch. I draw my magic from the flame and feed it with the fire of my soul. My flesh may be on its last legs, but my magic is strong. Even if it burns my power to a cinder in the process, Ellen will have her trip to Graceland. Do I make myself clear?"

A shutter fell across Clara's expression. "Crystal. Ellen's wants come before your own needs, or mine for that matter, as I need my sister in my life for a long time to come." Spinning on her heel, Clara left the room. The annoyance of her passage hung like a dense gray fog, which was probably why Mag never noticed the extra weight that fell into the sleeve of the peasant blouse she wore over bell-bottom pants.

Outside the door, Clara let her stern expression drop, allowed herself a slight smile of satisfaction, and reached into her pocket to finger the other half of the charm she'd just left with Mag.

Clara would know about it if her sister's power dipped too low and could step in to help. Not that Mag would thank her for it, but thanks didn't matter.

On the other side of the door, Mag sniffed once, then shrugged and rifled through the depths of her magical fanny pack until she found a small glass globe on a chain. Questing tongues of flame tickled her hand as she thrust the globe into the fire.

"Fill." She didn't bother with fancy words, just the simple order to set a glowing ember into the sphere. Mag didn't expect to need the extra boost provided by bottled—or in this case, sphered—fire magic, but it certainly didn't hurt to have it in her arsenal.

She felt strong enough for the trip, and if she wasn't, and this was her last magical hurrah, she'd burn herself out doing something nice for a nice woman. There were worse ways to get to the Summerlands.

But Mag wasn't ready to die and certainly didn't intend to do so while she had Ellen's spirit along for the ride, so she dumped the contents of her charm drawer into her fanny pack. Pre-made magic would help conserve her energy, so Mag decided to stop at the workshop behind the store and help herself to whatever looked useful from Clara's cabinet as well.

"Take this one." Clara reached around to select a charm made from a drinking straw. She held back a smirk when Mag jumped. "Drop this in any cup, and it will fill with the beverage of your choice." While she had it in her hand, Clara layered in a restorative spell so that any beverage produced would strengthen the drinker. Just one more way of protecting her sister without seeming to hover.

"Good one. Single-use?"

"Do I look new?" Clara dropped the charm into her

sister's waiting hand and selected a twist tie from the shelf. "Take this one, too. It's a companion charm to the straw. Put it on any flat surface, and tap it three times for a picnic lunch."

The second charm got the same protective layer added as the first, and Mag never noticed a thing. Inside, Clara whooped. Outside, she maintained a bored expression while she picked several more charms that she thought Mag would find useful and added extra magical layers to each. The last, a compass on a keychain, would bring Mag home if she got lost, even if she had no breath of magic left in her.

"I don't need that," Mag bristled.

"Neither do I," Clara pulled an identical charm from her pocket. "But I carry one anyway. Just in case. Seemed like a good idea, given how many times various magical attacks have targeted us. It's keyed to the Balefire. Just touch it and tell it to take you home."

"No heel clicking involved?"

"You can if you want to. Have fun." Clara offered a hug and was surprised when Mag hugged her back. "Call me if you need me, and bring me something from the gift shop."

Nodding, Mag waved, activated her invisibility charm, and took herself off to the hospital. As best as Mag could tell from a cursory glance at her chart, Ellen's condition remained the same. Only the hiss and click from various machines and the softest sigh of the patient's breath broke the silence.

"Let's do this." Still unseen, Mag moved closer to the bed and placed one hand on Ellen's heart, the other on her head. "Tethered soul, wake and be free, travel with me, so mote it be."

"Where am I? Who are you?" A shining ball of light rose from Ellen's body, hovered for a moment, then took her shape in glowing mist. "What's happening?"

"You're in the hospital," Mag answered the first question succinctly. "With a head injury."

"Are you my guardian angel?"

Huffing out a laugh, Mag allowed, "Witches don't qualify for halos, and if they did, mine would be tarnished. It's Mag Balefire."

"Why, so it is. I didn't recognize you with all that red hair. You look younger. How did you do that?"

"I didn't come to talk about my fashion choices. I've come to offer you the trip of your dreams. It won't be exactly as you planned, but I hope it will be close enough. Want to go to Graceland?"

"Right now?"

"Unless you have something else to do."

"I guess I don't." Ellen looked down at her spectral body. "Am I dead?" Then she looked back at Mag. "Are you?"

Mag laughed with little mirth and shuddered when she looked at the machines keeping Ellen alive. "Not yet, and I wouldn't want to go out that way."

"Me, either." Ellen shrugged. "But I guess we don't always get to choose. I'll take that trip. Even if this is nothing more than a fever dream or a death delusion, seeing Graceland has to be better than watching my life pass before my eyes."

Mag grinned. "You're casting with coven on that one." She unzipped her fanny pack, and pulled out a vial, then a pair of tweezers. Swathed in layers of thin blankets, Ellen's body barely took up any space in the bed. Her face was nearly as pale as the bandages surrounding her head. Better get this show on the road, Mag thought, before it's too late. With Ellen's hair covered, Mag exchanged the tweezers for a pair of nail scissors and, with a delicate touch, took a sliver of thumbnail, which she dropped into the vial for later.

"That's it, then. If you're ready now, just take my hand. This will be a fast trip."

"Are we flying on a broomstick?"

Mag revised her plan for the return trip. "Is that something you'd like to do?" What could it hurt at this point? Ellen's prognosis wasn't good, and if, by some chance, she pulled through, Mag could wipe her memory. Or get Hagatha to do it since she was better at that sort of thing.

Ellen clapped her hands. "Yes, please."

"Okay, we'll work that out later. For now, just hang on tight." Mag took Ellen's hand and shifted them to a remote spot on the banks of Mud Lake. She'd killed her second, or maybe her third, Raythe here. There'd been so many, it was hard to remember.

"Where are we?" Ellen had done enough research to know she wasn't on the hallowed ground where Elvis had tread. "This isn't Graceland."

"It's not." Mag shook her head. "This is just a rest stop. I've got a spell to do here."

"More magic." Ellen's outline wavered. "I'm fascinated. I've always suspected there were true witches in Harmony, but you don't just walk up to someone and ask. That would be rude."

Nodding absently, Mag cast a circle to work in, then

rummaged around in her fanny pack for a straw doll and the vial of fingernail she'd dropped in earlier. "Stay inside the circle," she cautioned as she laid the doll in the center and began pulling out the rest of the elements she needed for the spell.

Ellen watched the process with great interest.

"You could make millions selling those on Etsy." She gestured toward the fanny pack. "I'd buy one. Great for the gal on the go."

Mag didn't need millions, but she appreciated the show of faith and bowed when Ellen applauded her ability to light a candle with her breath. It might be fun to show off a little, but she'd rather not give Ellen the wrong idea.

"Magic isn't free, and it isn't the answer to everything."

"I suppose not." Ellen watched avidly as the spell took shape. The doll expanded to match her size, and when Mag snapped her fingers, sucked in Ellen's spirit with a whoosh. Delighted, Ellen laughed. "Such fun," she declared, her giggle trailing behind as Mag shifted them both to a secluded spot she'd chosen a few yards from the corner of the property.

"The front gate's down that way," Mag pointed. "We'll tag along with one of the groups to get in." So saying, she dropped an obfuscation charm into Ellen's pocket. "This is your all-access pass. No one will notice us unless we want them to."

The sweet southern heat soaked into winter-chilled limbs, lending more flexibility to Mag's leg and hip. If she could get through a few days without having to flash back to Harmony for a dip in the pool, so much the better. Not needing to return would make it seem more like a true vacation. Feeling lighter in her soul, Mag ushered Ellen toward her dream vacation.

The days flew by in a blur. Ellen must have taken a thousand photos with the digital camera Mag conjured for her to use. They explored the grounds, stood in solemn silence over the good man's grave, and felt the hushed admiration of those who had come to pay their respects.

Assured her purchases would be sent home, Ellen bought out half the souvenir shop while Mag searched for just the right thing to take home to Clara.

On the third day, Ellen stood in the bathroom where the singer had lost his battle with addiction. Her form was ghostly to keep from being caught by the security cameras, and her face was a mask of sorrow. The upstairs rooms weren't part of the tour, and they weren't supposed to be there, but that hadn't stopped them. If Mag felt a twinge at breaking the rules, she justified it against knowing these could be Ellen's last moments on earth.

"Why didn't anyone help him?" Tears ran freely down Ellen's face. "All they did was take and take. Someone should have helped him. Someone should have been there so he wouldn't have to die alone."

Some of Ellen's mood transferred to Mag. "If it's your time, I want you to know I won't let you die alone." Uncharacteristically, she reached out to squeeze Ellen's arm. "Now that your nephew's gone, you'll have to settle for me."

"You barely know me," Ellen's eyes met Mag's. "And you've already done more for me than my own flesh and blood."

Mag shrugged, unable to think what to say since sentiment rarely came easy. "I'm sure Sam would have done his best by you if he was still here." She'd intended to lead Ellen to this topic at some point, and now was as good a time as any.

"I suppose you're right," Ellen's voice went gruff. "He'd have considered it a duty and probably buried me in the wrong clothes." Before Mag could put a lid on the tangent, Ellen had described her preferred clothing choices for a trip into the hereafter. It took a few moments to get her back to the topic of Sam Wayland.

"Did you meet my nephew?"

"Not as such," Mag admitted, "but I've seen him around the country club a time or two, and I know his ex-wife a little."

"Then you know he wasn't an easy person. Not in recent years, anyway."

"He'd changed, had he?" This wasn't the first time Mag had heard it said.

Ellen took a moment to frame her response, then sighed. "I feel as if I let my brother down by not being more nurturing, but Sam was grown when we lost his folks and didn't want any mothering from me."

"I'm sure you did your best."

"That's nice of you to say, but I can't help feeling I could have done more. He visited me a day or two before…it happened." Ellen wiped away a tear.

"Any idea what he wanted?"

"Just doing his monthly duty. Checking in on his old auntie." But Ellen took a moment to think. "Now that you mention it, something odd did happen."

Mag perked up.

"We'd just about run through a typical visit. You've got family. You know how those go. You've got your hellos and how have you beens, followed by ten or fifteen minutes catching up on recent events. Then it's another few minutes chatting about the weather before the awkward goodbyes."

That wasn't exactly how things went when Mag visited her niece, but Ellen probably didn't need to hear stories of fighting faerie godmothers and other wayward fae.

"This time was different? How?"

"Somewhere in the middle of the weather spiel, Sam pulled out his phone and announced he had to make a call, and he'd appreciate it if I would give him some privacy." Ellen's tone went sharp with disapproval. "That boy kicked me out of my own living room and then had the temerity to close the door in my face."

"Rude."

"You haven't heard the half of it. After all the door business, you'd think he would keep his voice down, but he didn't. I heard the entire conversation, and do you know what the call was about?" Ellen paused for effect. "His dry cleaning. What's so private about how much starch he prefers on his collars? As if anyone cares."

Whatever Mag had expected, dry cleaning wasn't anywhere on the list.

When Mag thought she'd learned all she could, Ellen surprised her by saying, "I don't mean to speak ill, but when he hung up, I opened the door, and I could swear he'd been rifling through the drawers of that Davenport I planned to sell."

Excitement drifted through Mag's blood like sparkling wine. "Interesting. Did you keep anything of value in it?"

"Nothing at all." With that, Ellen changed the subject back to Elvis. The rest of the day rushed by in a blur, as did the two that followed.

Once she'd dropped Ellen back off in her body, Mag went home. The cold had already begun seeping back into her bones.

"Did you have fun?" Clara asked as she clipped the blue suede shoe charm onto her bracelet. Mag had chosen well. Too bad she hadn't done the same for herself, as she'd returned sporting a pair of truly dated gold sunglasses with the singer's initial set into the nosepiece. Still, Clara let her gaze run over her sister. Mag had made it through the better part of a week without a spell. Moreover, she seemed lighter in her soul.

"You know, I really did. I'm beat. I'll tell you everything in the morning."

Chapter 18

Clara sat at the front counter of Balms and Bygones, contemplating the plan she'd been working on for quite some time. Her granddaughter, Lexi, had planted the seed when she'd told the story of how she'd helped him when the godmothers had knocked Santa and his sleigh out of the sky one Christmas.

If the jolly old elf's beard provided him the benefit of immortality as Lexi said it did, there might be hope for resetting the clock on Mag's age.

If—and it was a big if—she could get to the old fellow and talk him into snipping her off a whisker, Clara thought she might produce a miracle. The trick to it all would be keeping Mag in the dark until it was time to cast the spell. No sense in getting her hopes up too early in case the whole thing went south.

As for Clara, she could keep a secret with the best of them, but she'd need help from a problematic and unlikely source. Hagatha Crow was so old she'd outlived her verbal and emotional filters. Clara suspected they hadn't been well-established, to begin with, but whatever might have existed before was long gone to dust now.

When the local coven lured the Balefire sisters to

Harmony with the offer of taking over the leadership position, they hadn't bothered to add that Hagatha, the current leader, wasn't on board with the plan. The attempted coup had backfired harder than an engine needing a tune-up.

Instead of taking over the coven, Mag and Clara became Hagatha's glorified babysitters. They'd had their hands full between running damage control to keep the non-magical community from learning that there were true witches in town and busting up Hagatha's honey pixie playground.

Asking the ancient witch for help could be an absolute boon or go horribly wrong in all kinds of ways. Clara would take the risk for her sister and never count the cost. It certainly helped that Mag was preoccupied with solving the mystery behind Sam's death and Ellen's attack. Clara hated the means but couldn't help being thankful for anything to keep Mag busy while she set the wheels in motion.

As she was mulling over the possibilities, the bell above the door rang, and the sisters' friend and coven member, Juniper Honeywell, stumbled inside, looking slightly dazed.

"Are you all right, dear?" Clara asked.

A wan smile crossed the younger witch's face. "I will be after you offer me a cup of your world-famous peppermint tea."

Having just brewed a pot, Clara poured a cup, handed it to the harried-looking witch, and watched her drink it in two long gulps.

"You look like you could use a cookie too."

Curls bounced as Juniper shook her head. "If I ate

one, I'd eat a dozen, but right now, I'll settle for a refill on the tea. I have a little problem that's kind of a big problem."

Clara nodded. "Sugar and spice can be addictive."

Juniper sighed. "I hope I'll be as wise when I've been around as long as you."

"Age doesn't automatically equate with wisdom. Just ask Hagatha."

"No thanks." A shudder accompanied a frantic head shake.

"So what's the big problem?"

Juniper sighed again. "I'm experiencing what you might call a growth spurt."

Clara raised an eyebrow. "You're growing? At your age?" How was that possible? Juniper had to be well into her first century.

"Sorry. I'm an idiot. I didn't mean my body. It's my magic that's acting like a teenager on hormones."

"Tell me," Clara said simply. "Magic is meant to get more powerful with age and experience. And with repetition. That's why we're often called practitioners."

"This is not that," Juniper's hand shook. "I just want to be a normal witch."

Clara smiled. "Is there such a thing? I hope not."

"Anyway," Juniper continued. "Lately, my magic hasn't been working right. My spell-casting is out of control. It's like I'm using a machete to spread butter on my toast. Total overkill. Most recently, I went to light a candle, and the flare burned a hole in my ceiling. I got the fire out, but not before a cinder put a hole in my favorite blouse. Bringing fire is a witch's first spell. For it to go out of control like that is just…well, it's not normal."

"Have you done anything different lately? Do you source your own ingredients? Or do you shop for them? Maybe it's a supply issue."

Mouse-brown curls drifted in the wind as Juniper shook her head hard. "My granny taught me how to grow and dry my own herbs. I get my green thumb from her. I'm proud to be a kitchen witch, but there's more to me than that."

Because she felt the same, Clara nodded her agreement. "New cauldron? Check your wand for cracks lately?"

"No. And yes. My wand is in fine fettle. The only thing that's changed is my exercise routine. You don't think building muscle could be the problem?"

A frisson of energy tingled across Clara's skin. "Exercise?" She hadn't seen Juniper at the pool, but Fiona taught other classes there, and Juniper probably wouldn't be interested in the same classes she'd chosen to take.

"Advanced water aerobics."

The tingle turned sharp as needles.

"At the country club?"

"It's the only place in town that offers classes. Costs me a pretty penny in class fees since I'm not a member."

The news was too startling to be a coincidence, but Clara didn't want to give her thoughts away just yet. "The last thing the town needs is another Hagatha."

"I know," Juniper said with a sigh.

"But I don't think you need to worry since I have an idea that I think will help. Will you trust me enough to create a charm for you?"

Relief relaxed Juniper's shoulders, and her face cleared of worry. "I would. Of course."

"Wait here."

On her way to the workroom, Clara grabbed a necklace from Mag's marked-down costume jewelry section. She'd put the two dollars in the till and count it well-spent. For the sake of time and speed, Clara raised her hands like a conductor and prepared to do some serious magic.

Potion bottles flipped through the air to dribble droplets over the necklace, and when she was satisfied, Clara picked it up to imprint the final magic by calling fire. When she opened her hand, the deed was done, and the charm set. Only then did she notice Juniper peering around the door frame to watch the show.

"That was something to see. What's it do?"

"Call it a leveling charm," Clara lied without a single stab of conscience. To explain fully, she'd have to snitch on Hagatha. There would be fallout, and Clara could be right in the middle of ground zero. The lie would save her butt, and the charm should hold until she got hold of Hagatha and talked with the ancient witch about her meddling.

"I can't tell you how much I appreciate this," Juniper gushed as she dropped the necklace over her head. "I feel so much better already."

Juniper smiled and waved goodbye.

As the door closed behind the younger witch, Mag came in through the back, looking quite flushed and flustered.

"Sorry. I got distracted with something."

Clara walked over and took a sniff. Mag smelled of

pool water. "So I smell. Feel better?"

"Like a million bucks," Mag also lied. It seemed to be the flavor of the day. The trip with Ellen had taken more from her than she wanted to admit. Even to herself. "Slow day?"

"We had a rush this morning that seems to be over. Now that you're here, I'll take a belated lunch break."

"Try not to snore."

"I said lunch. How is it you heard nap?" Clara couldn't help but chuckle.

"Whatever," Mag fluttered a hand. "Take the rest of the day. You took care of the place while I was gone. It's only right I handle things today." For Mag, that was an effusive thanks.

"Okay. If you're sure, I've got an errand to run. It should only take an hour or two."

"Go," Mag ordered. "I need to check my inventory and make sure you didn't undersell anything while I was gone."

"You sell one ugly chair cheap, you never hear the end of it." Clara detoured upstairs for a coat and escaped before Mag could continue the lecture. Before she tackled Hagatha, Clara needed to ask Gertrude for a favor.

Skipping lunch turned out to be a good idea since Gertrude couldn't resist plying her guests with treats. In this case, she served what she called Festive Finger Food—a selection of delicate sandwiches cut into the shape of Santa's head. If Clara found that slightly creepy, she didn't offer the opinion. This favor was a big ask, and she needed all the goodwill she could generate.

"There might be something more you could do for my

sister, but it's delicate." Now that the moment was upon her, Clara had trouble getting out the words. "But since we're talking about Mag's situation, I don't mind admitting that there's more going on than age-related illness."

Gertrude nodded and poured more chocolate from a pot shaped like a Christmas tree. "She's fading. Her life force is weakening."

Surprised anyone else had noticed, Clara continued. "It is, and she doesn't think anyone knows, but I have eyes, don't I? She's resigned herself to an early death, so it's up to me to save her. I've been working on a spell to reverse the Raythe damage, and I'm getting close, but I've realized I need a very special ingredient. In fact, the entire spell depends on that one thing, and you're the only one with a chance of helping me get hold of what I need."

Flattered, Gertrude's hand went to her heart. "Margaret Balefire is a legend. I consider you both to be my friends. If there's anything I can do to help, you have only to ask."

"I need a whisker from Santa's beard."

The carols playing softly in the background made that scratching-record sound, then went still—probably for the first time in decades. Every clock in the house stopped.

"You need a what?"

"You heard me. Can you get me some face-time with the head elf?"

Gertrude shook her head, then tilted it and pinned Clara with a gaze. "Maybe."

"Would it mean cashing in that favor I know you've

been holding onto so tightly?”

“What if it did?”

Clara sighed. “It’s for Mag, so I’d still ask, but I’d understand if you said no. I need a pinch of immortality for this potion, and I do have other, costlier options, so I won’t press if it would cost you something precious.”

“Then it’s a good thing it won’t. Still, you’ll need to amp up your Christmas spirit, and even then, I won’t make any promises.”

When one of his elves had ended up half-dead in a snowbank, Gertrude had been instrumental in getting the little fellow home where he belonged and, in the process, earned a favor from the big guy himself.

Clara’s heart lifted. “All I need is for you to arrange a meeting, and I’ll take care of the rest.” Old Gertie wasn’t the only one with good deeds on the old fellow’s books, but she was the one with access. “As long as you can do that without costing you his friendship or favor.”

As the house sprang back to life, Gertrude nodded, the relief evident in her smile. “That’s the easy part. He comes around whenever I’m testing new cookie recipes. As you know, he’s *the* cookie connoisseur. Last month, he gave his stamp of approval to my cheesecake sugar cookies with salted caramel drizzle. I’m not sure I can top that recipe, but I’ll try.”

Feeling relieved, Clara let Gertrude prattle on while she ran over the vague basics of the spell in her head to make sure she wasn’t missing any other major ingredients.

Chapter 19

Before her second massage appointment with Fiona, Mag called the hospital to check on Ellen and learned her condition hadn't changed. Was that good news or bad news? At this point, only time would tell.

She suffered through the kneading and the stretching by running the facts of the Sam Wayland case through her head. Since her conversation with Ellen, Mag had become more convinced that Ellen's attack might be related to Sam's death. It only made sense, given their family connection. Maybe, she thought, she'd been looking at everything from the wrong way around.

Once Fiona had finished her torture routine, Mag figured she'd take a quick spin through the hot tub, then head over to Ellen's for some light snooping.

Meanwhile, since the shop was closed and both sisters had the day off, Clara decided she'd put off the visit to Hagatha long enough. If a flare of fear turned her guts watery, she could ignore it on Mag's behalf.

Visiting Hagatha Crow without an express invitation was not something one did on a whim. However, since Hagatha had very little use for modern conveniences such as phones—unless she could bend them to her will and use them to make trouble—showing up on her doorstep was the only way.

The rumor you could conjure Haggie by saying her name three times was only a myth. Clara hoped.

After selling her last place to Mag and Clara, Hagatha moved into a three-bedroom ranch-style house so she wouldn't have to navigate stairs or waste magic avoiding them. Of modern design with vertical siding painted a boring beige, the house certainly didn't scream *a witch lives here*.

That, Clara supposed, was part of what had drawn Hagatha to the property. That and the fact it was more secluded than her old place in town, so she had a better chance of getting away with whatever shenanigans she could cook up. The previous summer, she'd set up a hive of honey pixies that got out of hand and caused chaos for the entire town. Hagatha maintained she'd acquired the pixies to study their mating habits, but that hadn't stopped her from harvesting plenty of their magical honey.

After the honey pixie debacle, Hagatha had beefed up her magical security measures. Clara neatly avoided a huge spiderweb that dropped out of nowhere, dodged a nasty encounter with an enchanted stinging nettle plant, and made it a point not to step on a flat rock that fairly reeked of magic. What might have happened if she hadn't? She didn't want to know.

"Hagatha Crow. It's Clara Balefire. Can I come in? I'd like to ask you a favor."

Her voice as rusty as an old screen door hinge, Hagatha answered from inside. "I don't do love potions."

"Then, I guess it's a good thing I do just fine in the

love department. I'm here to talk about my sister, Mag. Can I come in?"

Even with a set of tennis balls covering the feet, the slap of Hagatha's walker echoed on ahead as she came to the door, opened it, and gave Clara a measuring look. "What's wrong with Mag?"

"Nothing," Clara said, then amended, "or nothing new, anyway."

Saying so to Mag might result in a fight, but given their love for creatures of all types, Hagatha and Margaret Balefire were a lot alike. Worse, Clara thought, was that magical cryptozoology wasn't the only commonality the two witches shared. If she survived long enough with her present outlook intact, Mag stood a very real chance of ending up just like Hagatha. Cranky, prone to magically chaotic outbursts, and just generally lacking so much as an ounce of give-a-crap.

"Then what's the problem?" The open door framed a stooped figure wearing what looked like a crocheted blanket pinned strategically to cover her body. If she got any closer, Clara worried she might see things through the weave that she really didn't want to see. But she needed Hagatha's help, so told herself to suck it up and kept her eyes at face level.

"I've been working on a spell to return Mag to her true age and vitality, and since you're the most experienced witch I know," Clara laid it on thick, "I wanted to get your opinion on the spell's ingredients."

But Hagatha tilted her head and, Clara noticed, didn't offer an invitation to come in from the cold. Fine, they'd discuss this on the porch. "You'd need some essence of immortality. Only way I know to get that is to make a deal with the devil himself.”

“I was thinking more along the lines of Saint Nick, but I’m open to suggestions.”

Hagatha went still for a moment while she thought.

“You got an in with the big guy?”

Clara grinned. “I might.”

“Well, then. That’s a new angle on the problem. You’d still need a piece of the Raythe that bit her, but there might be a way. What’s it got to do with me?”

“A couple of drops of pixie honey to start, and If you have a minute, I’d like to run my idea past you and see what you think.”

“Now, Clara, you know those pixies are back in their own world. How could I possibly have access to their honey?”

“Now, Hagatha, we both know you do.”

Hagatha cast a glance into the darkness of the house behind her. “If you expected tea and cookies, you won’t get them.”

“I didn’t come for a snack. I came to help my sister.” Hoping this wouldn’t be a one-way trip, Clara stepped inside.

If there were a witchy version of world records, Hagatha would probably take one for her age alone and probably another one for the number of questionable spells she’d cast in her lifetime. Clara wasn’t sure what she expected the inside of the ancient witch’s house to look like, but nearly normal definitely wasn’t on her list.

It should have been.

Other than a stack of cauldrons near the stove, a prodigious collection of broomsticks in one corner, and a curio cabinet containing some fairly creepy items,

Hagatha lived like everyone else. Clara wasn't sure if she should be relieved or let down. Still, the place, as had been mentioned, was clean, and Hagatha looked as healthy as anyone of her advanced age could look. And yet, none of that was the reason for the live-in care.

Left to her own devices, Hagatha tended to create magical mischief.

Oh, who was she kidding? Clara thought, even with supervision, Hagatha could throw down the crazy magics with the best of them, and she wasn't above creating non-magical chaos, either. She'd certainly outlived her filter. Worse, Hagatha thought it was time to bring magical abilities out into the open.

In her heart of hearts, Clara almost agreed, but she'd already spent a fair number of years as a statue, and her bucket list did not include hanging, drowning, being actually stoned, or burning to death. Whether benign or wicked, witchery should probably remain shrouded in a certain amount of darkness. Just for safety's sake.

Hagatha stomped across the living room and settled herself in a recliner covered in so many crocheted blankets, Clara couldn't see its original color and said, "Let's have it, then. What's the big plan? And what's old Nick got to do with it?"

"First, I need to ask a question if that's okay."

"You can always ask."

"Why did you spike the pool with what amounts to a healing potion?"

Surprise wrote itself over Hagatha's features but only briefly before she schooled them. "Who said I did?"

Balefire witches are born knowing how to play with fire, but poking at Hagatha was a sure way to get burned. Clara prayed to Hecate for safety, pulled a vial from her pocket, and then showed Hagatha the crimson drop inside. "That's your blood, is it not?"

Until then, it hadn't occurred to Clara that Hagatha might see this visit as a form of blackmail. Her blood turned to ice in her veins. "You did a good thing, Haggie. Part of why I'm here is to thank you for it, but Mag's losing her battle more quickly than I think she expected. If you can help me, I'll be forever grateful."

With Mag's life on the line, groveling wasn't too big a price to pay. Not when it put that self-satisfied look on the ancient witch's face. To garner more favor, Clara dropped the vial of blood in Hagatha's lap. "This is all I have. I got it from distilling the potion down to the basic ingredients to see why using the pool helped Mag so much. A stupid witch might use your blood to force you into doing something to help, but I'm not a stupid witch. No good deed should be rewarded with perfidy."

Her face an unreadable mask, Hagatha studied the younger witch until Clara felt the need to squirm.

"I do a great many good deeds. I just don't bandy the list of them around for public consumption," Hagatha's voice deepened slightly. "It's bad for my image. The potion helped Mag, you say?"

"You know, I could get to like you." Clara slid forward until she sat on the edge of the sofa. "It did. It also amplified Juniper Honeywell's magic to an unsafe level. Was that the original intention? To create chaos by boosting magic?"

"You give me credit for being more devious than I am."

Clara just about choked.

"Not even possible." Changing the subject seemed prudent, so Clara ran through the recipe she'd been working on and outlined what she hoped Hagatha would be willing to contribute. "Will you help me?"

All business now, Hagatha considered what she'd heard, but Clara's heart sank when the older witch pursed her lips in a faintly negative way.

"For a price." But when she named it, Clara balked.

"No."

"Not even if I promise to only use it for good?"

Through narrowed eyes, Clara assessed the old witch. "Spit on the oath, and you've got a deal."

When the deed was done, Hagatha went on as if she'd meant to help all along. Maybe she had. "It takes a flexible mind to think of using quartz dust to create a time-release potion, but without a piece of the Raythe, no matter how good your spell is, it won't last."

"Mag mentioned something about that, too. Unfortunately, she burned the Raythe and danced on the ashes. I don't suppose ashes would work."

"Not without the blood of the mother." Sounding far more educated than she usually spoke, Hagatha launched into a magical alchemy lesson that spun Clara's head. "But if you're willing to shed some of the red and dip a toe into the dark, there's a way."

It wouldn't be easy, but Hagatha's magical theory couldn't be faulted. Intrigued, the old witch spent two hours helping Clara refine her plan. Rising to leave, Clara asked the question she probably should have asked earlier, "Where's your niece? Shouldn't she be home by now? It's long past lunchtime."

"My niece is…on vacation."

Hearing the pause, Clara wondered if Hagatha had needed a second to come up with the right term or if something else was happening. Something sinister. Even at her most helpful, you couldn't put anything past Hagatha.

"She left you here alone?" Heading toward the door, Clara couldn't let it go. "Where'd you say your niece went for her vacation?"

"I didn't," Hagatha said and then cackled. Could she be any more of a stereotype? Or worse, a stereotype with an unpredictability factor of at least a hundred.

"I don't need a keeper." Hagatha circled a hand to indicate the room around her. "See, the house is clean. There's nothing to worry about."

A smart witch might have taken Hagatha's words at face value. Or would that be a dumb witch?

While she decided which witch she was, Clara walked closer to the curio cabinet and looked at the contents. The way a person displayed their keepsakes, she thought, said a lot about them. In Hagatha's case, the curio cabinet cemented Clara's opinion that the old witch hadn't been playing with a full deck of Tarot cards for quite some time.

Jumbled across the shelves were everything from a relatively new-looking doll to a chunk of something Clara had to look closer at to identify.

"Is that a piece of pizza crust?" She pointed to the offending item.

"So what if it is?" Hagatha scratched the back of her neck. "Why do you want to know?"

"No reason. It's just an odd thing to keep on display, I suppose. Quite random."

"I guess," Hagatha's eyes sparkled with mischief, "you're not as quick as your sister."

Clara took offense. "I'd like to think I am."

When Hagatha flicked a finger, the recliner footrest came up. "Then you'll figure out the right question to ask, won't you?"

It took only a moment's thought before Clara did. "Whose pizza crust was it?"

"Let's just put it this way, if Dante had asked before sampling off my plate, his version of hell would have only had six circles."

"So this is a memento?"

"Sure." Hagatha humored me. "I guess you can call it that."

"I'm sorry I asked."

A flicker of movement drew Clara's eye back to the doll on the top shelf. She was no expert by any means, but she didn't have to be to see the exquisite detail worked into its features and dark, pin-straight hair. Even the jeans it wore were perfect in miniature, with creases worn light at the knees.

And then, the doll blinked.

Clara turned to Hagatha, her expression both shocked and furious. "Where did your niece go for her vacation?"

Hagatha shrugged. "She's not my niece. She's my sister's great-granddaughter."

Clara tried to do the relative math in her head but didn't get very far. "I still think that makes you her great aunt."

"Whatever," Hagatha flapped a hand at Clara. "She said she was sick of me and needed time off. She said she wanted peace and quiet, so that's what I gave her.

She's fine."

"She is not fine." Indeed, the doll's expression had altered so slowly that the change was nearly imperceptible, but it didn't take magic to see the terror written across its face. Clara tried the curio cabinet door and found it locked. "This is not how we treat family. Unlock the door and let her go."

Eyes rolling, Hagatha held out an empty palm, snapped the fingers of her other hand, and a small, ornate key appeared. She tossed the key to Clara, who caught it neatly and fitted it into the lock.

"Honestly, Hagatha. This is the worst thing you could have done. It's a gross misuse of power. You know the rede we live by. We don't use our magic to bring harm to others." As gently as she could, she lifted the doll from the shelf, set it on the floor, and muttered an apology to Hagatha's niece.

"Harm, shmarm. She's fine. Not hurt a bit, and if you think this was the worst I could do, you don't know me very well." Still, with a finger snap, the deed was done, and instead of a doll, a pissed-off woman stood in the middle of the floor.

"I'm out of here," the young woman spit fury.

Hagatha shrugged a bony shoulder. "Go, then. Ain't nobody stopping you. I never said I needed a glorified housekeeper or a babysitter. I can take care of myself." Now that the teaching portion of her day had ended, Hagatha reverted to her habitual speaking pattern.

Hands on her hips, the niece, whose name Clara couldn't pull to mind, rounded on her aunt and wagged a finger. "I'm not your housekeeper, glorified or otherwise, nor your babysitter. I'm family and agreed to this living arrangement to get to know you better. Maybe to learn something from the great and legendary Hagatha Crow. All I've learned so far is you're a mean old crone and one nasty bitch of a witch. There, I said it out loud."

A lesser woman might have backed down at Hagatha's appraising look. Her great-grand-niece, or whatever, did not.

Clara thought the tirade over, but the younger woman took her by surprise, kicked the sofa, whirled, tilted her chin, and let go with a few more zingers.

"I'm sure you'll be happy to see the backside of me, but it didn't have to be this way. I actually liked you, Aunt Haggie. Maybe you should think about that when you're busy pushing people away."

When Clara glanced at Hagatha, she wasn't sure what to expect. Cold anger, brewing magical ire, maybe, but not amusement. And then Hagatha spoke, "Oh, get over yourself. I didn't know you were a fan. You can stay."

"My name is Clara Balefire," Clara saw an opening and took it. "I'm pleased to meet you."

"Bessamina Balmoral." Hagatha's niece rattled off a mouthful of a name and took Clara's proffered hand. "I've heard of you. I mean, who hasn't, right? You're keepers of the flame, and your sister hunted Raythes. Part of the reason I agreed to come here was the chance to meet Mag Balefire. She's a legend, but more, I've been working with a coven out of Boston, genius types, you see, and we've been developing a potion to detect certain types of dark magic. I'd love a chance to run our research past your sister. Get her insight."

Clara glanced at Hagatha and read jealousy on her face. Wasn't that interesting, she thought.

"You should have come by the shop. We could have talked shop." Clara chuckled at her own pun.

"I thought I had more time," Bessamina turned to glare at Hagatha. "I thought we'd settled into a groove with this living together thing, but I see now I was wrong."

"What is it they say these days? Take a chill pill," Hagatha responded.

"Nobody says that anymore, and they haven't for years." Even Clara knew that much.

"Whatever. That stuff runs together when you're as old as I am." Hagatha pushed forward. "You don't have to leave, 'Mina. I promise I won't use magic on you again."

But Bessamina was already shaking her head. "That's a start, but I need more, or I'm gone."

"What more?" Hagatha's eyes narrowed.

"No more ghouls in the pantry." Bessamina began ticking off her list of demands. "Or spiders in my bed. I want my best cauldron back, and if you enchant another one of my brooms only to make left turns, the deal is off. Do you agree?"

Hagatha waved a hand impatiently. "Yes, yes. No more shenanigans. You have my word."

"And you'll teach me?"

"I'll test you, and if you pass the tests, then yes, I will teach you."

Clara wasn't sure if this was good news or bad but left the pair to work things out for themselves.

Meanwhile, as Clara stepped back onto Hagatha's porch, Mag pulled up in front of Ellen's house across town.

Two steps from the van, she heard someone say, "Hello."

Turning in the direction of the sound, Mag saw the electric wheelchair first, and then the woman bundled in a puffy jacket topped by a fuzzy blanket patterned with what looked to be the phases of the moon. From beneath a flop-brimmed hat peered friendly green eyes. This must be the other neighbor. Mag tried to remember if Ellen had mentioned a name, but nothing came to mind.

"I'm Mag Balefire," she said. "A friend of Ellen's."

"Rebecca Moore," the woman replied and waved Mag closer. "Have you any news?"

"I called the hospital before I came over. They said she's resting comfortably but still in a coma."

As Mag stepped onto the porch, a furry, brindle-and-white face popped out from the folds of Rebecca's blanket. Dark eyes blinked at her.

"Does your dog bite?" Being somewhat small herself, Mag knew mighty hearts often came in small packages. "It's a chihuahua, right?"

Nodding, Rebecca smiled again. "Her name is Mia. She's friendly enough."

Because Mia seemed to expect such treatment, Mag leaned down to offer her hand for a sniff. Mia wiggled her way out from under the blanket, then flipped over to stick her belly in the air for scratches. Mag complied.

"Do you know if they're letting people see Ellen? I don't like to think of her lying there alone." For the first time, Rebecca's smile faded fully away.

"Family only, but if you speak to the older nurse, she's less of a stickler and will probably let you in. I'm sure it would do Ellen good to have a friend by her side."

Without seeming to ask any probing questions, Mag skillfully led Rebecca into a retelling of what she'd seen and heard on the day of Ellen's attack.

"It sounds morbid, but I wondered if she sensed her pending doom."

Pending doom? Melodramatic much?

"What do you mean?"

"Well, only she'd changed her will the day before, hadn't she?"

If she had, it was news to Mag. News she thought Ellen would have mentioned during their trip to Graceland. "What makes you think that?"

Taken aback by the sharpness of Mag's tone, Rebecca frowned. "Sam went into the house with a manila envelope and came out without it. I assumed he was there on legal business, and she'd been talking about making some changes, so I just thought…but maybe I'm wrong."

"Did you see anything on the day of the attack? Anyone going in or out, I mean."

"I'm sorry." Rebecca shook her head. "I had an appointment in Bangor that day, so I wasn't here. Did you check with Miss Nosypants across the street?"

"I did. No luck."

Because she couldn't stick around without concocting an explanation, Mag thanked Rebecca for talking to her, then headed back home to think over what she'd learned. Snooping could wait until later.

Chapter 20

Having gained Hagatha's approval of the spell, Clara decided today was as good a day as any to track down Santa Claus. According to Gertrude, she had to travel to the Fringe, take the corner seat at a certain diner, order hot chocolate, and add a drop of diluted Christmas spirit. If her inner child and Gertie's mix were strong enough to make Clara glow, Mr. Kringle would join her.

"Order him a hot chocolate with cinnamon and marshmallows. That's his favorite," were Gertrude's final words on the subject.

To keep anyone from Harmony from spotting her on this mission, Clara returned to Port Harbor to use the Fringe portal there instead of the one behind the community center where the Moonstones held their meetings.

Since the day was sunny, she took a minor detour to do some window shopping while marveling at the hustle and bustle of the busy city compared to her sleepy little town of Harmony. Port Harbor's cobblestone streets ran through areas featuring historic charm and the latest fashions for those who could afford them. The buildings here had tall brick facades and large windows. The day's sunlight reflected off whitewashed walls, giving the street an ethereal glow.

Maybe it was just the city's energy, or perhaps only the holiday season, but lights seemed brighter here, the colors more diverse and upbeat. Gliding from place to place, some people smiled with happiness. Others scowled at the sight of crowded streets. The city bustled as snow and ice failed to chill the air enough to stop people from coming and going.

A block before the portal alley, Clara spotted a pair of boots that stopped all forward progress. The leather gleamed a beautiful, deep black under gold buckles and laces. The low heels looked comfortable enough to wear for hours. Maybe even comfortable enough to dance in.

She didn't need new boots.

But they were really good boots.

Boots she didn't need.

Deciding the inner argument could go on forever, Clara entered the shop and ran her hands along the texture, admiring the craftsmanship and the buttery feel. They'd be just perfect for her next date with John.

She really needed new boots.

"You need those boots," the shop clerk echoed Clara's thoughts, his cheerful smile hard to resist. Clara smiled back. "I don't say this to everyone who comes through the door, but you have a vibe. You know what I mean? Like you and those boots are a perfect match."

"What are you? The boot whisperer?"

He blushed. Clara found the response charming in one so young. The clerk couldn't have been more than twenty.

"Naw," he said, "But I know what I know."

"I think you might be right. Do you have these in nine

and a half?"

Ten minutes later, her wallet a great deal lighter, Clara owned a pair in black and another in a rich brown with red overtones. She probably should feel guilty for shopping while on a mission, but for once, she refused to allow guilt to steal the joy of the moment. There'd be time enough for sorrow if she failed.

A brisk wind picked up the remnants of an old paper bag, sent it skidding ahead of Clara as she stepped into the shadow of a deep doorway, turned her back to the street, and sent the boxes of boots home so she didn't have to carry them with her before making her way toward the narrow space between two tall buildings.

Taking a deep breath, she checked that no one had followed her into the alley, then stepped over the mound of snow that had built at the portal's edge. The air went from winter chill to summer heat and carried the scents of cotton candy and something darker.

Not tempted by the carnival atmosphere, she skirted the gaily striped tents and dodged past a clown juggling what she hoped were doll heads and not something worse. Keeping to the rear of the main event, she looped around and came out on the road north. If memory served, the diner was about a mile and a half away, so she shed her jacket and used a shrinking charm to make it small enough to fit in her pocket before setting off briskly.

Sweat plastered dark strands against Clara's head as the heat slid over her. More moisture dribbled down the furrow of her spine. Gertrude had to be mad to suggest hot chocolate in this heat. All Clara wanted was a glass of lemonade, cool and refreshing, but when she settled at the table, she did as she was told.

Surprisingly, the chocolate soothed her parched throat, and when she added it, the spirit potion tasted of sugarplums. When Clara closed her eyes to savor the moment, she heard excited voices and the sounds of paper tearing, and she smelled pine needles.

Growing up, she'd enjoyed similar sights and sounds during Yule. Small tokens exchanged, treats in the kitchen, pine burning in the fireplace, and a mixture of cedar and rosemary purifying the house for the ritual of welcoming the returning light were all fond memories for Clara. She missed her mother but knew well enough that those types of thoughts were not the ones that would call the old elf to her table, so she pushed them aside and concentrated on letting joy permeate her soul.

"May I join you?"

Clara's heart skipped a beat as a hand came down on her shoulder. She nodded to indicate he was welcome and said politely, "By all means." She caught the eye of her server, a cyclops in a gingham apron, and gestured to have a second cup of chocolate brought to the table. "I was hoping you would."

"You're Clara, right? Daughter of witches, keeper of the flame, saver of wayward elves, and grandmother to the Fate Weaver who returned my reindeer."

"That would be me." At least he hadn't mentioned that Lexi had had something to do with losing those reindeer, at least indirectly. So long as he focused on the good, he might be willing to grant her the boon she sought.

"Gertrude sends her best wishes." Because she'd promised, Clara got that out of the way and was encouraged when he let out a quiet laugh and his rosy lips turned up in a smile.

"Gertrude is made of best wishes."

"It is her best feature."

Santa looked up from his cup of hot cocoa and smiled warmly. "Well then," he said, "Friend of Gertrude, what can I do for you?"

"Do you do that with everyone?" She knew she should get right to the point because Mr. Claus was a busy man at this time of year, but she couldn't stop the question from popping out. "Turn everyone into labels, I mean."

Brows that looked like bushy white caterpillars disappeared under the brim of his hat. "I suppose I do. Helps with making the list, don't you know? No one has ever pointed it out before."

Clara took a deep breath and launched into the tale that forced her to beg a personal favor. She explained Mag's plight and how her sister had selflessly fought against the darkness and didn't deserve for her life to be cut short. "I've been working on a potion that I think will cure her ills, but I need a very special ingredient to restore my sister to her proper age. An ingredient I can only get from you."

Santa chuckled softly before replying, "What might that be?" The smile fell right off his face when Clara answered.

"A whisker? You have no idea what you're asking."

"I think I do." Clara let go of everything except for her love for her sister and the desire to see her healed, which she let show on her face. "I know your whiskers hold the secret to your timelessness, and I hoped that if you saw fit to give one to me, some of that power would translate to Mag and help her regain what was taken from her during a valiant fight. My sister is no saint—she'd be the first one to tell you that—but she was trying to save witchkind, so she deserves to be saved. Whatever your price, I'm willing to pay. I'd give my life for hers just as she would do for me."

He waved her offer away with a mitten-clad hand. "That's commendable, but not what I meant."

"Are you going to give me what I need or not?" Her patience had limits.

"I'm leaning that way as long as you understand the consequences."

"Then tell me because I'm desperate to save my sister."

"My whiskers are the seat of my power. All of my power. Do you understand?"

Even fuddled with worry, Clara's mind was quick enough to get his meaning.

"You mean she might be overwhelmed with the desire to give away toys once a year?"

This time when he chuckled, he put some ho ho ho behind it.

"Could be. I can't say whether my love of children gives the whiskers their magic or if it's the other way around. The risk is, I think, acceptable since it takes an entire beard to keep me going, so whatever effect your sister might suffer should be minor."

"We'll take it and offer our gratitude."

"You'll understand if I consider us even. You will get no more favors from me, and I expect you to keep this transaction confidential."

"Deal." Clara held out a hand to shake on it. She felt the weight of the world lift off her shoulders. "I can't thank you enough. Hey, is this how you converted Gertrude? Did she get a whisker?"

Taken aback at first, once he considered, Santa let out another long laugh. "That one never needed any of my help. She's a natural convert." He reached up and plucked one white whisker from his beard before handing it to Clara with a twinkle in his eye. "Here you go," he said. "May it serve you well."

"Thanks!" Clara said to air empty except for a wash of twinkling motes. Her heart felt so light she nearly skipped the entire way back to the portal.

Back in the city's chill, Clara shrugged her coat back on and detoured to the house she'd turned over to her granddaughter before the move to Harmony.

"Gran." The spitting image of her grandmother—minus a few shallow wrinkles—Lexi enfolded Clara in a hug. "Did I know you were stopping by?"

"Sorry. Unplanned visit. I hope that's okay."

"This is your house as much as mine. I want you always to feel welcome here." Lexi narrowed her eyes. "Is everything all right? You're…unsettled." She finally found the word that seemed right.

"Your mother?"

Once a troubled teen, later a volatile adult, Sylvana had given her mother and daughter a run for their money before transforming herself into a white witch through an act of utter selflessness no one had thought possible.

Lexi waved a graceful hand. "Borneo, I think. Or maybe that was last week. I can't keep up. She and my father are hardly ever home these days. Can I get you something?"

Clara shook her head. "I've just had hot chocolate." She let herself be drawn into the living room and settled on the sofa in front of the fireplace that hid the family workrooms from view. "The house is quiet today."

"The godmothers are working out of the new building. They'll be home at the end of the day, but I'm enjoying the peace now. Now, tell me what's wrong," Lexi held her grandmother's hand as she sat beside her. "You're scaring me."

"It's Mag. She's not doing well."

Sympathy etched itself into worry lines between Lexi's eyes. "Is it…the end?"

"I hope not. That's why I'm here, but now that I've come, I realize I have no right to get you involved in dangerous magic."

Lexi sucked in a breath. "Dangerous magic? Or dark magic?" There was a difference, as she'd come to know far too well during her adventures.

"Shades of gray, at least."

"To save Aunt Mag?"

Clara nodded.

"I'm in. What do you need me to do?"

"Just like that? Don't you want to know the details?"

Rising, Lexi reached into the fireplace letting the flames tickle along her hand as she found and pulled the handle to open the workshop door. She turned with eyes still blazing from the fire's light. "If you're doing it, I'm doing it. Aunt Mag's family." So saying, she walked through the fire, leaving Clara to follow. "Family is everything."

While they gathered what they needed, which included a trip to the kitchen, Clara explained the mission.

"Let me get this straight. You're traveling to the back of beyond, where you intend to search for, and if found, use blood and enchanted pool water to reconstitute a piece of the Raythe that tried to kill your sister?"

"When you put it that way, it sounds—"

"Like something a Balefire witch would do. Mother would not approve." Lexi grinned. "At least not anymore."

"I suppose not," Clara returned Lexi's smile. "But she would enjoy our positions being reversed."

"Probably." Lexi sobered. "Be honest. What are the chances we'll find something?"

Her expression going bleak, Clara admitted, "Not great. I've been to the site before. Mag did a thorough job of destroying her enemy, but I didn't have Hagatha's pool water potion before. Even then, I think the odds are low, but I have to try."

"I'm going with you. Don't even bother to argue. It won't change anything."

"I wasn't planning to. Playing with Raythe pieces and parts isn't something I take lightly. I'll appreciate the backup."

As soon as Clara finished loading up what she thought she might need, she held out her hand for Lexi's and took them both to the scene from Mag's VCR tape.

The passing years hadn't removed the psychic smear of true evil from the narrow mountain pass where Mag almost met her death. Clara shivered as the sensation washed across her skin with the same revulsion as if spiders crawled under her clothes.

"Creepy, much?" Lexi also shivered and shuddered.

"Let's get this done. I don't want to be here any longer than necessary. Hagatha gave me some good pointers, so I'm hopeful we can finish the job with minimal fuss."

"She's the cantankerous one?" Lexi hadn't had the pleasure but had heard plenty of Hagatha stories.

"Hagatha Crow puts the whack in whackadoodle, but I've learned she has a softer side, so I don't think I'll find her quite as intimidating from here on out." While she talked, Clara walked in a circle to get her bearings and compare the current landscape with what she had seen on the tape. "It's grown up some, but I think this is where the main fight went down."

Shuddering, Lexi nodded. "I think you're right." She moved to an area where nothing grew. "Soil's black."

"This is it. I'm sure of it." Clara pulled ingredients from her pack. "Set the candles, please. Black on the inner circle, white to contain. They need to be marked with blood."

Nodding, Lexi used her ritual knife to score a line across her palm. As she set each candle, she called on the powers that be to make the spell strong. "Done," she turned to see that her grandmother's eyes had gone dark with purpose and magic.

"Light within dark, dark within light, ashes burned in haste and might."

Clara took up a handful of blasted soil and let it run through her fingers.

"Rise to me, take form and shape."

The wind rose and whipped Clara's hair back from a

face gone sharp with power. How easy it would be, she thought, to take all that the darkness had to offer, but that wasn't the Balefire way, so she resisted the impulse.

A cloud of ash filtered up from the ground to swirl and take on the hazy shape of what had tried to kill Mag Balefire. Clara shivered with the effort it took to hold the magic together. "Get the filter ready."

"Terra's gonna be ticked." But Lexi couldn't help a smirk as she dropped a filter into the commercial-sized, fairly new coffee maker she'd stolen from the kitchen. She filled it with the container of water Clara had spiked with a dose of Hagatha's pool potion—minus the pixie honey and the older witch's blood replaced with her own.

"Terra will have to get over it." With a flick of her wrist, Clara sent the Raythe-shaped ash cloud into the filter. Lexi slammed the filter and housing home, fed the power button a spark of magic, and set the coffee maker to brew.

"I've cast a few weird spells in my time, but this is one for the books," Clara observed as disgusting black filled the carafe below the filter.

"Double the ick factor." Lexi wrinkled her nose and stepped back as the scent of reconstituted Raythe filled the air. "What are we supposed to do with that when we're done?"

Sighing, Clara admitted. "Send it to Hagatha."

Lexi cocked a brow. "No way that could go wrong on so many counts."

"She took a spit oath to do no harm. It'll hold. I trust her. Mostly."

Minutes ticked away while they watched for the final

drop of water to make its way through the filter. When it did, their eyes met above the machine. Now came the moment of truth. Her breath clogging her throat, Clara pulled the filter housing from the unit and looked inside as Lexi did the same. Neither noticed the pain when they bumped heads.

"Son of a narwhal," Clara breathed. "Do you see it?"

Amid the muddy ash clinging to the formerly-white filter was nestled a tiny sliver of unburnt bone and a small clump of what looked like beef jerky—if jerky was made from black meat, anyway.

"Don't touch it with your fingers," Clara warned, pulling out a bespelled vial, which sucked the bits from the filter when she released the stopper.

The job done, both witches sighed.

"Let's get out of here," Clara said.

"Just a minute." Calling balefire into her palm, Lexi closed her eyes and concentrated until the flame went white. "I want to cleanse the ground."

"I'll help." Clara followed suit. "Do you mind if I go straight home from here? I need to start testing right away."

"Go. Give Aunt Mag my love, and tell her I'll skim by for a visit in a day or two. In the meantime, if you need a white witch, I can get word to Sylvana in an emergency."

"Let's hope it doesn't come to that." Clara hugged her granddaughter, and with a whisper of magic was gone.

"Let's hope," Lexi said as she did the same.

Chapter 21

While Clara got to work on her spell, Mag Balefire sat across a pub table from Penelope Snow, and hell didn't even freeze over. There might have been a flying pig sighting, but Mag wasn't bothered about it. Penelope had asked for this meeting, after all. Any flying pig fallout was on her head.

Mag wished.

Penelope let out a deep sigh and absentmindedly twirled her straw, her almond-shaped eyes wide with worry. "This business with the death of Sam Wayland is getting out of hand. We all know Hagatha is at the heart of it. You have to do something."

"Why?" Since it was there, Mag sipped ginger ale and blinked twice when the bubbles tickled her nose. "Why do *I* have to do something when you're the one who screwed up?"

"Excuse me?"

Penelope could put on the doe eyes all she wanted. The show of innocence didn't move Mag. "You staged the worst coup in the history of coups. Besides, isn't Hagatha's lawsuit dead in the water anyway? Literally."

"What a horrible thing to say."

If Penelope thought shame would work on Mag, she

was sorely mistaken. "Or did Hagatha find someone else to run with it?"

Condensation ran down the side of Penelope's glass as she yanked out the straw, then chugged half the liquid down.

"She didn't, and I'll thank you for not giving her any ideas. Half the coven has been brought in for questioning, and we're all suspects."

Mag squirted a generous amount of ketchup on the fries she'd ordered. "And half the town had a motive." The ratio of people with anything nice to say about Sam Wayland was around one in five. Mag might have found that sad if she'd been a philosophical person. Since she wasn't, she turned her attention toward figuring out which of Sam's haters had taken the final step.

"Is that why you invited me here today? To talk about my failings?"

"No," Penelope sighed. "I have a personal matter to discuss. A very delicate personal matter."

"You mean like woman stuff?" Horrified, Mag held up a hand to stop any further conversation. "Clara's better with that kind of thing. Why don't we call her?"

"I don't need Clara. I need a magical badass, and that's you. No offense to your sister."

"None taken, I'm sure." Mag wasn't sure of any such thing, but Penelope had piqued her curiosity. "What's the big problem?"

Leaning forward, Penelope pitched her voice low. "I've had some unexpected magical bursts over the last month or so. In fact, it's possible I killed Sam Wayland with one of them."

"You have my undivided attention."

Under such scrutiny, Penelope had some trouble getting her story out. "You're a fire witch, right?"

As Mag's affinity with fire was well-known, she circled a hand to indicate Penelope should get on with it.

"My strength lies in earth-based magic with an emphasis on potion-making."

"This isn't a job interview. I don't need your resumé."

Penelope puffed up. "I wasn't giving it to you. I was trying to explain what happened the other night. If you'd let me finish."

"Go right ahead." Almost negligently, Mag circled her index finger in the air to create a sound-deadening barrier over the table. "And quit whispering."

"Fine," Penelope continued in her normal tone. "I was at the country club with a couple of friends on the night Sam died."

That got Mag's attention.

"Supper in the lounge followed by a quick steam and then a dip in the pool. We stayed until closing, and everyone else left, but I stayed behind to harvest some yellow dock seeds for a tummy-soothing potion. There's a patch behind the clubhouse that's still tall enough to stick up through the snow, and I find them to be more potent at this time of year."

Mag nodded.

"The snow was up to my knees, and I didn't feel like wallowing, so I figured a little spell to shake the seeds loose wouldn't hurt anything. I've done it a hundred times before, and nothing crazy happened, but this time, it was as if my spell was amplified to a hundred times its normal strength."

"The earth shook?"

"Like a bomb went off. Knocked me off my feet, and that's what got me wondering. Maybe it knocked Sam off his feet, too. Maybe that's how he banged his head, and then it was just bad luck that he fell in the pool."

The young witch raised her face so that Mag could see the doubt and sorrow in her eyes. "I didn't mean any harm."

For the first time ever, Mag felt sorry for Penelope. Drat the girl for making herself so vulnerable.

"Did you go back into the club after?"

Penelope shook her head.

"And did you find Sam and purposefully tamper with the evidence by cleaning up the blood?"

"No, and how do you know any of that actually happened? The police haven't been especially forthcoming."

"Let's just say I have my sources and leave it at that. You didn't kill Sam Wayland."

"You're sure?" A deep breath whooshed out on a sigh.

Mag nodded. "A hundred percent. Since you're off the hook, who else had a motive?"

Penelope gestured around the room before speaking. "Just about everyone here had strong feelings about the man, but Jessica Hayes hated him with a passion. She held a deep-seated grudge against Sam Wayland because he represented her ex-husband in their divorce case. Sam dug up some dirt on her, then called a secret meeting where he pressed her to let her ex-husband get away with most of the business they built together."

Mag leaned forward, her interest piqued. "What makes you think she might have snapped and killed him?"

Penelope shrugged. "I don't know that she did," she said hesitantly. "But I know she spent every penny she had on her defense, and she wasn't the only one."

"I'm sure that's true of any attorney."

"Maybe. There's Cassandra Bane, too. Why any witch would want to spend time doing paperwork or learning mortal law is beyond me, but she worked in his office as a paralegal." Penelope signaled for another rum and coke. "Until he let her go without cause and then refused to give her a reference."

"Why?"

"He said she'd signed his name on court pleadings. She didn't."

Always the devil's advocate, Mag said, "How can you be sure?"

"Because Cassie's no idiot, and her magical gift lies in being able to discern truth from lies. Maybe that's why she went into the legal field in the first place."

Penelope swigged the last of her drink and continued, "About a week after she took the job with Sam and Claudia, she asked me to help her craft a special ink that she put into every pen in the office. It seemed she was right to be cautious because a few weeks ago, Sam accused her of signing something she shouldn't, and when she proved him wrong, he fired her."

Mag nodded slowly as Penelope finished speaking. That explained the ink she'd found in Sam's casket. Even so, Jessica Hayes and Cassandra Bane went on her shortlist of those willing to give Wayland what he deserved. Or not, because Mag didn't believe anyone deserved to have their life cut short. She'd rather see her enemies live to regret their actions.

"How does it work? The ink, I mean." Even if the ink hadn't been involved in a murder investigation, Mag would have asked. She loved hearing about a good piece of magic as well as the next witch.

"Tap the signature twice and speak the name of the person who wrote it. If you speak true, the ink remains black, if not, it turns red."

"Good one. Forge proof ink."

Penelope preened at the praise.

At the end of the meal, Penelope walked Mag out to her van. They hadn't become friends, but no longer were they antagonistic toward each other. Mag decided she could live with that. Since the hospital was only a short detour from the pub, Mag decided to stop and see Ellen on her way home.

"Excuse me," Not intending to be rude, a nurse shoved past Mag as she walked down the corridor toward Ellen's room and the chorus of alarming sounds that couldn't mean anything good. Two more nurses followed the first, their expressions guarded.

Dismayed, Mag broke into as fast a walk as she could manage using a cane and having knees that didn't want to bend like they used to. Before she got very far, she was sure her heart would burst out of her chest. Not even pausing at the nurse's station, she beelined for Ellen's room to find a doctor standing at the foot of Ellen's bed, a grim expression on his face as he monitored the beeping machine that displayed her vitals. Mag's heart sank. She'd arrived too late. Ellen had already gone to be with the angels.

But then a noise caught Mag's attention. A faint gasp rose from the bed. Ellen's eyes fluttered open. Her gaze took a moment to sharpen, then landed on Mag. The slightest smile curved Ellen's lips as she croaked something that sounded like "Graceland."

The nurse smiled at Ellen, saying, "Looks like today's a day for miracles. Welcome back."

While the nurses worked quickly to make Ellen comfortable, Doctor Gregory took Mag aside. "Are you family?"

"Friend, but Ellen didn't have any family in the area, so one else is coming. I'm the one who found her, and I'd like to hear what you have to say." When he began to cite privacy rules, Mag didn't hesitate and changed her tune, adding just enough magic to make sure he believed her claim of being Ellen's cousin. If she had to pay for casting a spell to cloud his mind, so be it.

"These types of cases can sometimes land us in unexpected territory. We didn't expect Ellen to survive, and I can't say why she's awake right now. You need to prepare yourself for the possibility that this sudden recovery won't last."

"She could relapse?"

He nodded. "Relapse is one possibility. Another is that we sometimes see a burst of vitality before the final moments. We'll monitor her closely for the next few hours."

Keeping her gaze riveted to Ellen's face, Mag qualified the statement. "You're saying you think she could still die."

He nodded. "Or she could make a full recovery. Nothing about Ellen's case has been...normal." He paused to find the right word.

"How so?" Mag already had an idea but needed

confirmation.

"On arrival, she presented with signs of healing inconsistent with the severity of the injury, and then, a few days ago, she experienced a profound change in brain wave activity. I thought we would lose her, but as suddenly as her levels flattened, they picked right back up."

Mag knew she could take credit for both of those anomalies but had no intention of telling Doctor Gregory what was none of his business.

"I wasn't dying," Ellen croaked but didn't open her eyes. "I went to Graceland."

The doctor arched a brow but didn't comment. Neither did Mag.

"When can I go home?" Ellen slitted one eye open and put the doctor on the spot.

"Let's see how things go for a day or two, shall we? I'll schedule a new scan, and depending on the results, we can talk about transferring you to the rehab wing. You'll need some PT before I feel confident about sending you home. Maybe a week or two at a care facility to complete the transition."

"I'll die before I go to a nursing home." Ellen glared at the doctor, the set of her mouth radiating defiance.

"We'll see." He made no promises.

Mag stayed by Ellen's side for a while longer, watching the nurses fussing over their miracle patient. Before she left, Mag leaned in close and whispered softly into her friend's ear, "You're a tough old bat, and so am I. You get better now. Together, we'll figure out who did this and why."

"We'll call the number you left if anything happens."

The nurse informed Mag as she opened the door.

"Thanks."

On the way home, Mag fretted over the state of the investigation into Ellen's attack. She'd paid far too much attention to Sam Wayland, and now that Ellen was awake, she might still be in danger.

Tomorrow would be soon enough to return to the hospital and get some answers. After all, if anyone knew why someone would do such a thing, surely it would be Ellen herself.

Chapter 22

When a puff of foul-smelling smoke rose from the cauldron, Clara's pulse jumped. The first stage of the potion was ready, but would it work? What if it didn't? Her chances of slipping Mag one potion were pretty good, but two? Probably not. If her sister ever figured out Clara's intentions, there would be hell to pay.

"We need a way to test the potion," she absently stroked Pyewacket's fur. "Any ideas?"

Pyewacket slid gracefully to the floor, then shimmered into her human form. "It's specific to Mag, so you'd need to test it directly on her, wouldn't you? Like physically?"

Nodding, Clara admitted, "Without her finding out about it."

"We're witches and familiars, not miracle workers."

Clara acknowledged the truth with a nod.

"Only one way." Pyewacket pointed out what her mistress already knew. "Hair or fingernails."

Clara sighed. "You know how Mag is about keeping her pieces and parts from ending up a commodity."

There was a booming market for bits of witch. Some sold hair and fingernail clippings for extra cash, but Mag and Clara weren't hurting in that department. Being

Balefire witches, their hair and nails would command a premium price and could be used for stronger spells. For that reason, Mag tossed all nail pairings into the fireplace and cleaned her brush with magic flame every time she used it. Getting hold of so much as a strand wouldn't be easy, but it would be the perfect test subject. If the spell worked, the hair should show the effects quite readily.

The more she thought about it, the more Clara knew she needed at least one strand of Mag's hair. But how to get it without Mag knowing what she was up to? That was the problem.

"What if we give her a sleeping potion with dinner?"

"Better off talking her into taking one on her own." Pye considered. "But then, you'd have to get into her place once she was asleep."

Mag slept with the sure knowledge that no one would sneak up on her in the dark. If she accidentally set off her own alarms a time or two, that was the price she paid for a sense of security. Being family, Clara wouldn't trip the booby traps. At least not under normal circumstances, but if she went into Mag's room with intent that could even remotely be considered malicious, she was screwed.

"We could wait until she takes a shower and try to get a few hairs out of the drain," Clara suggested.

Pye nodded in agreement. "That might work, but it's risky because we'd have to cast a spell on the drain to keep her from remembering to clean it herself. You know she's been off her game lately, but not that far off it. She'll know. We'll get caught."

Clara sighed, doused the fire under the cauldron, and

sank into her chair to think. The answer had to be there somewhere. She just had to find it.

"We could read Jinx in on this. He has more access than we do."

Before the words were out of Clara's mouth, Pyewacket was already shaking her head. "He'd tell. And not even out of worry for her welfare but out of concern for his own fur. He only has two lives left, and he's terrified she'll cost him one of them before he's ready."

"This should be good news for him, and he should want to help. If I can return what the Raythe took from her, he'd be guaranteed a longer life."

All tawny hair and skin, Pyewacket made a picture as she sat cross-legged on a large pillow near the fire. "You think so? I don't. Mag is who she is. You give her back her youth, and I promise she'll go out and find something else dangerous to spend it on."

That was a point Clara had not thought of before and one that showed Pyewacket was an astute judge of character. While Margaret Balefire considered herself an enigma among witches, anyone who knew her well could have predicted her response to regaining her vitality. Clara cursed herself as a fool for not realizing what might happen sooner.

"Maybe you're right, but what would you have me do? Only give her back enough to keep her tame? To prolong her life a little, but not enough for her to be truly happy?"

"Well, if you're going to be all sensible and stuff, I guess you're right, but we can't bring Jinx into this. I feel it in my whiskers."

Clara conceded and got to work thinking of another way to get what she needed, but Mag was a hard witch to fool.

"Charm the hairbrush? Or her nail clippers?"

"Maybe."

"You could just tell her what you're up to."

Under Clara's steady gaze, Pyewacket shrugged. "No, I can see why that won't work. She puts on a good front, but there are vulnerable places under all the bluster."

Now, Clara paced the room. Days of tracking down obscure ingredients, calling in favors, carefully blending and mixing the potion—and doing it all behind Mag's back had taken a toll. Yes, it would have been easier with her sister's cooperation, but getting Mag's hopes up and not delivering was Clara's biggest fear. No, that wasn't entirely true because dead sister certainly trumped ticked off or disheartened sister.

"Okay, enough dithering. This is a practical problem with a practical solution. We need some of Mag's hair, and getting it from her house is not an option."

A solution began to suggest itself, but it was devious at best and plain mean at worst.

"What I need to do is get her to wash her hair here where I can charm the drain to capture several strands and send them to a safe place."

"That could work." Pyewacket had also begun to pace. Both women stopped and looked at each other. "I think that could work, but how?"

When Clara merely stood and looked at her familiar for a moment, Pyewacket caught on. "You wouldn't."

"I would. But only because it's important."

"I hope you know what you're doing."

Clara sighed. "Me, too."

Arriving home, Mag was so full of Ellen's potential recovery she let Clara talk her into coming upstairs for a soothing toddy without a single qualm.

"That's fantastic news," Clara poured the drink into a pair of thick mugs, handing one to Mag. "Have you eaten? I made spaghetti."

Since Clara's red sauce was a favorite, Mag admitted she could eat.

"Don't be skimpy with the sauce, either."

"I wouldn't dream of it," Clara said as she fixed Mag's plate. "The more, the better."

Half a minute later, Mag blinked out at Clara from behind a curtain of dripping red noodles.

"I'm so sorry. How utterly clumsy of me." Clara's lips twitched. "Let's get you right into the shower, shall we? Before that sauce sets in and turns your hair funny colors. Pyewacket will work her magic on your clothes, and we'll have you set to rights in no time."

Before she could catch her breath, Mag found herself standing under a steaming spray with a bottle of Clara's best homemade shampoo and wishing her place had such good water pressure.

In the kitchen, Clara held up an empty vial and watched as several white strands appeared.

"It worked," she murmured to Pyewacket as she filled a new plate. "Looks like we're in for a long night."

"What on earth are you wearing?" Pyewacket changed to human form to ask the question as she entered the workshop later that evening.

Clara looked down at the lab coat she'd charmed to be impervious to anything short of nuclear war. She didn't think it looked that weird. "It's a protective garment."

"I meant your head."

"Oh." With a gloved hand, Clara patted the leather helmet and goggles she wore along with a fairly modern respirator. Not a single inch of her skin showed. "We're working with volatile magic here. I didn't want to contaminate the potion."

Keeping one eyebrow cocked, Pyewacket muttered a shielding spell that worked just as well as Clara's protective gear. Probably better.

"My way's more fun."

"Whatever you need to tell yourself," Pyewacket said. "What can I do to help?"

Careful to preserve the contents, Clara dragged the stopper out of a vial containing the sliver of Raythe bone and handed it over to Pyewacket.

"If you wouldn't mind powdering this," Clara got out a stone mortar, then handed Pyewacket a matching pestle.

"Ice method, or fire?"

The tools had to be sanctified before Pyewacket could use them to grind up the chunk of singed bone.

"Good question," Clara patted her familiar on the arm with encouragement. "What do you think, Pye?"

It was a test.

"You're Balefire witches, so fire seems appropriate."

"That's my thought, too."

Clara watched as her familiar ignited a small flame in the palm of her hand. She carefully held the mortar above the fire, moving it slowly back and forth until the flames had touched every surface. Then, she did the same with the pestle and set them aside to cool.

"I think that's good." Clara dropped the bone shard into the bowl.

Pyewacket began to grind the yellowed mote between the stone pestle and the mortar wall, using all of her strength to crush the chunk into tiny fragments. Clara watched with a critical eye, ensuring that not even a single mote of dust contaminated the powdering process. They were dealing with a very powerful potion, and this was an even more powerful ingredient. Any mistake could have disastrous consequences.

Once the morsel had been reduced to a fine powder, Clara produced a second bottle. "Be careful with this one. It's reconstituted, so it will go to paste. Might be sticky."

For her first test, Clara set aside a tiny scoop of the powdered Raythe bone. If that didn't work, she'd try the paste and, as a last resort, use a quartz-tipped stirring stick to blend a measure of both.

"Here we go," Clara chose her smallest cauldron, barely bigger than a coffee cup, and set it on the tiny brazier she'd made specially to fit the gently rounded bowl. Like a conductor standing before an orchestra, she lifted her arms and began to chant as she pointed toward various ingredients, using magic to lift and spill each one into the tiny cauldron in the order she hoped would work.

"Stop!" Pye grabbed Clara's wrist. "You're messing it up. It's Raythe powder, then the infernal elf hair." Santa Claus wasn't on Pye's list of favored people for reasons she refused to share with anyone, so she tended to refer to him by a series of slurs.

"You're right." Clara quickly swapped the order, then

grinned when the potion turned pink and glimmered as if made from liquid glitter. "Gimme a hair to test. Quick."

"I live to serve." Pyewacket carefully extracted a flyaway strand and placed it on a slice of black obsidian. Clara snapped a dripper cap into the top of the potion bottle and tipped it over the hair. She forgot to breathe as a single drop slid free.

"Is it working?" Leaning in close, Pye's shield took the brunt of the minor explosion as the hair flashed and shriveled. "Oh," she said. "I guess not." The pungent scent of skunk filled the air. "Pugh."

Scowling, Clara picked up the container of bone powder and blew across it with a gentle puff to send motes into the white balefire she'd conjured into her other palm. The tiny cloud of dust took the shape of a skunk silhouetted in flame.

"I guess that wasn't Raythe bone after all." Clara conjured a large fan to waft the skunk scent into the fireplace, where magic smoke carried it up and out the chimney. "Looks like we'll be using the paste."

Pyewacket redid her shield but kept her distance when tarry black met glittering pink. Sparks flew out of the cauldron, whizzed in a funnel shape, then filtered back into the potion.

"That's encouraging."

"So's the fact that I don't smell anything disgusting." With a wave of her hand, Clara bottled the potion, added a dripper top, and called for another hair to test.

"Moment of truth." A droplet fell. Somewhere, a bell rang. Clara's head buzzed with the force of magic.

"Holy tuna casserole." Pyewacket breathed, then let out a strangled sound as Clara snatched her up into an enthusiastic hug. "It worked. Let's go dump it on her right now."

When she would have rushed from the room, Clara grabbed her familiar's arm. "Wait. We need to give this a day or two. Just to make sure the effects aren't temporary."

"But," Pyewacket began to argue, then realized Clara had a point. "I'll be at Lexi's if you need me," Pye said. "You know I can keep a secret, but this is more than just a secret. You call me when it's time."

Clara nodded and was soon left alone to contemplate the disk of dark stone holding one perfect, lustrous blond hair with reddish highlights.

"Maggie," she sighed.

Chapter 23

Armed with a jar of Clara's pain-relieving salve and fortified from a soak in pool water, Mag began her day with a trip to the hospital to check on Ellen. She found her friend propped up in the bed, wearing a smile bright enough to put the sun to shame.

Mag couldn't help but respond in kind. "You scared me," she said.

"Scared me, too." Ellen waited until the nurse had taken her breakfast tray. "It happened, right? Graceland wasn't a dream, and you're a witch. You don't have to worry. Your secret's safe with me."

"If I thought any different, I wouldn't have taken you."

"Then we're friends? True friends?"

"For life." No one was more surprised than Mag to discover she meant the sentiment and that the truth of it warmed her heart. "Do you need anything?"

"Now, you see," Ellen said, her eyes twinkling, "That's a problem. The ambulance crew didn't think to grab my purse, so I've been locked out of my house. I don't suppose you know a spell for that."

"I can get in." And had, but Ellen didn't need to know that part. "What do you need?"

"My own clothes, for a start. You'll find pajamas in the second drawer of the tall bureau in my bedroom, and my bathrobe hangs on the back of the bathroom door."

"Pajamas, check. Bathrobe, check."

"My purse, of course."

Mag nodded.

"And in my nightstand drawer, there's a book." Ellen blushed. "If you could wrap it in the pajamas, that would be good."

"Will do," Mag said, tilting her head. "And did you get a chance to review your new will? I could grab it while I'm there if you didn't."

Ellen wrinkled her brow in confusion. "What new will?"

"Wasn't that the reason for your nephew's visit? You didn't mention your will when we were at Graceland, but your neighbor said Sam had an envelope with him when he went in and not when he came out. She assumed you'd updated your will."

"No." Ellen closed her eyes and pictured the day. "But I didn't see him come in, so he could have set the envelope down somewhere and left it behind."

Call it witch's intuition, a hunch, or a gut feeling, but Mag felt the case breaking wide open.

"Would you like me to look around for it while I'm there?"

"Go right ahead. I'm curious, too."

Since Ellen's fingers had begun picking at the blankets and she looked like she needed a nap, Mag excused herself and headed back to the van. The drive back to Ellen's seemed longer than it should have, but she finally pulled up out front.

"Any news?"

Mag spun to see Rebecca rolling down the road. The way the wheelchair handled the terrain got Mag considering whether to get one for herself soon.

"Plenty, and it's all good. Ellen's awake. By tomorrow, I expect she'll be ready to receive visitors. She's much improved and has asked me to bring her some things from home."

Beaming, Rebecca said, "That is good news. The best I've heard in days. Give her my best, would you?"

"I will." Mag was eager to get inside, but she wouldn't begrudge a moment of her time. "She'll be glad to know you're thinking of her."

After a few moments of polite conversation, Mag feigned unlocking the door and let herself into Ellen's empty house. First, she used her breath and a steady stream of magic to remove the fine layer of dust that had settled.

Then, she headed for the bedroom, found a cloth bag in the closet, and filled it with Ellen's requested items—including the romance novel in her nightstand drawer. On the cover, a woman in red stood, her dress billowing in the breeze, while a man in tight pants gazed at her longingly. Mag flipped through a few pages before tucking the book into a pajama-wrapped cocoon. Spicy, she thought.

With that chore out of the way, Mag stepped into the living room, where Sam had purportedly carried on an in-depth conversation about his dry cleaning. A quick search of the room turned up nothing that looked like papers or an envelope. The tickle in her belly ramped up a notch.

What had Ellen said about Sam's final visit? Mag closed her eyes to replay the conversation in her head, then opened them to stare at the desk Ellen had planned to sell. The one she thought she'd seen Sam looking through.

"Let's see what you have for me." She opened the first drawer and found it empty. Same with the rest. "Okay. If that's how you want to play it." She pulled the side drawers out again, checking each one against the others for differences in depth, length, or width. All were the same, so she turned her attention to the center drawer, which was deceptively shallower than it should have been.

"Got you. Now, where's the latch?"

Mag wiggled and jiggled the drawer front. When nothing gave, she pulled the whole thing out as far as it would go and bent to look at the underside.

"Sneaky," she muttered, conjuring a magnifying glass the size of a saucepan. It took a solid five minutes before she finally located the pinhole set into the dovetail detail on the left-hand side. Away went the magnifier to be replaced with a wickedly sharp hatpin, which she jabbed ruthlessly into the hole.

Mag heard and felt the click as the false bottom dropped down. A brown envelope fell into her hands.

"Hot damn," she said. The temptation to open the envelope and have a look was nearly overwhelming, but Mag banked her eagerness as she locked Ellen's front door behind her and drove home. It wouldn't feel right to solve this mystery without Clara, and there'd be plenty of time to drop Ellen's things off at the hospital later.

She had to wait a few minutes longer than she wanted while Clara bundled up a customer's purchases.

"Where's Pye?"

"Port Harbor. Why?"

"Someone needs to watch the shop for a few minutes. I've found something that I think will break the Wayland case wide open, and I waited for you so we could go through it together."

"Jinx is closer."

"So he is," Mag closed her eyes and murmured his name.

"What?" Jinx appeared out of thin air. A gorgeous white long-hair in his cat form, he looked more like someone's accountant in his human one. "Are you hurt?"

Mag rolled her eyes. "No, I'm not hurt. Mind the shop, would you? We need to go out back for a few minutes." Already headed for Clara's workshop, Mag tossed her final order over her shoulder. "No discounts."

"You know he only does that to tick you off."

"It works." Dragging the envelope out, Mag tossed it on the table. "Sam had this with him the last time he visited his aunt. I found it hidden in that Scottish desk she planned to sell."

"You should take this to the police, Mag."

"And so I will, once we've had a good look at what's in there."

Clara's lips firmed as curiosity fought with duty. Curiosity won. "Fine. We'll look and figure out the best way to handle whatever we find."

"Open it,"

Using magic to undo the seal, Clara did and pulled out

a bundle of legal documents.

"Definitely not Ellen's will," Mag noted when she looked at the first page.

"This looks like some sort of financial agreement between Claudia Scanlon and Ben Worthington," Clara read from the paperwork.

"Who?"

"Claudia was Sam's law partner."

Mag waved the explanation away. "I know that. Who's the other guy? Name rings a bell, but just barely."

"Ben Worthington is the membership guy from the club. We met him the other day."

Light dawned. "Right. This case has too many suspects and too little hard evidence."

Clara continued scanning through the pages. As she looked at each one, she passed it along to Mag, who did the same. "I think this is a lease of some sort. Maybe the answer is here if we can figure out what we're looking at."

They worked their way through the stack twice before Mag tossed the pages down in frustration. "What do we know about this Worthington guy?"

"Not much," Clara admitted, "but I bet Gertrude knows everything except his shoe size. I'll go call her and see."

Alone again, Mag flipped through the documents one more time. If she ignored all the whereofs and heretofores, it seemed Clara had been right. Worthington's family had held a long-term lease on the club's back nine.

"Worthington's from a prominent family." Clara

returned a few minutes later. "Landowners mostly, but that's not newsworthy. What is, is that he was on the board at the club up until last month when he "stepped down" to take over as membership coordinator."

Considering, Mag tilted her head. "Scandal?"

"Not according to Gertrude, so if there was, he found a way to keep it super quiet. I swear if a mouse farts in Harmony, Gertrude hears about it eventually."

Mag picked up the relevant sheet and handed it to Clara. "You were right, I think. Ben's great-grandfather granted the club a leasehold on part of the golf course."

"For 99 years at a nominal fee with a purchase requirement when the lease ended." Clara nodded. "That's what it looks like to me, too."

"And isn't next year the club's hundred-year anniversary? I heard someone nattering on about the plans for a big party to celebrate."

"That's some interesting math." Clara's eyes narrowed as the implications began working through her head. "It's too big of a coincidence that Worthington takes a lesser role in club affairs in the same year the board needs to decide if they want to purchase the land."

"Maybe he decided he didn't want to sell." Mag began to pace. "And they demoted him."

"Maybe the board decided not to buy the land, and he stepped down in protest. It could go either way."

"Why would the club give up access to twenty acres they're already using unless Worthington tried to gouge them on the price? Seems to me it would be a big blow to lose a section of the course. Isn't golf at the heart of what pulls in those equity memberships? I think it's more likely that Worthington tried to shake them down."

"I still don't see what any of this has to do with Sam's death. Wouldn't it make sense to kill Worthington instead?"

Mag couldn't see a clear connection. "We're missing something."

"Obviously. We need someone fluent in legalese."

"I know just the person. Not sure why I didn't think of her sooner. Get that infernal phone of yours back out and call Penelope Snow. Ask her how to get hold of Cassandra Bane."

"That won't be necessary." Clara scrolled through her contacts list. "I have her number. You've probably waited on her before. She's one of my best customers."

"Must pay cash, or I'd have seen the name on a credit card slip."

Distracted, Clara nodded and hit the button to make the call.

"Don't say anything over the phone. You never know who's listening."

Clara rolled her eyes and used a time-sensitive, frequent customer discount on Cassie's favorite line of personal care products to lure the younger witch into the shop.

"We close in half an hour."

"I'll be there in ten," Cassie agreed.

"I hope she knows something helpful. Otherwise, you're costing me a bundle."

"Call it payback for that barber chair."

Clara rolled her eyes again. "Let it go, Mag."

"You let it go."

The bickering continued until Cassandra's mile-long legs carried her through the door a minute earlier than the projected ten.

"I'm afraid we've lured you here under false pretenses," Mag said.

"You mean I don't get the discount?" Steel gray eyes snapped below a fringe of deep mahogany bangs.

"Of course you do." Clara glared at Mag. "Once you're finished shopping, we'd like your opinion on something. If you don't mind, that is."

"No problem."

By the time Cassie finished making liberal use of her discount to purchase a year's worth of supplies, it was closing time. As she flipped the sign to closed, Clara did the mental math and winced at what the discount cost her. Mag had better never mention that chair again.

"I hear you have an affinity for knowing when someone's telling the truth," Mag began.

Nodding, Cassie confided, "Plays hell with my dating life, I can tell you. Men lie about the weirdest things. I just don't get it."

Mag didn't give a fig for dating. All she wanted to do was solve the case. Cassie wasn't the only witch in the room that could spot a liar at fifty paces.

"Did you kill Sam Wayland?"

"No," Cassie said. Disgust colored her tone. "It was tempting, but I didn't."

Mag saw and felt the truth in the statement.

"And you studied mortal law?" Cassie nodded again, but her face took on a certain wariness.

"I did. Why do you ask?"

"We've come by a set of documents that we think might shed light on the murder, and we were wondering if you could look at them for us."

Now, it was Cassandra's turn to tilt her head as she assessed each sister in turn, starting with Clara. "Why would you bother shedding light for him? Sam wasn't a nice man. Maybe the world is better off with him gone."

"Justice doesn't care about naughty or nice. It demands that the scales be balanced," Clara spoke quietly. "And if we're right, an innocent woman nearly paid for his mistakes with her life. She might still be in danger."

Satisfied with the answer, Cassandra snapped her fingers. "Give me the papers, then."

Without saying more, Clara handed the pages over. Cassandra paused once or twice to read more thoroughly. The process took several minutes. When she looked up, her eyes had gone sharp—almost feral.

"Where did you get these?"

"From Sam. At least indirectly. He hid them in his aunt's house, and someone almost killed her to get them back." Mag had put that together as soon as the envelope dropped into her hand. It was why she'd added a layer of magical protection to Ellen's hospital room. If anyone walked through her door with ill intentions, Mag would know. "Why?"

Cassie fanned the documents out on the table and picked out the ones with Claudia Scanlon's signature. "These were dated weeks after Claudia left the practice."

"And?" Mag didn't get the significance.

"And, under the terms of their partnership, each attorney would retain any clients they brought to the firm. Ben Worthington was one of Sam's clients."

"Which put her in breach of contract," Clara said.

"Exactly," Cassandra nodded.

"What?" Clara responded to Mag's look of surprise. "I know stuff."

"So do I." Mag's chin tilted slightly. "Like, I know Cassandra suspected someone in the firm wasn't being truthful." She reached into her fanny pack and pulled out the vial of ink she'd taken from Sam's coffin.

Cassandra gasped. "Grave robber."

"Wasn't technically in the grave yet."

"Can you please stop talking in riddles?" Clara had no idea what was happening. "What is that?"

"Forgery detecting ink," Mag answered first. "Cassandra and Penelope brewed it up. Nice piece of magic, by the way."

The compliment pleased Cassandra and went a long way toward softening her annoyance. "I never trusted Claudia Scanlon, and she knew it, which was why she tried so hard to get me fired."

"How does it work?" Curious, Clara took the vial from Mag, noting that the smooth glass felt warm to the touch.

"It's pretty simple." To illustrate, Cassandra touched Ben Worthington's signature and said his name. The ink on the page flared red. "What the heck?"

Mag's spine tingled with excitement. "That means this is a forgery, right?"

"It does." With a furrowed brow, Cassandra tested Claudia's signature. The ink remained dark, but when she lifted her hand, she noticed a crescent of green ink where her fingertip rested on Ben's name. "No," she said. "That can't be right."

"What?" Mag leaned in close for a better look and bumped heads with Clara, who'd done the same. "Ow."

"Ow indeed."

"Claudia Scanlon," Claudia repeated with her finger firmly placed on Ben Worthington's signature. The slant of red flickered to black, then began to pulse between the two colors. "Son of a witch."

Chapter 24

"What does it mean?" Mag had a pretty good idea but wanted confirmation.

Excitement lit Cassandra's eyes. "It means Ben's signature is a forgery, but it's also not a forgery."

"Impossible," Clara scoffed.

Nodding to acknowledge the outburst, Cassandra touched Worthington's signature again and tested the only plausible theory. "Claudia Scanlon." The line of text went red. "Ben Worthington." Red flashed to black and back again.

Cassandra's eyes widened as her gaze met Mag's.

"Looks to me like you have one signature, but it was made by two people. How is that possible? A flaw in the spell?"

"I'm not a novice, and neither is Penelope. That spell was solid. We made sure of it." When Cassandra would have taken insult, she realized Mag wasn't casting aspersions but asking out of pure curiosity. "There's only one way to explain what happened. Two people occupying one body."

Mag's mind began to spin. "Takes some seriously dark magic to pull that off. Are you sure it wasn't a glamor?"

"Even the best glamor in the world wouldn't get past the spell on that ink. Claudia's one of us, you know.

"A Moonstone?" That was the first Mag had heard of it.

Cassandra shook her head. "No. A solitary witch." She tapped the sheet of paper. "The way I see it, Claudia Scanlon manipulated and took over Ben Worthington's body so she could forge his name on an agreement that not only grants her the right to negotiate on his behalf but also puts her in control of whatever money he gets for the land deal."

Mag was surprised to find she wasn't surprised by the revelation or the obvious conclusion.

"It fits." Her cane thumped on the floor as she paced and put her thoughts in order.

Following that logic, it didn't take a leap to realize Sam had probably figured out what Claudia had done. With him dead, they'd never know how he came to that conclusion, but it seemed clear that something had given Claudia away.

"Not to state the obvious," Clara said, "but the date on the purchase option is coming right up. What do you think she intends to do with Worthington once the paperwork is finalized?"

"You won't find her so easy to pin down," Cassandra said.

"No offense to you, Cassie, but this is why there are certain professions witches probably shouldn't undertake," Clara said. "What Claudia has done only illustrates some of the ethical issues with magic when it comes to human law."

"None taken," Cassie replied in a neutral tone. "As it

happens, I agree with you. I will admit I find mortal law a fascinating pursuit. But then, I have no interest in using the twists and turns of it to feather my nest."

"Well, we appreciate you taking the time to help." It was a dismissal even if Mag didn't come right out and order Cassandra to leave.

Cassandra did not take the hint.

"You're welcome. Now, let's figure out how to catch the dirty witch because as much as Sam Wayland had his less-than-decent moments, he didn't deserve to die."

Catching Clara's eye, Mag lifted her left brow slightly and acknowledged her sister's shrug with one of her own. It looked like the crime-fighting duo had just become a team of three.

Noting Mag's expression, Cassandra grinned. "I already know too much. You'll either have to kill me or let me help. I vote for the latter unless you're fond of pigeons."

Clara shuddered, remembering the feel of bird feet on granite skin. As the only witch who had ever survived to tell the tale of being turned to stone, murdering a witch wasn't on her list of things to do. Ever.

"Slipping into someone else's body is tricky magic." Mag's hip had had all the standing it could take for now, so she sat in the rocker Clara kept by the fireplace, ran over her memory of meeting Ben Worthington, and then put herself in Claudia's place. "Especially when it's a live subject. It's much easier for a soul to slip into a body that no longer has one."

"Just say a dead person, Mag. There's no reason to be delicate. We're all familiar with the theory of magical transmutation." With a finger flick, Clara conjured two more chairs. "Have a seat, Cassie. Once Mag goes into problem-solving mode, we could be here a while."

"Fine by me. I'd love to see how well the Balefires live up to their reputations."

"That all depends on who's spreading the rumors," Clara smiled.

"If you're ready to get on with it,' Mag raised her voice over the creak of the chair's rockers. "Are we certain Worthington's still alive?"

"He was at the time these documents were signed," Cassandra said. "And before you ask, Claudia knew about the forgery ink." Most of the color leeched out of her face. "Sam's death was my fault, wasn't it? I developed that spell because he accused me of signing his name to court documents that I wasn't authorized to sign."

It took a few minutes to convince Cassandra she wasn't to blame for the murder.

"I must have sensed something was off," Mag mused, "because I pegged Worthington for the murderer the first time we met. I just didn't realize he was a she. The way I see it, she's been keeping him under wraps since she faked leaving town."

"You mean as a prisoner?"

Mag nodded vigorously. "Either in or out of his body."

The shock brought Cassie to her feet. "She wouldn't."

Tilting her head up, Mag fixed her gaze on the young witch. "If we're right, and you know we are, she's already committed murder. What makes you think something like that would be beneath her?"

"If you put it like that, I suppose you're right. How do

we find out for sure? And what does she do with her body while her soul is in his?"

"Good questions. I guess you're not an idiot." For Mag, that was high praise. "Undisclosed location, protected by magic and her familiar. That's how I'd do it if I felt the need for a meat-suit ride-a-long."

"Which you never would because it's not your talent, and you take your oath to harm none quite seriously," Clara laid a hand on Mag's arm in support. "Shoving someone's soul aside while you use their body doesn't follow the oath, if you ask me."

"Then let's do something about it." The beginnings of a plan had already begun to form in Mag's mind, and it was a good one made better by the suggestions Clara and Cassandra offered once she'd laid it out for them.

Two long hours later, Clara picked up a clean rag, mopped the sweat from her brow, and surveyed the charm she'd just created with disgust.

"There's no way to key the spell to Worthington—or Scanlon, for that matter—without full proximity. We'd need hair, blood, or nail clippings for the charm to work remotely."

Confused, Cassandra tilted her head and gave Clara a look. "Full proximity? I'm not great with charms, so I'm not sure what you mean."

"She means the spell requires physical contact. Skin to charm."

Clara nodded. "Whoever deploys it will have to wear protection while they get up close and personal with Worthington's body."

"How personal are we talking?" Cassandra didn't seem eager to volunteer.

"Hand or arm will work fine."

After a moment's thought, Mag said, "I'll do it. You can handle the rest?"

"Don't insult me, Margaret."

The mission was delayed by a few minutes while Mag retrieved a pair of gloves from the vintage clothing area of the shop, and Clara adapted some spare earbuds for communication. "There," she said as she tucked one in Mag's ear. "Tap it once to turn it on, twice for off."

"I got it," Mag palmed the completed charm, picked up her cane, and ignored the momentary weakness that stole over her limbs. "Let's do this." She shifted them all to her favorite storage closet at the club, where Clara handed Cassandra an invisibility charm.

"I'll want that back when this is done."

Cassandra merely grinned, then went on ahead to check that Worthington was in his office. She returned minutes later. "Phase one is good to go. He's right where we want him, and I've made sure he is alone. Or she. Whatever."

As they passed the front desk, Clara glanced into the alcove where a laser printer merrily spit out sheets of paper like they were confetti, and a harried young man punched buttons on the control panel to try and make it stop.

"Good one." Mag approved as Clara knocked on Worthington's door and opened it without waiting for permission.

"I'm sorry to bother you, Mr. Worthington, but I wonder if you'd mind answering a few more questions about your membership policy," Clara said. She felt Cassandra's body brush past her, then heard a whisper through her earpiece.

"I'm set."

Worthington didn't rise to greet them and barely bothered to wipe the annoyance off his face. "If you'd make an appointment for later in the week, I'd be happy to answer any questions you might have. I'm late for a meeting."

"Lie," Cassandra whispered in Mag's ear.

She'd known it wouldn't be as simple as a handshake. "We are truly sorry to bother you," Mag said. "But we were hoping you could provide us with more information about your membership levels. I'm considering whether or not to take up golf as a hobby."

Having dressed up for the occasion, Mag wore what she considered typical old lady garb, including a fluffy shawl knitted from pink yarn to match the protective gloves. Anyone with half a brain would see the sharp intelligence in her eyes, but Worthington only saw what she wanted him to see.

"You can request a packet from Mr. Daily in the front office. That should answer all of your questions. Now, if you don't mind, I'm late for that meeting."

But Mag did mind. She minded very much. "Your young Mr. Daily seemed a bit preoccupied. Something seems to have gone wrong with your printer."

Sighing loudly, Worthington rose and circled the desk.

As he approached, and Clara slipped on her Elvis

sunglasses—she'd cast a charm on them for clear vision—Mag saw her opportunity and put forth an Oscar-worthy performance.

"Oh," she let her eyes roll back in her head. "I feel funny." With that, she pitched forward, forcing Worthington to catch her before she fell. In the process, she slapped her gloved hand on his bare wrist, and the charm made contact.

Through the glasses, Clara saw a woman where a man had been. "Suspicion confirmed," she didn't bother to keep her voice low.

"What?" Claudia Scanlon said as Mag's body sagged in her arms.

"And go." Clara gave the order.

Things happened fast. Cassandra dropped the invisibility charm. Her sudden appearance distracted her long enough for Mag to say the spell that would trade Claudia's body for Worthington's soul.

"Now," Cassandra's shout saved Mag from a nasty curse but not from being tossed to the floor. Her exclamation of pain shot Clara's temper to the boiling point.

The force of her magic stirred Clara's hair. Fury darkened her eyes. One look at features gone so sharp and hard they could have been chiseled from granite had Cassandra stepping back.

"Ligabis, Ostium, Carcere." Clara's spell ripped the air. She suffered a moment of deja vu when Claudia muttered a counter curse.

"Oh no, you don't." Raising herself on one elbow,

Mag pointed at Claudia and cast a stunning spell. Cassandra had the same idea because both spells hit the murdering witch at once. She went stiff as a board just as Clara's binding rendered her harmless.

The whole operation took under five minutes.

"Maggie!" Clara dropped to her knees. "Are you okay?"

"Sorry, Clarie, but I don't think so."

Chapter 25

"Get Mag's bed to the workshop." Clara used her mental connection to Pyewacket as she knelt beside her sister. "Put it right in front of the fireplace."

"On it."

"Pye," Clara's voice remained calm Despite the fear and sorrow jumping in her belly. "It's time. Tell Jinx what he needs to know."

Already risen from her velvet pillow near the fire, Pyewacket shivered off her cat form and took the human one that would be more helpful. "Is the spell ready?"

"All but the final ingredients." Whether it would be enough or not, they were about to find out. Clara wasn't sure she could live with the consequences if she failed. "We need Lexi. Sylvana, too. Can you get the word to them?"

"Consider it done. We'll be ready."

Today would not be the day she said goodbye to her only sister. Not if Clara could help it. She looked up at Cassandra. "I have to go. Can you handle things here?"

"It would be my pleasure. I'll get someone out to check on Worthington, too. Go and blessed be."

Past caring what happened to Claudia or Ben, Clara muttered an order for Mag to hold on, then shifted them both to the workshop and the waiting bed. Pyewacket had come through, as Clara had known she would.

In his cat form, Jinx dove under the covers, tucked himself as close to Mag's side as he could get—whether for his own comfort or to loan her his strength, Clara couldn't say. What's more, she didn't care.

"Maggie! You hold on."

All Clara wanted to do was stay in that bed and hold her sister tight, but there was magic to be done. Fresh pain hit Clara like a hammer. Buried under a layer of covers, Mag looked so small—so diminished with only her face showing, and she was pale, too.

"Leave me alone," Mag barely had enough breath to force words through cracked lips, but there was still a bit of fire in her soul. "Let me die in peace."

"The hell I will. You're not dying today."

"It's okay, Clarie. I'm ready."

"Well, I'm not. I don't know who I'd be without you, so shut up and let me help you. I've been working on something."

"Won't help." Where most might consider Mag a pessimist, she thought herself a realist, and death was about as real as it got.

"We're coming," Clara heard Pyewacket's voice in her head as she leaned down to kiss Mag on the forehead.

It wasn't easy to walk away from Mag's side, but Clara needed to get things ready, so she waved a hand to clear a small table, dragged it next to the bed, and laid out her tools. A blessed bowl joined her ritual knife next to the potion bottle. She could have placed the candles in a circle around the table using magic, but the working would be stronger if she did it by hand. Once placed, she ringed each candle with five crystals and waited for Lexi and Sylvana to arrive. The rest of the ritual and spell depended on them.

Clara didn't have long to wait. Sylvana arrived first, her shock of silvery white hair still a surprising sight even this many months after her transformation. Lexi popped in right behind her mother. Both wore faces grave with worry at the sight of their beloved aunt.

"Get in the circle." Clara wasted no time and allowed none for her daughter and granddaughter. "I need your blood."

Sylvana's worried expression turned to shock."Since when do you condone blood magic?"

"You know very well that all magic carries the essence of both light and dark. Blood magic can be light if done for the right reasons, and I don't have time to debate any of this with you. Step inside the circle."

When Sylvana did, Clara lit the candles and called on the spirits of her ancestors for guidance. Magic filled her with an unearthly light when she raised her hands. "Let the spell begin."

Grabbing Sylvana's hand, Clara poised the knife over her daughter's palm and waited for the nod of permission which Sylvana gave willingly. Lexi followed suit, and when it was her turn, Clara welcomed the line of fiery pain as her essence welled up to spill into the bowl. Taking blood from Mag caused more than a twinge of conscience, but it had to be done.

"That's enough." She offered a spelled white cloth to Sylvana, another to Lexi, and wiped away the cut on Mag's hand first and then her own with a third. "Now, we call the Balefire." Flames of purest white burst to life in each cupped hand.

"Blood to fire." Her voice booming, Clara sent her fire into the bowl. She motioned for Lexi and Sylvana to do the same. White fire flashed to crimson.

"Fire to prove."

Drawing the stopper free, Clara poured the potion she'd prepared into blood-colored flames. Spotlight-strong flares shot toward the ceiling while Clara's knees trembled from the force of the magic she had wrought.

When the light died down, Clara blinked until her vision cleared. The potion sparkled as she'd hoped it would.

"We need to get this into her. Jinx, you have to help hold her up." But Mag's familiar only quivered and buried himself deeper under the covers.

"I'll do it," Lexi rested her hand on her grandmother's wrist for a moment's comfort before sliding into bed with her aunt. Tears rolled unheeded down Lexi's face as she gathered the frail body into her arms. "Ready. And I think you need to hurry. She's barely breathing."

Clara sobbed but didn't take that all-important step toward the bed until Sylvana slid an arm around her waist. "Come. We'll do it together."

"Okay." Clara wasn't sure her feet would carry her, but with Sylvana's gentle guidance, she approached Mag and held the bowl to her lips. "Drink, Maggie. Please. Drink." The bowl tipped up enough to send a rivulet of potion toward Mag's mouth.

When the first drop of liquid touched cracked skin, there was healing. Just a little, but enough to send hearts soaring at the sight.

"It's working," Clara whispered through an unsteady breath. "Oh, Maggie. It's working."

Sip by sip, more potion disappeared down Mag's throat, her body strengthening and healing until she no longer needed help holding the bowl, and greedily drank to the last drop.

Sylvana kept an arm around Clara, adding more support when her mother's knees buckled, then guided Clara to sit on the edge of the bed while they watched Mag improve.

Wrinkles plumped. Her eyes cleared, and her color returned. Age spots faded, allowing freckles to show once again. When she smiled, her teeth gleamed whiter. It was a miracle. Clara's hand rose to press against her chest, where her heart felt like it might beat right out of her chest.

"It's like watching a movie backward," Sylvana grinned at Lexi. Lexi grinned back, and there were smiles all around until Mag screamed, and her body bowed up, her eyes rolling back until nothing showed but white.

"No!" Clara shouted. This couldn't be happening. They were losing her.

Time slowed. The air turned molasses thick as Clara reached toward her sister. She got hold of Mag just in time to support her sister's body while her mouth opened to release a cloud of darkness that writhed and formed the shape of a Raythe. Black and glowing darkly, pure evil rose from and over Mag like a shadow.

The shadow Raythe's mouth opened, most likely to offer some pithy comment.

"Oh! I don't think so." A halo of purest light formed around Sylvana as the white witch merely turned her head to look at the dark and menacing form. "Begone, evil spawn." A flick of her fingers shredded the black miasma to ribbons leaving nothing behind but a gentle warmth where icy darkness had been.

"Um, Gram," Lexi said.

Clara turned just in time to watch her sister's dandelion-fluff hair thicken and turn to a fall of burnished gold, framing a freckled face.

"That was some fine magic," Mag said, throwing off the covers. "I feel pretty good. What was in that stuff?"

Eyes wide, mouth open, Sylvana looked at her mother. "You didn't tell me you were going this far. No wonder you needed blood magic."

"What?" Mag took in the trio of astonished faces. "Do I have something in my teeth?"

"Not exactly." Clara conjured the mirror from her bedside table, holding it up for her sister to see. Mag looked, then did a double-take.

"Holy Hecate," she said. "I'm middle-aged. Guess I'll look better in that bathing suit next time I go to the club."

-The End-